Soul Corporation

Robert Collins was born in London in 1972. Having spent periods of his life in São Paulo and Italy, he lives and writes in London. *Soul Corporation* is his first novel.

For more about Robert Collins and *Soul Corporation* visit www.soulcorporation.com

Soul Corporation

Robert Collins

arrow books

Published by Arrow Books in 2005

1 3 5 7 9 10 8 6 4 2

Arrow Books
The Random House Group Limited
20 Vauxhall Bridge Road, London, SW1V 2SA

Random House Australia (Pty) Limited
20 Alfred Street, Milsons Point, Sydney, New South Wales 2061, Australia

Random House New Zealand Limited
18 Poland Road, Glenfield, Auckland 10, New Zealand

Random House (Pty) Limited
Endulini, 5a Jubilee Road, Parktown, 2193, South Africa

The Random House Group Limited Reg. No. 954009
www.randomhouse.co.uk

A CIP catalogue record for this book is available from the British Library

Papers used by Random House are natural, recyclable products made from
wood grown in sustainable forests. The manufacturing processes conform to
the environmental regulations of the country of origin

ISBN 0 09 946507 8

Typeset by SX Composing DTP, Rayleigh, Essex
Printed and bound in the United Kingdom by
Cox & Wyman Ltd, Reading, Berkshire

Thanks to: Lu, Lisa, Charlotte, Jules, Jack, Bill, Pete, Jonny, Doug, Nikola,
Andy, Susan, Raschid, Anna, Jerry, Nat, Serena, Bill A., Anna S., Lucy D.,
and Vic.

For Cleusa and
Alan

I

iVerts

FMCG

'What's your name?'

Kristin barely turned round before choosing her answer.

'Piss off,' she said, and swivelled on her stool.

The guy stood in front of her, confident, drunk, his eyes wide and glassy. But it was Esh he was staring at, a meek-looking friend behind him, the two of them gazing at Esh as she sat at the bar with her back turned.

'Where are you from?' the drunk guy asked.

Esh stayed where she was, fingers resting on her near-finished drink on the counter, legs stretching to the ground. In the dim light of the bar her face looked almost angelic, pale skin striking beneath her crop of dark hair.

'I thought I told you to piss off,' Kristin reminded him.

'Your friend not speak for herself?'

'She doesn't need an asshole like you bugging her.'

'I'm not talking to you.'

'Yeah?' said Kristin. 'Well, I'm talking to you.'

As sedate as he was, the guy was finding it hard to

ignore Kristin's interruptions. He turned his languid eyes towards her and looked her up and down.

'The fuck are you?' he snorted. 'The night shift?'

Kristin took a calm look over herself.

'Let me see,' she said.

This guy didn't scare her. She knew how under-dressed she looked. She was in her house jeans and sweatshirt, and Esh was in a T-shirt and Khakis. Neither of them was wearing make-up. Neither of them had their hair fixed. They'd just walked the five hundred yards from Kristin's parents' house, a couple of streets off Oxford Street, to have a quiet Saturday night drink at Dusk Junkie's. Now the bar was filling up with excruciatingly trendy people, but the people who ran Dusk Junkie's had known Esh and Kristin for a long time, and always let them in no matter how they were dressed.

How anyone would come up and start hitting on them now was beyond her. That was the thing, though. Esh could have dressed in fish-stinking sackcloth and every guy in the bar would still have wanted to talk to her. But Kristin didn't mind. That was just the way it had always been.

'That's right,' Kristin replied. 'We're the cleaners. We're just getting hammered before we start our shift.'

The guy chuckled.

'What do you really do?'

'We're investment bankers.'

He sniggered.

'Really?'

'Yes.'

'What area?'

'Structured corporate finance.'

The guy grinned, not knowing whether to laugh or believe it. He gazed thoughtfully into Esh's back. Whatever was going on in his head, his eyes weren't giving much away. Even he wasn't sure which way his mood was going to go.

Slowly, he turned his eyes back to Kristin.

'Don't piss me off, all right?'

'Leave us alone,' she said.

Eyes swimming, his lip started to curl. He raised his finger at Kristin, and suddenly, unexpectedly, jabbed it between her eyes.

'Dave!' she cried.

Dave the head barman looked up from the end of the room and motioned to the bouncers. Undeterred, the guy pressed his finger against her forehead.

'Twat.'

Esh turned round.

She curled her fingers around his hand, gave it a little twist, and instantly he skewered to the floor.

The suddenness of her movement startled his friend into alertness. He gaped at his drunk friend on the floor, one arm raised absurdly in the air as Esh kept him down.

'If I let go of your friend,' she told him, 'he'll probably get up and start acting even more of an asshole than before. So I'm just going to let him cool off. Okay?'

The silent guy nodded, looking at Esh in admiration. She was taller than him, looking back at him with beautiful dark eyes.

'Everything all right?' Dave called anxiously, running over with the bouncers.

They stopped and looked at the guy on the floor.

'Yep,' said Kristin. 'Looks like we're fine.'

Dave didn't take any chances, and had the bigger two of the bouncers pick the guy up and pin his arms behind him.

With sudden surprising strength, the drunk guy struggled, loosening the bouncers' grip, and managed to take a quick swing at one of them before the third bouncer stepped in and punched him in the gut. All three of them pinned him down, and with the guy tussling between them, they led him through the bar as the crowd in Dusk Junkie's looked on. The bar was buzzing, music and voices mixing with the ads and video clips on the iBoards, suffusing everything with shafts of vibrant colours and glowing light. But the commotion was enough to attract everyone's attention.

The drunk guy's friend trailed behind him, still silent, and turned to take one last look at Esh before he too was chucked out unceremoniously onto Oxford Street.

'You okay?' Dave asked.

Esh shrugged, and gave him a nod.

'Fine.'

'Do you do martial arts?'

'No.'

'Are you sure?'

She'd floored a guy it had taken three of his bouncers to escort from the bar.

'Yes,' she said curiously. 'Why?'

Dave shook his head.

'I'll get you girls some drinks,' he said.

He walked off, and Esh resumed her place on her stool.

'Thanks, Esh,' Kristin told her.

She leaned over and kissed Esh's head. The two of

them turned to each other, belated nerves now making them grin.

'How do you do it, Esh?'

Esh shrugged again. She didn't know. She'd never used physical strength on anyone before, really. She'd just got off her stool the moment she saw the guy attacking Kristin and, without processing the situation, floored him.

'On the house,' Dave said.

He slid two freshly-made Mohitos across the counter. 'With apologies from the management.'

He left them, and returned to his paying customers.

Taking a breath, Esh and Kristin turned to each other and raised their glasses.

'The future,' said Kristin.

Esh smiled and clinked glasses.

'The future.'

She and Kristin had been at school together since they were four. Fifteen years later, it was a Saturday night in August, on the main drag of Oxford Street, and they were still each other's only friends.

From their very first day at Ford, they'd never been the gregarious, mixing-with-the-gang types. Withdrawn and uninterested in anyone, the two of them had gravitated towards each other and had never ventured any further.

Throughout their time at school the teachers had showed them off to the rest of their year as prodigies, driving Esh and Kristin further into their exclusive and private world. They might have been classroom freaks, but when it came to tests and exams Kristin and Esh outclassed everyone.

They'd started so differently.

Kristin's family had always had money, living in a four-storey house in Portman Square where Kristin had been born. Her dad was a lawyer. Her mum was a financier. Kristin's siblings went on to become City professionals, but Kristin still stood out, the more so because no one had really expected the young afterthought of the family to echo the success of her brothers and sisters. She could have gone to Ford whatever had happened, but she attended the school on as much merit as Esh.

The difference was that Esh had never been destined to go to Ford.

She took a sip of her Mohito and looked around. Dusk Junkie's was filling up slowly, the crowd gradually moving around her and Kristin as they sat on their own at the end of the bar. On the far side of the long room, the floor-to-ceiling iBoards glowed on the bar's walls, blaring with videos and ads. On one of the screens, Esh saw the boys from FMCG prancing around in the video for their new single, 'PollyGonnaRocka', a tie-in for the latest Sneaker Store campaign. She watched, stunned as ever by how mystifyingly crap the video was and how successfully FMCG sold their product. They'd been so perfectly styled to bring out the Sneaker Store endorsement, the entire video synched to enhance the 'Sneakers' motif.

'Jesus,' she sighed.

'FMCG?' Kristin asked without turning.

She knew that sigh.

Esh leaned forward to glance outside, idly surveying the busy crowd on Oxford Street. Shoppers, tourists, teenagers out for the night, all thronging through the street, weaving in and out of shops. Every now and then a couple of trams thundered by, street-guards momentarily stalling the steady stream of people to let them pass safely. The SkyBoards above shone so brightly it seemed as if they were only metres away. Orbiting in space, each SkyBoard stretched a hundred miles long and transmitted huge advertisements across the world, leaving narrow strips of night between one slab of brightness and the next. The giant mosaic of ads for Interface, Bank, Sneaker, Juice, and the rest of the endless roster of products and services that beckoned to the crowd below, moved above in a luminescent canopy, adding to the intensity of the iBoards and the building-size video-walls across the Sneaker Store and Khaki Company.

Esh turned her head slightly to take in the queue outside Dusk Junkie's, steadily trickling into the bar from behind the transparent iBoard that fronted the premises. The iBoard played a Japanese cartoon to the outside queue, casting red, green and yellow pools of light over everyone already inside.

'I'm hungry. Let's get some fries,' Kristin suggested.

She called over a barman, asked him to bring them a couple of bowls.

Esh sipped her Mohito.

Dad was a professor at Imperial, Mum taught physics at UCL. Education meant more to them than anything, but neither of them had ever made enough money to consider sending Esh to somewhere as exclusive as Ford.

She realised that, beneath their close bond, she'd always felt a bit sorry for them. She'd often found herself pitying them when she looked at the simplicity of their lives, and her own, compared to the other girls at Ford.

Only recently had she come to understand what Mum and Dad's financial humility really was. Deep down, they'd have loved to have money. They'd have loved to have sent her to Ford on their own earnings and given her everything she'd wanted. But in the end money just wasn't as important to them as their personal happiness, their careers. They lived for what they did. Even at the weekends they were always working in their studies, in the tiny terraced house in East Stratford they'd shared since their marriage.

So little seemed to have happened in their lives. They'd never gone anywhere. Every holiday Esh had ever been on, bar a stay in Normandy with Mum and Dad when she was two, had been with Kristin's family. They included Esh on their yearly trips without even thinking of asking Mum and Dad for a contribution. Or maybe they'd never had the heart to ask for money that probably wasn't there.

Esh remembered her parents and Kristin's parents meeting once and the guilty embarrassment she'd felt at her parents exuding their pious bookishness beside the glamour of Kristin's mum and dad.

From early on, Esh had always been treated as one of Kristin's family. Kristin's parents could see as well as Esh's that Kristin and Esh were an odd couple, but that was okay. Esh and Kristin made each other happy. They didn't squabble and lose their tempers like a lot of children did. They had a silent understanding through which they never infringed on each other's space, and Esh had quickly become a member of Kristin's family.

But inside herself, through her whole adolescence, Esh had never lost the feeling that she was different, not just in terms of intelligence and physical ability, but in terms of money. However much she hid behind Kristin's self-assurance, she felt constantly aware that she was the scholarship girl from East Stratford who'd come to join the ranks of Ford.

Mum and Dad both did jobs they loved, and had reached the top of their professions. But they'd never made wild financial successes of themselves, they'd never left their roots. They were modest, tidy people who praised Esh for doing so well at school. But Esh couldn't deny that their small lives depressed her, and sometimes made her feel as alienated at home as she did at school.

Kristin was the only one who didn't make her feel odd. Kristin was her bridge. Together, they kept each other safe inside a world that seemed to find no place in the world around them.

'Fries. Times two.'

The barman landed the bowls in front of them. Without giving Esh the chance to open her mouth, Kristin told the barman she'd pay, and transferred her Account details via the bar's Interface. Immediately, the price of the fries showed up in her EyeScreen and she confirmed the sale, triggering the debit to her Account.

'Thanks,' Esh whispered as Kristin slid one of the bowls over.

'Don't mention it.'

They sat eating their fries at the end of the bar, while the glowing space of Dusk Junkie's thrummed around them.

Esh had been scouted by Ford's special bursary

scheme at the age of four. When they found her at her local primary, they immediately gave her a scholarship. There was nothing she couldn't do. Gymnastics, running, swimming, volleyball, tennis, fencing. She did everything better, faster and with more poise than anyone else at Ford. She mastered everything she touched, there was no intellectual challenge she couldn't overcome, no sporting discipline she couldn't perfect. She was tall, strong, fit, lithe, and entirely in a class of her own.

She was becoming increasingly aware of her own alienation, though, and the more the world opened up around her and Kristin, the more keenly she felt their isolation within it. In nineteen years, they'd never been out with anyone. Partly it came from going to a girls' school and partly it came from being the two most academically pressured girls in the school. But it wasn't just that. It was the nature of their relationship, that magical exclusivity that kept them secure. On the rare occasion when they'd kissed a guy, they'd treated it as something drunken and prankish, a mishap that they'd probably never repeat. Life and school had pushed them hard, and Esh and Kristin had always been preternaturally advanced for their years. But they'd arrived at the age of nineteen almost completely innocent.

'Hey, cool it, buddy.'

A line of people was crowding round them, causing Kristin to dig a defensive elbow into the person right behind her, who'd leaned round to get to the bar.

'I'm trying to eat some fries,' she said.

Esh turned her head. The guy behind Kristin was cute, and Kristin would never know it. Esh exchanged a glance with him as she ran her hand around her wrist, feeling a bruise coming up after pinning the drunk to the floor. She gave the guy a smile, and turned sheepishly to the bar.

Things were about to change. They'd soon be starting their jobs, and life was waiting for them with all the rewards they had worked to achieve. This was what school had been about. Sitting the FTDs in May, obtaining their results, and getting those jobs at the Corporation Bank.

The Fast-Track Diploma results had been posted at the end of July, published to attract future employers. This was Esh and Kristin's final chance to shine. It was the moment Ford had prepared them for. Just getting a place on the FTD had meant sitting a series of exams so stringent that most candidates failed. But out of the two hundred most exceptional candidates in the country, in the nationwide FTD league, Kristin had come second, and Esh first.

Just like that, they'd suddenly become the brightest prospects in the country. Within hours of the results coming out, they both received a call from Julie Trebeck at the Corporation Bank telling them that they'd been placed at the head of the Bank's graduate fast-stream programme. It was an unspoken Bank tradition: snatching up the top five performers in the FTDs every year. As a signing bonus, they would each be bought a residence in the centre of London, paid for by the Bank. The rest of their pay package read like a long menu of gourmet extras: a car of the graduate's choice, medical cover in one of the Corporation's clinics, guaranteed retirement bonus, a holiday home after ten years, full school fees for children, two twelve-month maternity-leave entitlements, and all of this beyond the basic pay package of the Corporation Bank, which no one in the world could match.

For the next thirty or forty years, Esh would have to work out of her skin for the largest financial institution on the planet. But she would earn a salary so far beyond anything Mum and Dad had earned, she'd be able to change their lives instantly. It made her as proud as it did embarrassed.

Yet now that she was here, somehow it seemed almost too easy. Perhaps it was just a side effect of it all being over, but everything had gone so smoothly Esh felt as though it had all passed in a dream, as if she'd barely had to try.

She peered wistfully into the rippled surface of her Mohito, watching it catch the spot lamps behind the bar.

She and Kristin had come such a long way. Everything lay ahead of them. Bar perhaps a couple of boyfriends. Was that what was missing? She couldn't put her finger on it, but she felt adrift, like a balloon someone had let go into the sky.

Kristin licked her fingers as she finished her chips. She pushed her bowl aside, ignoring everyone crowding round her at the bar, and calmly took a sip of Mohito. She could hardly hear herself think. The entire room was packed with people, loud with laughter and shouted conversation, the iBoards pumping out adverts and music along the wall. She touched her middle finger and thumb together as the bar squeezed in around her. The microchips in each fingertip connected, and Interface immediately appeared in her EyeScreen. She whispered a message, inaudible to the bar around her, but picked up by her internal Ear Mic, and sent it to Esh.

An instant later, Esh was in the middle of draining her cocktail as the message icon appeared in her EyeScreen. She touched her finger and thumb together to open it.

'*Get The Hell Out Of Here?*' Kristin's voice spoke through the tiny chip in her Ear.

Esh put down her cocktail, turned to Kristin, and laughed. They both stood up, chuckling, and snaked out of the ruck of people through Dusk Junkie's.

Before them, the long transparent iBoard outside the bar played a movie trailer. On the street, the Saturday hordes teemed past beneath the iBoards over every shop. Everything was speaking, flashing, moving. Esh and Kristin were young, free, and living in the most exciting city in the world.

The bouncers parted for them to come through.

'See you,' said one of them who'd picked the drunk guy off the floor.

The other bouncers grinned behind him.

'If you're ever looking for a job,' he told Esh, 'you know where to come?'

'Sure,' she smiled.

And she turned to walk with Kristin through the Saturday crowds.

The Khaki Girl

The air was warm, even at close to midnight. Thousands of people were streaming along the central pedestrian reservation, queuing at bars and restaurants, shifting in and out of the shops along the long tunnel of light that was Oxford Street, with its blazing iBoards and the light of the SkyBoards shining above them.

Esh saw the biggest iBoard on Oxford Street towering over the Saturday night crowds. It was the giant, transparent video-screen outside the seven-storey Sneaker Store, playing FMCG's video for 'PollyGonna-Rocka' fifty feet above the crowds.

'They're everywhere, Kristin.'

'What?'

'They're everywhere!' Esh shouted.

Kristin still didn't hear her. But it didn't matter. She'd heard it before. Esh found the four members of FMCG – George, Larry, Dirk, Dwight – the most cringe-making foursome on the face of the planet. Like a roll call of the world's best-loved consumer products – Juice, Heaven, Sneakers, Dream – they shifted more product in endorsement deals than any other media entity in the world. And they didn't even exist.

They were Digital Animates, computer-enhanced images designed to look like real human beings, and when you saw them turn up on the stage of the Music Awards or the Fall Oscars, or in a live television interview promoting their new single, or goofing around in the 'Making Of' for their new video, the thrill and fascination of watching came from knowing precisely that they weren't there. Never had four guys bereft of flesh and blood been so globally adored.

'PollyGonnaRocka' still boomed out from the giant iBoard over the Sneaker Store, drowning out the rest of the noise on Oxford Street.

'Jesus,' said Kristin, pointing at the iBoard. 'These guys are everywhere.'

'I know!' Esh shouted.

'You know something?' said Kristin. 'I think I fancy Dirk.'

He was the dark dreamboat, the one almost every girl fancied.

'He doesn't exist, Kristin.'

Kristin shrugged. Who cared?

She looked up at the iBoard, and it immediately connected with Interface. Every minuscule movement made by her eyeball constantly transmitted to NetSync through the EyeScreen Projection Chip in her retina. NetSync knew exactly where she was, and what she was looking at. As soon as she'd glanced at the SkyBoard, Interface had sent the ad to her Ear and EyeScreen: *'Sneakers In Your Size 34 – Featured In "PollyGonna-Rocka" – Are Waiting In Store For You Now'* said a wheedling voice in her Ear.

'What do you think of these Sneakers?' Kristin asked, pointing at the iBoard. Esh looked up, and the same ad connected to her own Interface, showing a thumbnail image of the Sneakers in her internal EyeScreen.

'*Esh – We Have Sneakers In Your Size 38 Waiting In Store. Say "PollyGonnaRocka" To Buy Now.*'

'I think they're crap,' said Esh.

Kristin instantly touched her finger and thumb together and whispered ' "PollyGonnaRocka". Home Delivery.'

'You bought them?' Esh guessed.

'Two pairs,' Kristin told her.

Esh shook her head. She'd never understood why Kristin bothered asking before she went ahead and bought something anyway.

Just a couple of blocks ahead, she caught sight of the second biggest iBoard on Oxford Street. It was the enormous video-wall outside the six-floor emporium of the Khaki Company, and on the screen was the Khaki Girl, the company's global face, looking laid-back, pure, and ineffably cool.

'Hey, your heroine,' Kristin joked, pointing out the iBoard.

'Not funny, Kristin.'

The Khaki Girl bent down to scratch her knee on the forty-foot video screen. She looked completely unaware of looming so majestically above Oxford Street, a twenty-two-year-old American girl who appeared at movie premieres, went to launch parties, and never got into trouble. The ethereal, beautiful Khaki Girl, the embodiment of Khaki purity, was compellingly, alluringly real: it was her very reality which made the story of the previous Khaki Girl so tragic.

Twelve months ago, clandestine footage of the Khaki Girl jacking up heroin on a marble bathroom floor had suddenly shown up on the Net, on iBoards, even on SkyBoards. The image of her injecting herself, one pale leg stretched out in front of her, the other bent underneath her, had stayed in people's memories for a long time. However hard the Khaki Company fought to contain the story, millions of people accessed the illegal images which someone had recorded and posted on the Net.

They were called 'iVerts'. No one knew who created them. No one knew who had the ability to infiltrate them onto the SkyBoards. Somewhere out there, some gang of uncatchable pranksters were sending out shocking images in the middle of genuine ad broadcasts, and the authorities had never been able to find them. The iVerts kept coming. They flashed up so quickly people were left wondering whether what they'd seen was real. But in the case of the Khaki Girl, the footage had been all too genuine.

A month later, she was dead. Every time Esh saw the new Khaki Girl on an iBoard or a SkyBoard now, she felt a shiver. They'd been almost the same age, their lives ahead of them. And then suddenly the Khaki Girl's was over.

'I want to go into the Khaki Company.'

Kristin started leading Esh towards the store.

'Kristin, it's ten to one in the morning.'

'I know. But I need some jeans.'

'Now?'

'Yes.'

Kristin dragged her on one of her stubborn shopping missions. For a girl who didn't really care what she looked like, Kristin certainly loved shopping. Esh sighed, and looked around the glowing shopfronts. Everything was made of light. Above them, a sea of luminous SkyBoards floated across the night.

In the zenith of the sky, she spotted Marcus: the global face of Interface, a Digital Animate like FMCG. Every time she saw him, she sensed a quality of authenticity about him that she couldn't explain. He didn't seem artificial to her, but utterly real. If Kristin thought she fancied Dirk, then Esh, secretly, had always fancied Marcus. It had only been a few years ago that she'd finally managed to convince herself that he was simply an amalgamation of data, just a patchwork of polygons and skin-tones.

He was beautiful, though. He seemed to be a living, thinking being in his own right, a little kooky, a little naive, unselfconscious, unafraid of being out of the ordinary.

In that instant, the sound of his voice spoke in her Ear.

'*Let's Go Places You've Never Been,*' he said.

It felt as if he were looking straight at her, speaking to her alone, and she had to quickly remind herself that he wasn't real.

'Hey, Esh,' he said. '*You Want To Upgrade To Interface 9.9?*'

A text version of his speech scrolled across her EyeScreen as an ad for the upgrade appeared in the vision projected onto her retina.

She touched her finger and thumb together.

'*Fade,*' she said, making the ad instantly dissolve.

'Esh, get your eyes off Marcus for a second.'

Kristin had caught her in flagrante, but decided to spare Esh further humiliation as she led her into the Khaki Store.

All around, Khaki ads began arriving through Interface in Esh's EyeScreen. But until she started earning her salary at the Bank in a month, she could afford nothing.

'*Esh! Update The Pair Of Khakis You Bought In January With A 10 per cent Discount If You Buy In Store Now. Or Choose Home-Delivery By Saying "Khaki" Now.*'

Esh ignored it, and followed Kristin to the jeans section. They weaved through scores of people to the rail, where Kristin quickly pulled out three different styles and took them to the changing room. Esh sat down as Kristin tried them on.

'What do you think?'

'They're good,' Esh responded.

She glanced at the jeans. Immediately an ad popped into her Interface.

'*Esh – Get These In Size 10 In Store Now.*'

'*Fade,*' Esh whispered, touching finger and thumb.

'Okay,' said Kristin. 'I'm taking them.'

'Which?'

Kristin held them in her hand.

'All of them.'

Despite her yen for shopping at one in the morning, Kristin was mercifully quick about it. They traipsed to the payment Interface, Kristin bought the jeans, and they resurfaced onto the iridescent lightscape of Oxford Street.

They turned towards Kristin's house through the seething mass of shoppers. As they walked, data constantly appeared in Esh's EyeScreen. The barrage of information annoyed a lot of people, but Esh had always loved it, ever since she was a kid. She felt a cerebral rush at the information coursing into her vision, constantly updating itself on EyeScreen: the time, the news, temperature, her location. It was a buzz, the world experienced through Interface, everything responding as soon as she set eyes on it. Everything about her – her position, her sightline – was being constantly logged onto the Net through Interface.

She looked up at the sky, feeling the thrill of being alive and happy. She linked arms with Kristin, and thought what a good place London was to be, as she gazed at the giant moving parade of SkyBoards.

'Things are cool, aren't they?' she said.

'They are,' Kristin replied.

Esh's eye wandered automatically to Marcus's face in the Interface ad. He wasn't real. But she couldn't help it. He looked so good.

Suddenly, his face flickered. His features morphed into the face of the Devil, his teeth stretching, horns popping from his skull, hair turning to flesh, and eyes drawing into sinister slits.

A headline flashed above his head.

'*Fucking Satan Boy!*'

Esh shook Kristin.

'Quick. iVert.'

She pointed.

'Where?'

Kristin looked up, but it was too late. The iVert had gone.

'I can't believe it.'

'What happened?'

'They turned Marcus into the Devil and called him "Fucking Satan Boy".'

Kristin burst out laughing.

'Jesus.'

'I know!'

No one else on Oxford Street seemed to have noticed, all flocking through the central pedestrian reservation beneath the light of the SkyBoards.

Targeting Marcus meant the iVert creators were going after big game. Nothing could match the sight of the Khaki Girl shooting up heroin on a bathroom floor, but calling Marcus 'Fucking Satan Boy' was a coup.

'Was it cool?'

'Incredible,' Esh said.

They walked through the crowd, arm in arm, searching the sky for another iVert. But none appeared, and Esh watched the screen featuring Marcus's face as it floated to the horizon, and towards the States.

23

Second

Esh opened her eyes, and touched her finger and thumb together. Interface booted up in EyeScreen. 09:39. No messages.

She got out of bed and walked down the corridor to look in on Kristin.

Kristin lay dead to the world, as lifeless as a mummy.

Esh went to the kitchen, and fixed some tea. Next door, she heard Kristin's parents sitting in the drawing room, talking and reading the Sunday papers.

She stood by the big window in the kitchen looking out over Portman Square. The day was beautiful, the sky crisp and bright, shining behind the transparent SkyBoards and making their broadcasts meld softly into the blue.

She sipped her tea and thought about going home. She hadn't seen Mum and Dad all week. Kristin would stay in bed at least another couple of hours, and she felt too energetic to hang around. So she had a shower and decided to go home, leaving a message on Interface for when Kristin woke up.

Gone Back To Stratford. See You Later.

She called 'bye' to Kristin's parents and stepped out into the sun. The air was cool. The silence of Sunday hung around her as if the world were populated by no one but herself.

Walking down to Oxford Street, it was almost unrecognisable. The multitudes had gone, and it was just her, a few service teams cleaning the street from last night and a scattering of early Sunday shoppers.

Her tram appeared along the street and she stepped inside the empty carriage. Interface told her that it had deducted her fare as she sat on one of the back seats and eased herself in for the journey. She brought up her Music and Movie files and looked through them on EyeScreen. But it was too beautiful outside to watch films.

Out of the West End, the tram rose over the ground on its monorail and passed by her old school in the City. She saw the Ford clock tower jut out from the streets. Suddenly, she experienced a strange nostalgia. She'd only left a month ago, but already Ford felt as if it was becoming nothing more than a memory.

She'd never return to school. She'd left for ever now. Turning away, she saw the glass edifice of the Bank appear in the distance, vast, and gleaming in the morning sunlight as they rushed over the City streets.

Just then, a call came through on her Ear.

The caller's ID showed it was Julie Trebeck. Esh frowned slightly, glancing at the Bank's giant glass roof. Calling on a Sunday? She sighed, and touched her finger and thumb together, revealing Julie Trebeck's image in her EyeScreen.

'Esh.'

'Hi.'

'How are you?'

'Fine.'

Julie was acting disturbingly perky.

'Is everything okay?' Esh asked quickly.

Julie simpered, and scuttled round her desk.

'Er, well,' she said, and Esh's stomach sank. 'We've had some bad news.'

Esh sat up: Mum and Dad? Immediately, she realised how crazy that was. Why would Julie Trebeck have been calling about Mum and Dad?

'We've just set a major reshuffle in motion,' Julie said. 'It's been cooking in the States for months apparently, but we've only just been told. You're practically the first person to hear this. We're having to cut the fast-stream. I know this is going to be a huge disappointment, but it's come all the way from the top. It's just the aggressive nature of the market. You're an outstanding candidate, Esh. I'm going to give you a personal reference, you'll get another job, you don't need to worry. But we're not going to be able to take you in September. I'm sorry.'

Below her, on the right, the Thames sped past as Esh groped for words.

'I don't believe it,' she said finally.

The morning was too bright suddenly, the light glaring off the windows.

'I know,' said Julie. 'Things like this happen. It goes company-wide. We're forced to nip and tuck, and the fast-stream are the first to go.'

'You're cutting the fast-stream?'

'Well,' said Julie. 'We're skimming from the top.'

Esh stared past her EyeScreen at the river, forgetting Julie was there.

'Who else are you losing?'

She watched the bridges passing.

'No one,' Julie Trebeck answered. 'Just you.'

Esh couldn't gather her thoughts. Her entire being refused to believe what had happened. In just an instant, a single phone call had taken away everything. The dream of a new life, a home in the city.

She no longer had a job.

She'd been so sure of her life. In that moment she realised how much she'd never even questioned her future. It had all been laid out in detail, the most certain thing in her life. And suddenly it was gone.

What was she meant to do?

A sudden restructure in the Bank. They'd skimmed the graduate intake. But no. They'd only skimmed her.

She touched her finger and thumb and called Kristin.

Kristin took ten seconds to answer.

'Esh.'

She sat up in bed, looking into the iCam on the wall across her room.

'Where are you?'

'On my way home.'

'Oh yeah. Your message is here.'

Kristin rubbed her eyes.

'What are you up to?'

'I just got a call from Julie Trebeck.'

'How come?'

'I've just lost my job at the Bank.'

Kristin suddenly woke up.

'I don't understand.'

'They've done some kind of reshuffle.'

'You sure?'

'Yes.'

'Shit,' Kristin said. 'They're getting rid of us.'

'No, Kristin. It's just me.'

Kristin stared at her through the iCam.

'This isn't right, Esh.'

'I know. Listen, I've got to go.'

'Are you okay?'

'I'll call you later.'

Esh pressed her finger and thumb together and ended the call.

It felt as if everything in her life had suddenly turned unreal.

In East Stratford, she got off the tram. Walking out of the station, she felt weightless and leaden at the same time, following the streets and turning the corners without thinking or looking up.

What happened next?

She reached the beginning of her road, and began the walk home, moving unconsciously past the line of cars along the pavement.

The street was silent. Everyone was tucked inside.

She felt the same sensation she'd always felt here. Living in East Stratford was like existing in an in-between world, far from real life. The Bank had been her chance to escape. But no longer.

She noticed a car parked on the street that she'd never seen before. She stopped to look at it. It was parked just outside her house.

A long black limo, bodywork glinting in the sunshine. Esh saw her own reflection curved in its tinted black window.

She bent down and moved near the glass, but couldn't make out anything inside. Across the street, she saw Mr Vespucci gawking at her through the white net curtains of his front room. Esh gave the limo another look and turned to her front door, where Interface logged her in and opened it for her.

'Hi,' she called.

Nobody answered.

She walked to the kitchen, and noticed three coffee cups sitting on the kitchen table.

'Grandad?' she said, walking into the kitchen.

Sitting at the table with Mum and Dad was a woman with beautiful translucent green eyes. Her black suit spoke of elegance, sophistication, and wealth.

She rose up gracefully.

'Esh,' she said.

She put out her hand.

'My name is Estella.'

She was American. In her fifties, maybe, with a radiantly youthful glow.

'It's a pleasure to meet you.'

She held Esh's hand for a moment in her own smooth fingers.

'Is this about the Bank?' Esh asked with a flicker of hope.

Estella let go.

'Not entirely' she said, and looked into Esh's eyes, her expression bright, her body language relaxed.

'Something wrong?' Dad asked Esh.

He'd seen her face.

'I got a call from the Bank,' she replied, glancing sideways at Estella, uncomfortable about telling her parents in front of this stranger.

But she didn't need to.

'There was a last–minute recalibration in the Bank's hiring policy,' Estella cut in from behind.

Mum and Dad looked up.

'I don't understand,' said Mum.

'I've lost the job,' Esh told her.

Mum and Dad turned to meet Estella's open gaze.

'I was aware of the position the Bank had offered you,' she told Esh. 'You were their prime recruit, the most dazzling candidate in the FTDs. But they are no less prone to the vagaries of the market than anyone else.'

Her clear, green eyes glowed at Esh.

'I'm afraid that's why they lost you.'

'Who are you?' Esh demanded, abandoning any semblance of politeness.

Estella looked at her levelly.

'I'm from the Corporation.'

She stared at Esh, then glanced at the table.

'Shall we sit?'

Esh looked over at Mum and Dad, and remained standing. They didn't seem to know any more about this than she did.

She turned, to see Estella sitting casually at the table, crossing her long legs, her elegant presence almost unnatural in her parents' kitchen.

Sighing, Esh finally pulled out the last chair from the table.

'I've been dying to meet you, Esh,' Estella told her.

'We too have been watching you for a long time. The Bank were not the only agency on the planet to notice you. The Corporation has taken great interest in you.'

Estella fixed her eyes on her.

'I have an offer for you. The unexpected loss of your job at the Bank will prove to be a happy coincidence, I believe, as it allows me to make you this proposal.'

She spoke warmly and animatedly, hiding a layer of icy reserve Esh couldn't help sensing, the aura of someone absolutely sure of their place in the world.

'I'm well-acquainted with what a fast-stream position at the Bank can offer a young person like you,' Estella said. 'There are few careers more prestigious or rewarding. But I believe your career in the City would have limited you. You are a woman possessed of an exceeding appetite for discovery. You would have found yourself at the top of your profession all too soon, and I believe that would have frustrated you. Your extra-ordinary abilities mean that you need to continually surpass your boundaries. The Bank would not have nurtured that side of you. They'd have paid you, and demanded great things of you. But in the end you would have been nothing more than their servant. I believe you are destined for something far more important.'

She sat forward.

'There is a product the Corporation has had in development, secretly, for a long time, Esh. Something that has the power to change the world, and which requires a very special kind of campaign to launch it. We have looked long and hard to find the right person for that campaign. But we believe we have finally found her.'

'What is it?' Esh asked.

'I can't tell you,' Estella replied. 'The nature of the product demands an exceptional level of secrecy until it is launched, something we wish to happen as soon as possible. I am able to make you an offer on no more than financial incentive, though I can guarantee you one thing. If you become the face of our product, you will take part in the most exciting and important technological event of our time. We are not advertising perfume or hair-dye. What we are offering you is the chance to participate in the most significant product launch of our time.'

Estella looked at Esh with her clear, green eyes, and Esh could suddenly see how important this moment was, how long Estella had waited for it.

'Why me?'

'There's no one else like you, Esh. We have looked for a long time for all the things you possess. We needed somebody who displayed every gift nature could have bestowed on them, someone who stood head and shoulders above their contemporaries. We have studied you and observed you, and you are that person.'

'What would you need me to do?'

The corners of Estella's mouth turned delicately upwards.

'We wish to use your image to advertise our product. You would be given a residence in LA where you would shoot the campaign, and long-term we would need you to travel the world to promote the product, with a home in any territory you visited in order to provide you with as normal a life as possible.'

An emotion blossomed in Esh, familiar, like the excitement of working at the Bank.

'How long would you need me?'

'Seven years. Beyond that time we are unable to plan the product's marketing. But seven years would guarantee us your services for the campaign's important first phases. After that time, your contract would be negotiable. Depending on our mutual wishes, you could stay or go.'

'I'd be free?'

Estella smiled, and nodded.

'The value of what we are offering you is not merely commercial. The significance of the product is universal. This is an incomparable opportunity, one which would allow you to see things and visit places you may never have otherwise experienced. You would have access to a life that you can barely imagine now, and you would be involved in one of the most important social events ever staged. You are the only person whom we wish to act as the face of this campaign, and your fee is intended to reflect that fact.'

Estella looked at Esh for a moment, then turned to Mum and Dad behind her, as though asking their permission. When she turned to Esh, she told her what the Corporation had decided to pay her.

As her words rang, a small tremor passed through the little group, barely noticeable, and Esh, Mum, and Dad sat back.

'Your homes would be supplementary perks,' Estella continued. 'As would be a number of items. You would have a jet at your permanent disposal.'

Esh couldn't say anything.

'You'll need to think about this,' said Estella. 'There is a certain time factor, as we would need to know by the end of the week. But you should be given a chance to think this over properly.'

Estella looked into Esh's eyes.

'I'm going to give you the details of our lawyers in London.'

Immediately, a contact icon appeared in Esh's Interface, carrying the logo of a City law firm and the name 'Ilana Johnson'. The image hovered in Esh's EyeScreen, then filed itself away in her address book.

'Call them with any questions,' Estella said. 'And, when you're ready with your decision, we'll be waiting.'

Grandad

'Kristin, what do you think?'

Esh could see Kristin making coffee in her kitchen, awake now, and moving around in her usual, sparky time signature. She sat on the kitchen table and faced the iCam.

'I think it's the craziest thing I've ever heard.'

'But it's incredible.'

'What are your options?'

'I could say no.'

'And then?'

'Find another job in the City.'

'Which appeals how much?'

Esh was silent.

'Not as much as doing this.'

'What do they want you to do?'

'Go to LA and shoot an ad campaign.'

'For?'

'We don't know.'

Kristin took a sip of coffee.

'What if it's for cat pie?'

'Cat pie?'

'It could be anything, Esh.'

She knew that. It was a risk.

'I think their budget probably extends beyond cat pie.'

'It does sound like something huge. You know you'd be famous.'

It was the one part Esh hadn't managed to compute. Being famous. All she could imagine was having a house in LA.

'Do you definitely get out after seven years?'

'Yes.'

'Then you're rich for the rest of your life?'

'Yes.'

Kristin sipped her coffee, staring into the distance.

'So you'll be twenty-six, free, and you'll have all the money you could possibly need?'

Esh thought about it for a moment.

'Yes.'

Kristin nodded, and took another sip of coffee.

'I don't know, Esh. You're going to have to point out the catch to me.'

Mum and Dad seemed more rattled by the offer than she could readily understand. Were they just concerned about her future? She wondered whether it wasn't to do with the amount of money being offered, because she knew that to them this money was obscene. It didn't fit into their world; it was almost wrong for one person to have so much.

'You have to think about what you really want,' said Dad.

'What do you mean?'

'That money comes at a price, Esh.'

'What price?'

Dad looked down at the table.

'They'll want their money's worth,' he said.

'As would the Bank,' Esh reminded him.

'Yes,' said Dad. 'But this is just that much more, isn't it?'

Esh didn't speak. He was right. This was many orders of magnitude more. But didn't Dad see that was the point? The Corporation dealt in a world of proportions unthinkable to anyone else.

'Mum?'

Mum tried hard to conceal her disapproval.

'You have to do what you want,' she answered.

'Yes, I know.'

'But I think you're taking a risk.'

This was so frustrating. All Mum and Dad did was point out the obvious. How could they manage to look so miserable right now? This money would change their lives. They could have anything they'd ever wished for.

'It's too much,' said Mum, shaking her head. 'I just worry.'

She peered at Esh across the table.

'Think hard,' she said.

Esh held back her thoughts, and didn't say anything more.

Esh turned right at the end of the street, at the third turning took the left for Grandad's house. Outside his door, Interface asked whether she'd like to make herself known. She put her finger and thumb together and whispered 'Yes.'

Grandad opened the door to her, smiling.

'Esh.'

He closed her in his arms.

'How are you?'

'I'm great.'

'How's Mum?'

Since Grandma had passed away nearly eight years ago, Mum and Grandad had never really got on. Grandad had gone into a state of near-silent shock after Grandma's death, and Esh had effectively acted as the go-between between him and Mum. Throughout that time Mum had never showed him much sympathy, even though he seemed lost, barely able to communicate without Grandma. Esh hated seeing him like that. He'd been so energetic, playful, affectionate. And then he went cold, as if he'd died on his feet, but Mum still shut him out. Esh had never managed to understand, not even when Mum complained that this proved how much Grandad's world had always revolved around Grandma, and had never included her. Grandad had been a terrible brute of a father, she said. Esh could see how fit, tall and strong he still was, but if he'd been brutal, it must have disappeared by the time she'd been born.

'She's fine, Grandad.'

He led her into the house. The house where Mum had grown up.

'How's Kristin?' he asked, walking towards the kitchen.

'Really well.'

Grandad turned to sit at the kitchen table. The kitchen overlooked the garden, just as it did in Mum and Dad's house. All the houses in the area were the same, identical but for the fact that they faced in different directions.

'Something's happened?' he said.

'How do you know?'

'I have eyes, Esh.'

He looked at her.

'Sit,' he said, pulling out a chair. 'And tell me.'

Esh sat down, looked at the floor for a few moments, and then told Grandad everything as he listened in perfect silence.

'What do you want to do?' he asked.

'I don't know what I should do.'

'What would you *like* to do?'

Esh looked up at him.

'You're scared, aren't you?' he said.

'It's such a big deal.'

'Of course it is.'

He eyed her.

'So what are you afraid of?'

'Of my life changing. Of doing something new.'

He gazed at her, and nodded.

'Listen,' he said. 'I want you to know something.'

He cleared his throat.

'When Grandma died, I felt as if my life had ended. Time stopped for me. I was completely numb, and then I was completely afraid. I was scared to be alive. I knew Mum never forgave me for how I'd been, but I had to make a choice, and it was very simple in the end. I asked myself whether I wanted to live.'

Esh watched the firm, strong lines of his face move as he spoke.

'Some decisions you can only make for yourself. With

the big decisions, it doesn't matter what anyone thinks. That's precisely why they're so hard. You have to discover what you want. And once you've done that, Esh, the decision becomes the simplest thing in the world.'

Grandad put his hand on her shoulder.

'I know you're scared, Esh. But you have nothing to be afraid of.'

She left his house, walked instinctively to the nearby park where she'd jogged almost every night of her adolescence.

There were plenty of people out in the sunshine, walking round the lake, having picnics on the grass. But Esh hardly noticed them, her mind racing towards LA. She could no longer stop the wheels in her brain turning, imagining what it would be like to be in California, to have her own house.

The path of her life had been so sure. Until that morning, when the Bank had changed everything, she'd never had to make a decision.

She could look for another job in the City, run the risk of finding something that equated to what the Bank had offered. But then she'd never know how the Corporation's offer would have panned out.

Going to LA, travelling around the world, meant living far from Mum, Dad, Kristin and Grandad. But she'd have enough money to see them whenever she chose, free to do anything she wanted.

If she stayed in London and followed the path that had been set out for her, she'd spend the rest of her life wondering what could have been. All she could keep thinking about now were the unexpected horizons, the endless possibilities, that the Corporation's offer might give her.

She had just this one chance. And with all the timidity that she felt in her heart, she still knew that she was dying to take it.

'Okay, Esh.'

Mum looked tenderly at her.

'I respect your decision.'

She meant it, Esh could tell. They were letting her do it, and suddenly their consent felt terrifying, because she had only her own will to stop her.

'Am I doing the right thing?'

Mum and Dad gazed at her across the table.

'The only right thing is what you want, Esh,' Dad grinned.

Helplessly, Mum suddenly smiled too.

'It's going to be incredible, Esh. It'll be amazing.'

'Hello?'

'I need to speak to Ilana Johnson.'

The front-desk assistant's image melted from her Eye-Screen and was immediately replaced by the law firm's logo. As Esh waited to be transferred, her heart beat hard, and then all too soon a pretty woman with a dark fringe appeared in her EyeScreen.

'Ilana Johnson.'

'Hello, it's Esh.'

Such an obvious thing to say.

'Yes, I know,' Ilana replied, seeing Esh's Identity in her EyeScreen. 'Do you have your decision?'

Somehow, Esh had expected more formality, more

circumlocution before they reached the nub of the matter.

'Yes,' she said.

Ilana Johnson waited.

'May I know what it is?'

Esh stared into the iCam in her kitchen. Mum and Dad were upstairs, leaving her to do this alone. She fixed Ilana Johnson's image in her Eye.

'The answer's yes,' she said.

Ilana's expression didn't change.

'I'll send over a car,' she said. 'You'll need to come over for us to explain the contract. It'll take a few days. If you're free right now, the car can be with you in forty minutes.'

Esh had the car for a week. A black limo, just like the one Estella had arrived in. Each morning, it took her from home to Ilana Johnson's office, where a team of five lawyers was assigned to her to explain the contract, while the Corporation's lawyers sat across the table.

Esh made their job easy. She quickly grasped everything, but it still took days just to cover all the aspects of the contract. How was she going to be paid? When, and in what denominations? Her freedom and her rights. The rights of the Corporation.

Finally, it was just a matter of tying up loose ends, trawling through the contingencies that the contract set out in relation to any possible occurrence.

At its heart, the agreement was simple. For the next seven years Esh would be contracted to act as the exclusive face of an unnamed product which the Corporation sought to market worldwide. In return, she would be paid her fee on the day the product launched, in just over a month's time.

At the end of the contract came a ten-page list of supplementary items that she would receive as part of her signing fee. Cars. Homes. Clothing. Furnishing. Staff. Security. Transportation. Legal cover. Medical insurance. And, as promised, a private jet.

She signed the contract on the Thursday following Estella's visit. The Corporation told her that she would leave London for LA on the following Saturday morning, which meant she had two nights left. The limo, they said, could remain at her disposal.

'Where shall we go, Kristin?'

Kristin sat at home on her bed, thinking. And as Esh eyed her through the iCam, she suddenly knew exactly what Kristin was going to say.

'GRID.'

Stairwell

The limo stopped in the narrow streets behind Oxford Street, where delivery entrances backed onto bins of commercial waste and figures lurking in the darkness. There were no iBoards or illuminations, just the light of the SkyBoards above. The limo left them at the end of the alleyway, as far as it was able to take them.

The limo's courtesy logo appeared in Esh's EyeScreen. *'Estimated Time Of Return?'*

Esh touched finger and thumb together.

'Three a.m.,' she said.

By the time they left GRID, they'd have no idea what the time was. But the limo would be waiting, whenever she sent out the message.

She climbed out of the car behind Kristin, and stood on the dark, deserted street. Closing the limo's door, she watched the car's red tail lights blink and it drove away, leaving them at the mouth of the alley.

Instinctively, they both went very quiet. They began walking along the alley, not seeing another soul, making them almost doubt that GRID was actually down here.

As they passed a long line of bins, Esh heard a rustle. She turned and glimpsed a huddle of five figures crouched in a doorway. She knew instantly that they were NAPs.

No Account Protocol.

She hated the term. It was the kind of cute government euphemism that specified 'Frontal Ballistic Trauma' to describe a bullet in the head. NAPs had no access to the Net, consequently neither to Accounts nor Money. When the Net had closed in, in a grand sweeping consolidation of Interface and the electronic transaction of Money, everyone had been registered on NetSync via the Identity implants in their Eyes and Ears. Paper money had been withdrawn from circulation, and the NAPs – homeless, unidentified, beyond government registration, living without electronic Eye or Ear Chips – had fallen outside the loop. They'd ceased to exist. They didn't have Identities, or Money, and didn't appear on any Net systems.

It was rare to see them in the centre of town, and she couldn't help watching with ghoulish intensity as they cowered between the bins. The police were notoriously efficient at moving NAPs out of view as soon as they were found. It was rumoured that they'd developed their own barter system by which they survived on the outside of the Net without electronic Money, through a sophisticated black market economy using people inside the Net who traded them food, water, medicine and supplies in return for illicit goods that NAPs had stolen from 'real people'. Everyone expected the NAPs to rob, maybe even kill you, just to extract the chip from your Ear and sell it on.

But those figures huddled in the doorway looked too pathetic to attack anyone. They didn't scare Esh. They were the ones who were scared, their frightened eyes following her as she and Kristin hurried past.

As they turned the kink in the alleyway, they saw GRID at last in front of them, its long queue stretching down to the club's entrance at the end of the alley.

'Did you see them?' Esh whispered.

Kristin nodded. 'They looked terrified,' she responded.

Joining the end of the queue, Esh felt a lingering sense of unease. She was flying to the States tomorrow morning. And the NAPs still lurked in the alleyway, with nowhere to go.

The owners of GRID could have put the entrance to their club anywhere in the West End, but instead they'd chosen the darkest, most inaccessible back-alley in London. It was probably part of its mystique, this back-water entrance to the most popular and expensive nightclub in the city. As Esh and Kristin waited patiently at the back of the queue they knew they could count on standing here at least fifty minutes before they were allowed in.

It would be worth it, though. GRID was unique.

The hospitality guy from the door walked along the queue, eyeing all the entrants, and stopped in front of Esh and Kristin.

His long sheepskin coat flounced down to his ankles, making him look even shorter than he already was. He pouted, clutching his arms together as if it were cold.

'You,' he said.

He pointed at them, his voice effeminately husky.

'What?' Kristin said, immediately bristling.

'I've been told to let you in. Follow me.'

The short man turned abruptly on his heels, and Esh and Kristin followed.

'Who called you?' Esh asked his retreating back.

The fronds of the guy's coat swished by his feet.

'The owner got a call to say you were coming.'

He led them to the entrance door, past the people in the queue gazing at them as they passed. They arrived at the club's entrance, and saw it set in its low arch in the alley's wall, no name or sign above it.

The bouncers parted, and Esh and Kristin stepped into the shaded entrance area, where they were waved past the payment Interface, towards the long journey down the staircase. Esh still didn't get it.

She and Kristin walked down the stairs to GRID's subterranean labyrinth. And then, at the last moment, a message came through on Interface, hovering on her EyeScreen, waiting to be opened.

She touched her finger and thumb together.

'*I Called Ahead To Get You Two In,*' read the message. '*Hope You Have A Good Night.*'

It was from Estella.

Esh closed the message. And then, without warning, Interface vanished.

GRID was the only place in town that could do it. The circuitry in its walls jammed Interface, severing the guests from the Net for the duration of their visit, so no one could make calls or transact Money, no one could trace their route round the club using a Net location system, or track down their friends. The entrance fee even bought customers a limitless bar tab, so that Money, for a night, meant nothing. It was a boundless labyrinth beyond the Net, a world without Identities.

The rooms of GRID were identical. They were all cube-shaped and connected to one another by a single doorway in each of the room's four walls. In the whole of the club, there wasn't a single room that didn't connect to another just like it, and inevitably it freaked people out. The GRID seemed endless. The further you travelled into its maze, the more trapped you felt by its symmetry. But eventually, you realised how the GRID organically shaped your night, led you wherever you happened to go, no directions to the loos, just a pure, simple puzzle.

They wandered through the club's caverns all night. They met a group of guys and got drunk with them, then went exploring, moving round GRID's identical rooms. And through it all, in the club's dayless world and with all the people they met, Esh kept thinking about LA.

Late in the night, Kristin said she was drunk.

'I want to go home, Esh.'

They wound their way on, into GRID's depth, and eventually ended up at the entrance. Esh stepped into the bright sunlight, watching Interface reappear in her Eye. She looked at the time. 07:23. 13 degrees C. Chilly in the morning sunshine.

Esh touched her finger and thumb to call the limo, but across the alley she noticed a tall, well-built man in a suit, with a bulky physique and tidily kept hair. An Interface message appeared in her Eye displaying his Identity.

'*Tony Dufranti: Corporation Security.*'

'Esh?' he said, coming over.

He was American.

'Yes?'

'I'll take you to your car.'

Esh was wary of him appearing out of nowhere. He was almost forty, with a responsible, military air behind the smart suit.

'Why should I trust you?' she said.

'I've been told by Estella to escort you.'

Esh looked around, seeing people emerge from GRID.

'Okay,' she said. 'I'll follow you.'

Keeping her arm round Kristin, she followed Tony Dufranti past the kink in the alley, and along the line of bins. Looking into the doorway they'd passed earlier that night, she saw that the NAPs were gone.

Her limo waited at the end of the alley, vapour trailing from its exhaust. The limo's logo appeared in her EyeScreen, authenticating the driver's Identity.

'Here,' said Tony Dufranti.

He opened the door for her and Kristin, and waited for them to get inside. Then he closed it, and climbed into the front with the driver. Behind the black partition hiding them, the back of the limo felt as dark as GRID.

'When are you leaving?' Kristin asked.

'In an hour.'

The two of them sat in silence, holding hands.

'I'm going to miss you.'

'Me too, Kristin.'

She squeezed Kristin's hand, as the leather seats creaked beneath them. Suddenly, the limo was slowing down, and pulling up outside the house in Portman Square.

'See you really soon, Kristin,' Esh said hopefully.

Kristin didn't reply. She reached over and hugged Esh. They gripped each other tight. Then Tony opened the door behind Kristin.

'Okay,' she said.

She kissed the tips of her fingers and pressed them to Esh's arm.

'See you soon.'

She climbed out and without turning moved towards her front door, Esh watching as she walked away.

Tony closed her door, and left Esh sitting in the quiet of the limo, alone.

The jet would leave at 08:45. Tony told her there'd be just enough time for her to freshen up and say goodbye to Mum and Dad, but not to pass via Grandad's on the way. They were running on too tight a schedule.

For the last time, Esh took a shower in her bathroom, and wrapped her towel around her before walking to her room to change. The Corporation had told her not to pack. Everything would be provided in LA.

Suddenly, she couldn't believe she was going.

The excitement she'd felt all week now turned to sadness. She didn't know when she'd be coming back. She looked at everything in her room, at the objects that had surrounded her forever, and she felt a longing and attachment to everything that she was leaving.

This was her room, and yet somehow it already didn't feel like hers any more, as though it was a part of her life that was over.

She gave it a last look, hair damp, and silently said goodbye, then left, and closed the door behind her.

*

She peeked through the glass panel in the front door.
The limo was waiting with a large, black SUV behind it.
She checked the time. 08:16.

Mum and Dad were in the kitchen, both holding cups
of tea. On the table, they'd left a third cup for her.

'Thanks,' she said, taking a sip.

She could feel their sadness, their awkwardness at not
knowing how to say goodbye.

'Your car waiting?' asked Mum.

Esh took another quick sip.

'Yes. I wanted to say bye to Grandad.'

'Is there not time?'

'They've said I have to go.'

A message arrived from Tony Dufranti.

'*Need To Leave In 2 Mins.*'

'We'll say bye to Grandad for you,' Dad told her.

He reached out and put his hand on her shoulder.

'Can't believe you're going,' he said.

He looked into her eyes.

'You're going to have a great time, you know?'

Suddenly a tear appeared in Dad's eyes. He pulled her
towards him, as if to hide it, and squeezed her.

'I'll be back soon, Dad.'

Dad held her, not saying anything. A second message
arrived from Tony.

'*Need To Leave Now.*'

'I've got to go, Dad.'

Dad relaxed his grip, and behind him Esh saw Mum
grinning, trying to control her emotion. She reached out,
and rested her palm on Esh's cheek, still hot from her
teacup.

51

'Let's go, shall we?'

She led Esh to the door. The three of them stood on the doorstep, looking out at the limo and the SUV. From the passenger door of the limo Tony stepped out and came towards her. Esh turned to Dad and Mum.

'Going to miss you so much, Esh,' Mum said.

She held her as if she would never let go. Esh felt strangely conscious of how much taller she was than Mum, how Mum had held her for years as a little girl, and now it was the other way round.

'I'll call you when I get there.'

Mum nodded her head in the crook of Esh's neck, and let go.

'Ready to go?' Tony asked.

Esh turned to the limo. Tony walked ahead of her and opened the back door, and as she ducked inside she turned to Mum and Dad, and saw them standing at the house with their arms round each other.

'What's in the car behind?' she asked Tony.

'Back-up,' he said, and closed her door.

He moved quickly to the back-up vehicle and climbed in, then the convoy immediately set off, driving rapidly down Esh's street, and turning the corner.

The SUV tailed them, never letting the gap of twenty yards between them grow. Esh watched the faint silhouettes of East Stratford passing through the misted glass. They sped along the main road out of London, presumably towards the airfield. Sitting alone in the darkness, she could feel the drama and intense security closing in.

What were they going to do in LA? What was the product? How long was she going to be living there?

A call came through on Interface without an ID. Estella? Ilana? She touched her finger and thumb together to answer.

'*Esh?*'

'Hello?'

'*They've got you.*'

It was an American voice, young, male, with no image.

'Who are you?' she said.

The limo swung round a corner.

'*We've watched you, Esh, for as long as the Corporation have watched.*'

He whispered in her Ear as if he were right beside her.

'Who is this?'

'*We want to help you.*'

The limo left the main road, Esh glanced out of the window, and saw that they were driving across the wide, open tarmac of an airstrip.

'*They screwed up your job at the Bank so they could get to you,*' the voice said.

'Who are you?'

'*Take care, Esh. Send my love to LA.*'

The limo pulled up beside a white private jet.

'Hello?' Esh said.

But no reply came from her Ear.

Tony and two other men in suits jumped from the SUV and came over to her door. Tony reached in to lead her out, but she ignored him, climbing out unassisted.

Who'd called her? How had he known about her job at the Bank?

She looked at the resplendent white jet. It looked so small compared with an airliner, so vast for one person.

'Let's go,' said Tony.

The two men behind him had equally imposing physiques. They followed her towards the jet, bunching around her. At the top of the jet's stairway stood a fourth man who looked just like them.

Tony followed her up the stairway, and she turned to look up before entering the plane, as if saying goodbye to English sky.

The SkyBoards blended with the daylit sky. Marcus, Interface, Larry, George, Dwight and Dirk were filling the heavens.

Tony and the two other guards came up behind her. She stepped into the jet, felt the crisp veil of air conditioning drape over her, and the four men in suits led her into the jet, closing the cabin door behind her.

II

The Creative
Pagoda

LA

'Good morning.'

Esh turned round.

A short, plump woman with black hair pulled into a bun stood in front of her, wearing a white dress.

'My name is Maria,' she said, with a light Hispanic accent.

'I'm Esh.'

'I know,' said Maria, smiling white teeth and looking at Esh with a pair of big, beautiful eyes. 'You're English?'

'Yes.'

Maria scanned her face.

'Would you like some breakfast?'

'I'm okay.'

'Not hungry?'

'I ate on the plane.'

Maria nodded.

'If you'd like coffee, yoghurt. Just let me know.'

Esh smiled in acknowledgment. Maria turned and walked across the entrance hall's floor, disappearing down one of the house's corridors.

*

Alone in the living room, Esh turned to the view, wandering past the armchairs and sofas in the room towards the giant window that circled the living room in a continuous arc. Beyond it lay a sanded wooden deck bordering a sparkling swimming pool, and just behind it a parapet running the length of the house, shaded by a line of tall trees concealing the house from view. On the other side of the trees, a sheer wall dropped a hundred feet down the hillface on which the house and grounds perched.

She glimpsed LA in the distance, through the tiny gaps in the trees, shimmering far below like a mirage.

The living room reminded her of the inside of the jet, everything simple, pale, and sparse. A wide staircase circled in the middle of the room, through which Esh could see the hallway down which Maria had disappeared.

It had taken a full half-minute to reach the house along a sweeping drive. Esh had looked through the car's tinted windows as they drove through the grounds and had seen a garden filled with trees, a vast lawn rising either side of them with sprinklers watering the grass.

They'd entered the complex of mansions through an enormous pair of steel gates on the highway. Along the compound's private inner road, she hadn't been able to see any of the other mansions. They were all hidden behind individual gates, and the high red wall that circled the entire compound. Sitting in the back of the SUV and gazing out, she'd hardly believed she was in California, surrounded by the four men in her security team whom she'd been introduced to on the jet: Tony, Mikey, Clive, and André.

In front of her, she saw the house rise up over the lip of the lawn. She gawped at it through the SUV's windscreen. A shining, pale object trapped in the green of the garden, enclosed by the high red walls, windows glinting in the morning light, across two enormous floors of glass and steel.

'Whose is that?' she asked.

Tony Dufranti turned to her and smiled.

'Yours,' he said.

'Do you like it?'

She turned around again. This time, she saw a man standing in the entrance hall of her house with his hands in his pockets, smiling.

He looked as if he'd just stepped off a yacht. His hair dark, his clothes casual and sophisticated, looking in command of his surroundings.

'This is yours, Esh,' he said. 'Make any alterations you want. Redecorate it. Re-landscape the garden. Take out the pool. Do whatever you want.'

Esh glanced at the high interior of the room.

'It must feel strange to you.'

'Yes,' she replied.

'It'll take time,' the man told her.

He was good-looking, smooth, dark skin, and surprisingly blue eyes.

'I'm Heavey.'

He smiled.

'I'm the campaign director. We've been waiting all week for you. While you were signing in London, we were here, starting work, hoping you'd make it.'

Esh tried to smile back, but didn't know what to say.

'Have a good flight?' he asked.

'Yes.'

'Good.' Heavey smiled.

He took his hands from his pockets.

'Come on. We'll get Maria to bring us some coffee.'

'Thank you, Maria,' said Heavey.

She left them, and walked back into the house. It was warm as they sat under a parasol beside the pool. Esh looked in EyeScreen. 21 degrees C, it said.

'Maria doesn't usually do this,' Heavey said. 'It's just that the other staff haven't arrived.'

'Other staff?'

'Felipe, Miguel and Fontàn,' Heavey said. 'Your gardeners. They arrive at eight, just before Isabèl and Manuela, who come at half-eight to clean the house. Maria briefs them on their duties before discussing the day with Mano. He's your chef, and he gets in at half-seven. If there's anything you ever require just tell Maria. We'll be letting you know on a daily basis when and where you're needed. But for personal stuff like the kind of food you want in the refrigerator or what kind of flowers you'd like around the house, just let Maria know. That's what she's there for.'

Esh listened to the near silence of the garden and the grounds, the quiet private road outside her gates.

'Who lives around here?' she asked.

'In the compound?'

Esh nodded, and took a sip of coffee.

'Stars of the major campaigns.'

'Anyone I'd know?'

Heavey peered at her.

'Everyone you'd know.'

He looked at her with a reserved smile, signalling that they'd reached the end of the conversation.

'Where do the staff live?'

'We have a unit for them,' Heavey responded. 'Outside the compound. Maria's the only one who lives here with you. She has her own quarters in the house. After nine o'clock, though, you won't see her. You'll be free to enjoy your privacy.'

Heavey smiled, and picked up his coffee cup.

'Can I ask something?'

'Of course.'

'Why all the bodyguards?'

Heavey found the question quaint.

'It's just standard for our principals. A lot of money has been invested in you. It's only natural to want to protect that investment.'

He shrugged it off.

'Where do you live?' Esh asked.

'Not far,' he said, gesturing beyond the trees. 'The Hollywood Hills.'

Esh turned to look. Through the trees, down the side of the hill, there was nothing at the bottom of the drop but a no-man's land of scrub, rendering the house practically unassailable.

'And where will I work?' she asked.

She turned to Heavey, and saw him already smiling.

'Nowhere,' he said. 'We've built it all next door.'

He walked her down to a steel-plated door in the middle of the garden's ten-metre high wall. As they reached it,

Esh noticed an iScan inset discreetly in the doorplate. Heavey turned to her.

'I'm the only person apart from you who can enter your garden. Other than us, no one comes through this door.'

He looked for approval in her eyes, and then turned to the iScan. The door opened with a click, and Heavey pushed it back.

They stepped into a large shaded courtyard, far bigger than anything Esh could have expected to find behind this nondescript door in her wall. Wide swathes of sunlight criss-crossed in front of them around a group of small buildings, each no bigger than a cottage, connected by a network of paths.

'This is the Creative Pagoda,' Heavey said.

Above them, a strange, transparent roof covered the buildings. Esh tilted her head, and watched it change colour, like the surface of soap bubbles.

'We can't be seen from the sky,' Heavey said when he saw how intrigued she was. 'We're effectively invisible.'

She looked up, angling her head to watch the strange chromatic changes.

'Come on.'

Heavey led her along the path through the cluster of buildings.

'Where are we?'

'This is where we make the campaign.'

A giant glass building appeared in front of them. People were working inside beneath a long gallery over the main open space above which dozens of screens broadcast TV channels.

A door slid open as they approached.

'This is the Hub,' Heavey said.

There was an intense hush of concentrated murmurs and whispers inside. Heavey directed her towards the staircase leading to the gallery above the room. Walking a little way along the gallery, Esh watched the groups of people working below, before Heavey led her into a room constructed of glass on their left.

She pushed the door shut behind them, and saw Heavey take a seat by the transparent wall, on one of two sofas in the room.

'Have a seat,' he said.

He crossed his legs, reached his arms back across the sofa. As he gazed at the Hub, Esh took a seat and turned to look with him.

'This is where it all happens,' he said.

Some way along the gallery, a group of people were having a meeting in another conference room.

'This is the crew,' Heavey said, waving a hand. 'Everyone who works on the campaign.' She watched the colony of people living next door to her house. 'Everyone gets driven here in the morning. They're all security-cleared, since we bring them in every day.'

'No one lives in the compound?'

'Just you,' Heavey replied.

There must have been thirty people or more working in the Hub. They all looked young, dynamic, focusing on their tasks in the transparent building.

'You don't have to go anywhere,' Heavey said. 'We've constructed everything so we can minimise any risk to you.'

'What risk?'

The room felt quiet, as if the Hub wasn't even there.

'When the campaign starts,' Heavey said, 'you're going to get very famous. In one night, you'll go from sitting there unknown to being globally recognised. It's impossible for you to imagine what that will be like.'

Esh gazed into the Hub and tried to picture it.

'You'll never walk down a street without a crowd following you. You'll never appear in a public space without a group of people gathering around you. People will stare at you, Esh, not because they're rude, but because you'll be an exhibit to them, a creature none of them has ever seen, someone they won't even believe they're catching in real life.'

Esh peeked at the crew moving round the building like ants.

'The campaign launches in three weeks,' Heavey said. 'It'll run for seven days, until we eventually unveil the product to the world.'

'What is it?' Esh asked.

Heavey was looking relaxed and smiling, sitting on the sofa with his arms outstretched. There was something quietly, unnervingly serious about him. Esh could sense the determination in him as he diplomatically ignored the question.

'After the campaign kicks off,' he said, 'you won't be able to step out into the world without André, Mikey, Tony or Clive accompanying you. They're ex-service, the best, and you'll be very safe in their hands. As long as one of them's with you, no harm will ever befall you. Our insurance even stipulates that one of them must be with you at all times for your protection.'

'How about when I take a bath?' Esh asked ironically.

Heavey peered at her, and chose not to smile.

'Just when you step outside of this environment,' he responded.

He stared into the Hub, cogitating something.

'We've been very hard at work,' he told her, pointing at the crew. 'We have our airtime booked, our brand strategies in place. Everyone's been working around the clock to make this happen. We've been ready to launch at a moment's notice for many years, waiting for the appropriate individual to come along to front the campaign. And now we've found her.'

He stared proudly at the Hub, then turned to her.

'The people in the crew represent the top level of our global personnel,' he said. 'Worldwide, we have thousands of individuals working on the campaign, but the overview, the directives, come from here.'

Esh watched, captivated by the body of people moving beneath the myriad screens broadcasting in the room.

'In just under four weeks,' Heavey said, 'we'll have taken the planet from knowing nothing about the product to having it indelibly marked on their memories.'

Esh watched him looking intensely at his force of workers.

'And those thirty-four people are going to make it happen.'

He got up and led her to the window. Moving his index finger across the glass, he pointed out every member of the crew and told her their names, explaining each of their roles.

'There're two I'd like you to meet now,' he said. 'They're our senior creatives.'

Heavey accessed Interface in EyeScreen and made a call.

He walked back through the room and sat on the sofa. Almost instantly, a couple of young men came up from the Hub. They couldn't have been more than twenty–one apiece, charging up the stairs to the gallery.

'Gus and Nathan,' Heavey told her as they approached the door, omitting to specify which was which.

They walked in, dressed as formally as a pair of skate-boarders.

'Guys,' he said.

They stood looking at Esh, one fair, one dark.

'Someone I want you to meet.'

They looked vaguely at Esh, their expressions suddenly perking up.

'Esh!' said the fair one.

The one with dark hair was less impressed than his counterpart.

'This is her?' he shrugged.

'Yes,' Heavey nodded.

'Pretty normal-looking,' the dark guy concluded.

But the fair guy shook his head, grinning to himself.

'Look how she's looking at us,' he said. 'She's check-ing us out, man. Giving us attitude. It's perfect.'

They stared at her as though she was a piece of natural history.

'Yeah, she's kind of innocent,' the dark guy said, picking up his partner's train of thought.

'In a kind of *knowing* way.'

'Kind of gritty.'

'But pure.'

'Grainy.'

'Yet *real*.'

They'd reached a mutual understanding.

'See you later, Heavey,' they said.

Heavey watched them walk off, and chuckled.

'Great guys,' he said.

They moved through the Hub chattering to each other.

'Paid a lot of money for those two,' he added wistfully.

He snapped out of it, and turned to Esh.

'Any questions?'

'Yes,' she said, looking at him boldly. 'What's the product?'

Heavey gave her a mysterious grin.

'So you're intrigued?'

'Wouldn't you be?'

Heavey laughed.

'Good reply. I kinda expected that.'

'Why?'

'Because I've heard everything about you,' he said.

He smiled, and got up from the sofa.

'You've got the day off,' he told her. 'We'll start work tomorrow.'

She followed him to the door, realising that he hadn't answered her question about the product.

'Anything you'd like to do?' he said. 'You can make a request.'

He held the door as she thought about it.

'Actually, I'd like to go for a jog.'

It was before eight in the morning, she'd spent most of the night flying, but she felt brimming over with energy.

Heavey nodded his head.

'No problem,' he said. 'I'll let security know.'

*

Esh wandered round the house while her security team got ready for the outing. As she explored room after room, she couldn't believe this house was hers.

There was an indoor pool with a steam room next to it. There was a wooden hot tub in its own tranquil nook outside, surrounded by shrubs and herbs. On the far side of the house was a veranda clustered with bougainvillea overlooking the garden. Beneath the trellis sat a large round table with four big chairs around it and unlit lanterns on the walls.

In the living room she met Isabèl and Manuela, cleaning busily even though everything looked spotless. Isabèl was polishing the stairs, Manuela vacuuming the floor, both in crisp white dresses just like Maria. They smiled, and waved at her over the noise of the vacuum.

Upstairs, the eastern and western sides of the house were connected to each other via a long, white corridor. Sunlight poured in from an enormous window at each end. Doors opened along the corridor, letting in even more light.

Her bedroom lay at the end of the hallway, overlooking the garden. The floor was laid in cooling, green marble, and a gigantic sleigh bed stood against the far wall, with a basket of fruit sitting on top of its taut white linen. A note inside read: *Welcome Esh. From Maria, Mano, Isabèl, Manuela, Felipe, Miguel and Fontàn.*

She turned round. On one side of the room were four wooden doors in the wall. She immediately walked over to investigate, and touched her hand to them. The doors slid apart smoothly, revealing a secret closet.

Hanging on rails, neatly folded in spot-lit cubby holes, were more clothes than she'd seen in her life. She walked around, touching the labels, feeling how new they all were. Everything was in her size.

She walked out, grinning stupidly. Over by the bed she saw a doorway. She walked towards it, stepped in, and a light switched on automatically, lighting up a bathroom the size of the ground floor in Mum and Dad's house. It was enclosed by dark slate walls, with an open shower in the corner of the large white marble floor and a huge bath sitting imperially in the centre of the room.

This was hers. She grinned, leaning against the doorframe, staring at the bathroom.

In the corner, opposite the shower area, was a lavatory with a black wooden seat, matching the slate wall, dark against the starkness of the white floor.

It seemed so familiar; something about the set-up mesmerized her. Why was she staring at a toilet seat with such fascination? The black lid. The black slate wall. The striking white floor.

Suddenly, she knew what she was looking at.

It was the floor, the exact corner of the room, where the Khaki Girl had been filmed. The same white marble, the same black toilet, the dark slate wall. This was where she'd lived, and died.

'What do you think?'

Esh turned and saw Maria standing by the entrance to the bedroom. Shocked, she took a moment to respond.

'It's amazing,' she said.

'You like it?' Maria asked, smiling.

Esh nodded nervously.

'I love it.'

The grate

She found Mikey, André, Clive and Tony waiting outside for her in their track pants.

'Ready?' asked Tony.

The four men wore neatly pressed jogging gear, with
automatic weapons hidden beneath their clothes.

Had they been here when the Khaki Girl had lived
here?

'You take point,' Tony told Esh, pointing down the
driveway.

'Okay,' she said. And she set off.

She ran through the open gates of her grounds, took a
hard right, turned up the hill. Running alongside the wall
of her house, she felt a heat up in the air. It felt good
running through it. She passed a wooden gate in her wall
that must have led to the Hub.

Behind her, she heard the chasing patter of her
guards' feet. They never overtook her, never ran beside
her, specifically trained not to disturb her while she
relaxed.

She ran under the palm trees lining the compound's

road. Shade and sunlight alternated as she sprinted over the macadam. Not a car passed. No one appeared from any of the gates hiding the other mansions. She jogged through the breeze, the sun, and warmth.

The hill levelled off near the top, and then gently folded into an incline. As it descended, it began to follow a long, easy loop around the compound, the wind rushing even faster as Esh galloped downhill.

At the bottom of the hill, she saw the entrance she'd arrived through a couple of hours before in the SUV.

Two giant steel walls, twenty feet high, buffered the compound from the outside world. The two gates, she'd been told, never opened at the same time, the first opening to let you in, then penning you into the intervening space as the inner gate waited before letting you through. In the gap between the two walls, a guard had approached the SUV and leaned casually into the car.

'This the girl?' he asked.

There was a brief silence.

'Yeah,' Tony replied.

The guard glanced at Esh, then turned to Tony at the window.

'See you later, guys.'

He walked away slowly, to a sentry box by the inner steel wall where a second guard sat on duty. The first signalled to him, making a winding-up motion with his hand, and the inner steel wall slid open.

Esh ran past the wall, seeing it loom over her, and took the road uphill, following the compound's loop towards her house. On the uphill stretch she accelerated, climbing the last two miles with all her energy.

This was the most delicious run she'd ever had. When she saw her entrance gates ahead she sprinted. The warm, plant-scented air filled her, flooded her lungs. Her entrance gates opened automatically for her, making her think that Tony must have triggered them through Interface.

She ran up her driveway, towards the glass-and-steel house at the top of the hill, gleaming on her private horizon. Finally, she arrived at her front door, and stopped on the driveway, taking one deep breath to regain herself.

She turned around, and realised she was alone.

Where were the security guys?

At the bottom of her driveway, Mikey, Tony, André and Clive suddenly appeared through the gate, stumbling up the road, bending over trying to catch their breath, doing all they could not to vomit.

Tony doubled over in pain and looked up at her as he arrived at the house, shaking his head at the sight of her looking so perfectly unruffled, just a little rosy, standing calmly outside her house.

The others gave up on formality, and let themselves collapse on the driveway. They gasped on their backs, eyes closed, running with sweat.

Mikey mumbled something.

'Join the Green Berets.'

He smiled, arteries pumping in his neck.

Clive lay on his back, looked at the time on EyeScreen.

'Jesus,' he panted.

André turned his head to him.

'What?'

'We just ran eleven clicks in under twenty-eight minutes.'

*

Esh took a swim in the pool. She broke through the water's surface, body slipping in, and swam a hundred lengths. Twenty-five minutes later, she stood at the end of the pool, dripping.

Someone had moved one of the sun loungers so that it would be waiting for her as she came out of the pool. A white dressing-robe had been folded neatly on the lounger, and on the robe sat two white slippers. A glass of something golden and icy waited under a parasol on a little wooden side table.

Esh pulled herself out of the pool. She unfolded the soft, clean robe and wrapped herself in it, then lay on the sun lounger. Feeling the warmth of the sun, she took a sip of the icy drink. It tasted of limes, soda, and mint.

She breathed out, smiling.

Esh had a sauna, sat in the hot tub, and took a long shower in her bathroom, trying to ignore the fact that this was where the Khaki Girl had lived.

She opened her front door to the garden, and heard birds and crickets singing. Stepping outside, she walked across the lawn, feeling as if she was on holiday. In the far corner of the garden she saw three figures working in the shrubs: Miguel, Fontàn, and Felipe.

She followed her side of the wall. Its rust-red colour seemed warming and cooling at once. Nearing the wall's curve, she spotted a dip in the lawn. It dropped several feet to the base of the wall. Why? It couldn't be to drain the lawn, as the garden was filled with sprinklers, meaning that rain wasn't a regular occurrence. So why the ditch?

She walked over, took a closer look. A long section of the ditch was concealed by a line of bushes in front of the wall, in the middle of which also rose a tall tree, its branches arching over the other side of the wall.

Turning to see Felipe, Miguel and Fontàn at the far end of the garden, she checked that none of them was looking, and then walked into the clump of bushes. She turned, and saw that she was now completely hidden.

Crouching, she looked at the foot of the wall. At eye-level there was something she hadn't noticed. A small grate, built into the wall.

She put her hand against the red brick and slid down the edge of the lawn, shuffling along to take a look.

Through the grate, a wide flat lawn stretched off on the other side, partially obscured by a tree. The lawn rose towards a steel-and-glass house just like hers.

Suddenly, her heart stopped.

A face was looking at her through the grate.

'Hi.'

She stepped back, made out the features of a beautiful young guy.

'Who are you?'

'Who are *you*?' she asked back.

Their faces were inches apart.

'You're English?' he said.

'Yes.'

'What's your name?'

'Esh.'

She went into secondary shock. She'd seen this face a thousand times, knew it profoundly, couldn't believe it was real.

'Marcus?'

He smiled.

'Yes.'

'You're real?'

Marcus nodded. 'Seems so.'

'I don't believe it.'

'I can understand,' he said, charmingly.

He grinned through the grate, the face of Interface, as divinely beautiful as in the ads, except indescribably real, features alive, his eyes vivid with personality.

'I don't understand,' she uttered.

She'd floated from her body. She was having a conversation with Marcus.

'He's based on me,' he said, grasping her confusion. 'They said it would give him greater appeal if he came from someone real.'

Esh felt too giddy to say that's exactly what she'd always guessed.

'They shoot footage of me doing things, then model him digitally over the top. That's how they make it look good.'

Every time she'd gaped at the sky, kidding herself that he was genuine, she'd been right all along.

'You're just like him,' she said.

Marcus's expression saddened.

'I *am* him,' he replied.

'How long have you been here?'

'Five years.'

'*Five years?*'

'I was eighteen.'

'Where did you come from?'

'Chicago.'

'You were a model?'

'I was going to go to college. I'd just finished high school, then they spotted me. I wasn't sure what to do, but the money was crazy.'

He smiled, and Esh remembered his first appearance in the sky. She'd been fourteen, he'd suddenly cropped up everywhere, the most beautiful guy she'd ever seen.

'You've been here all this time?'

Marcus nodded.

'When do they let you out?'

'Never,' he said. 'Not while I'm on the campaign.'

'So how long are you going to be here?'

'As long as they need me,' he replied, with a smile of surrender.

He exuded gentleness, but the frustration of having been cooped-up so long shone through unmistakably.

'Who else lives around here?'

Marcus shrugged.

'I don't know. You're the first person I've met, Esh.'

She looked at him, trying to conceal how shocked she was. It felt impossible that he'd been here for so long without seeing anyone else.

'What about a girl who lived here? Did you know her?'

'She never came outdoors,' he said.

Somehow, it made sense.

'I think she was the Khaki Girl,' Esh told him.

Marcus's face suddenly registered it. He'd never known, even though she'd lived next door. Realising how isolated he was, Esh felt a horrible mixture of pity and dread.

'I can't believe they've kept you here so long.'

'Hey, I have to be secure,' he shrugged. 'What about you?'

Esh tried to pinch herself out of this dream, but the vision lingered.

'I was about to start a job in the City,' she said. 'Then I lost the job and this came up. Same story as you.'

Marcus's eyes gazed at her.

'What were you going to be?' he asked.

'A banker.'

'Banker?' he said. 'You have a mathematical mind, Esh?'

She nodded.

'Mathematical Campaign Star,' he said.

They looked at each other silently, smiling, two faces through the wall.

'What's your campaign, Esh?'

'I don't know.'

'You don't *know*?'

'It's a secret,' she said quietly.

'Secret?' he smiled. 'So they come all the way to London to find this beautiful girl for their secret campaign, and then bring her here?'

Esh grinned at him. There was something more appealing, even more satisfying and irresistible about him in the flesh than on SkyBoards all over the world. She couldn't believe she had him here, to herself.

'You must be pretty special, Esh,' he suggested.

Esh shrugged, looking at him quietly.

' "Esh," ' he said in a cod British accent. ' "The English Girl".'

Suddenly the two of them started laughing. They looked at each other, in hysterics, and for that moment she felt nothing but the two of them, the sound of the garden, and Marcus's face smiling.

A voice called out.

'Marcus!'

He turned to his house.

'Shit. Got to go.'

He turned back, and looked through at her.

'When will I see you?' she asked.

A strange emotion suddenly panicked her, as if she could never get enough of having him right here in front of her.

'Hey, we're neighbours,' he said with a grin. 'We'll see each other the whole time.'

'Marcus!' the voice called.

'Okay, okay,' Marcus muttered.

He smiled at Esh for a last time and took a step back.

'See you, Esh,' he said, and turned towards his house.

She watched him walking away. She couldn't believe it was him. A real guy, living next door. He was tall, his shoulders broad, his hair a little longer than in the commercials, but it was definitely him.

At the front of his house, he turned round again, looked at her tiny face in the grate, and smiled, giving her a brief wave. Then he disappeared into his house.

Maria arranged for Esh to have lunch out by the pool. Isabèl laid the table, moving the parasol to shade her from the sun. She sat waiting as Mano appeared from the house with a large white plate in each hand.

His dark, empty face looked a little malnourished, his frame slight beneath his pristine white suit. He could have been Heavey's age, yet he seemed so much older.

'Did you make this?' she asked as he laid down the plates.

Mano nodded. On one plate sat a diamond of grilled tuna with a twist of ginger. On the second lay a salad of leaves and nuts with a sweet dressing. They looked like the most delicious things she'd seen.

'Thank you.'

Mano poured her some water, then walked back to the house.

She ate alone on her deck by the pool. And she couldn't stop thinking about Marcus over that wall.

Safe

Heavey arrived in the evening, saying hello to Maria as she let him in and led him through to Esh, sitting in the living room watching TV.

'How was your first day, Esh?'

She turned off the TV.

'Great,' she said.

'You look so relaxed.'

Esh nodded.

'I feel good.'

Heavey looked her over with a genuine smile.

'Glad you had a rest.'

He stood before her awkwardly, hands in his pockets, studying the room as if trying to judge how her presence had transformed it.

'I was thinking,' he said.

He cast his eyes round the room, and turned to her.

'Shall we have dinner?'

Esh looked at him for a second.

'Sure,' she said.

'Great. I'll tell Maria.'

*

They sat on the veranda overlooking the garden, with its lanterns on the wall and the smell of the garden filling the air, just the two of them.

'I hear you outran the security guys,' he said.

He smirked at her, and Esh smiled back.

'Seemed so,' she responded.

Heavey nodded, visibly impressed.

'I hope the security aspect wasn't too off-putting,' he said. 'They just have a lot to consider. They need to plan everything, think through every step.'

Mano appeared at the door to the veranda with two large plates. Maria stood behind him, and followed him out to the terrace.

'Mano, this looks fantastic,' Heavey said as Mano served them.

Mano nodded politely, without speaking.

'How's your son?' asked Heavey.

'Very well,' Maria replied, not wanting to disturb the atmosphere. And then added, 'Thank you.'

With a small turn of the plate, Mano presented them with a risotto of pumpkin and saffron, with its own *salade tiède*.

'Well,' said Heavey.

Mano stood back, and he and Maria retreated. When they'd left, Esh looked at Heavey across the table.

'Maria has a son?' she asked.

'Little older than you,' Heavey replied.

Esh took a fork of risotto. Maria was someone's mum. It felt weird, though shouldn't have. It just made Maria seem more real.

'Where does her son live?'

Heavey chewed, then swallowed.

'Outside LA.' He pointed to the distance with his fork. 'Other side.'

'And what about Mano?'

Heavey kept chewing.

'What about him?'

'Does he have children too?'

Heavey nodded, then swallowed.

'Yes, he has a son,' he grinned.

'Really?'

'The same one.'

Esh watched Heavey grinning.

'Maria and Mano are married,' Heavey said.

He smiled for a while, then went back to his food.

'Married?'

'Husband and wife often are.'

'You said Maria's the only one who lives here?'

Heavey looked at her.

'She is,' he shrugged. 'They spend time together when they're on a break.'

'Mano doesn't live here?'

Esh put down her fork, as Heavey took a deep breath and let out a sigh.

'This is your house, Esh,' he said. 'Not theirs.'

That was all he had to say, and he promptly continued eating.

'I can't believe they're a family,' she said.

'That's the way we like to do things, Esh.'

It felt so peculiar, the thought of Maria and Mano never behaving like a couple in front of her, hiding behind their uniforms.

With a clink of satisfaction, Heavey laid down his

knife and fork, and brought his elbows onto the table.

'Esh,' he said, looking serious. 'I have something to discuss.'

'What?'

'The jogging issue. There's a related subject.'

Heavey's bright eyes grew a little sombre.

'Your security is extremely important to us,' he said, 'Not just because of the threat of physical harm to you, but because of the campaign's secrecy. Secrecy is one of our most important assets at the moment. It's the reason for your house and the compound, and the Hub next door. We're protecting you not just from danger, but from terrorist intrusion.'

Heavey gazed at her across the lantern-lit veranda.

'We have be very careful,' he said. 'As soon as the campaign launches we'll need to guard you even more fiercely than any other principal we have.'

Who did he mean? The Khaki Girl?

'I need to ask a favour,' he said.

She waited for his gambit.

'We have to take you offline,' he told her.

Esh watched his face flickering in the lantern-light.

'Sorry?'

'We need to delete you.'

She didn't know what to say.

'We want your Identity to effectively disappear,' he said. 'To erase your life history from NetSync, remove any trace of you from the Net, every CCTV shot of you, every Interface log, every trace you've ever left. We need to remove you completely, Esh, so that you're like a ghost.'

Esh took in the words as best she could.

'Why?'

'It's the most extreme security precaution we could ask for,' he admitted. 'It goes far beyond any normal request, we understand. But you would have our irrevocable commitment to turn your Identity back on following the launch of the product in four weeks' time. We've already had your lawyers take a look at this, and in principle they see nothing wrong with it, subject of course to your own decision.'

'You've been in contact with my lawyers?'

Heavey nodded.

Something had suddenly turned very odd.

'And you want me to disappear?'

'Temporarily.'

Esh looked down at the table.

'You want to turn me into a NAP,' she said, half to herself.

'God, no,' Heavey protested.

'But that's what I'd be.'

She looked up at him.

'It's different, Esh, very different. You'd have certainty it would be temporary.'

'I wouldn't have Interface, though.'

'No,' Heavey confirmed. 'You'd have nothing.'

Esh eyed him coolly.

'You want to take away my life, and then ask me to trust you to give it back?'

Heavey nodded.

'And what about my money?'

'It would be paid to you as contracted,' he said.

'But what if something happened?'

'What do you mean?'

'If my Identity didn't come back.'

'That won't happen, Esh.'

'Anything can happen,' she said, smiling. 'Isn't that why you made me sign a thousand-page contract? In case anything happened? That's what I'm thinking. What if the unforeseen came to pass?'

'It's not going to be like that, Esh.'

She was thinking, not listening.

'I want the money transferred to my parents,' she said.

'Why?'

'Before I do anything, I want my entire fee transferred to my parents on the day of the launch, regardless of what transpires.'

Heavey sat very still.

'Whatever you need,' he replied.

Why hadn't all this come up before? Why had Heavey suddenly produced this request now?

'This is crazy,' she said.

'It's as extreme as it gets, Esh. You have no idea what threat you'll be under, though.'

'I don't understand. I have nothing to hide.'

'We know,' said Heavey.

His face brooded in the darkness.

'We don't employ anybody without knowing everything about them,' he said. 'That goes for your house staff, for everyone in the Hub. They all have to be cleared. We know there's nothing to touch you. But it doesn't matter. We need to protect you from anything they might get hold of.'

'Who?'

Heavey didn't answer.

'Who?' she said again.

Heavey looked at her anxiously.

'The Team,' he said finally.

'The Team?' she repeated.

'The people who do the iVerts,' Heavey said.

'You know who they are?'

'Unfortunately we haven't a clue.'

'But they're called the Team?'

'That's what they call themselves.'

She hadn't seen Heavey look as serious as this.

'How?'

'They communicate with us, send us messages.'

She couldn't believe it, yet it was true. The Corporation had no idea who made the iVerts.

'What do they say?'

'Childish things. They're puerile, Esh. But even though I'm not allowed to admit it officially, they're powerful. They act with complete impunity, hit us with anything they want, whenever they want. They have an understanding of the Net that exceeds the detection of even our best trackers.'

He watched her with steely eyes.

'These are the people I'm talking about, Esh. The moment the campaign launches they'll be rooting around your life, trying to find out anything about you. They'll unearth everything you've ever done, and it doesn't matter what happens to you. You are a legitimate casualty in their war against us, and they've threatened every principal we've ever had. So far their reach has been minimal, but we live under the threat of their attack every day. I simply cannot let them harm you or jeopardise the campaign in any way. We can't take you off the Net for ever, but by deleting you temporarily we'll be able to protect you. And if we don't, we risk losing everything, Esh. Everything.'

He stared at her sadly.

Suddenly, Esh remembered the call in London, the anonymous American voice in her Ear. Had they found her already? Had they somehow got to her?

'If the Team hits us,' Heavey said, 'we all go. Party over.'

Esh thought of the house, everything she loved about it.

Heavey pushed back his chair and stood up.

'There's something I want to show you, Esh.'

Heavey took her through the hallways of the house, seeming to know its layout intimately. Had he been here when the Khaki Girl had been alive?

He led her down a corridor, then down a narrow set of stairs to the basement. At the bottom of the staircase a dusty low corridor led off towards a single door, wide, solid, and with a smooth white rubberized surface that looked like it was made from hardened plastic.

'Go ahead,' he said.

Esh made out the glint of an iScan beside the door. She stepped towards it, and it opened. Beyond lay a room glowing intensely with white light.

'No one but you can ever enter this room,' he said. 'We built it for you.'

'What is it?'

'A room for you to talk to your parents.'

Esh turned to him, looked into his eyes.

'So you assumed I'd accept being deleted from the Net?'

'No,' said Heavey. 'We built it in the hope that you would.'

He nodded to the wide, white door.

'Take a look.'

Esh turned, put her palm against the soft white rubber of the door's surface. In response to her touch, as if alive, the door glided back and opened to the glowing white room inside. She stepped in. The floor lit up below her feet, soft and bright. Walking along a minuscule corridor towards an open space, she noticed the walls were white and luminous, glowing, and reached out her hand to touch them. They were made of glass, and warm.

She heard a hiss. As she turned round, the entrance to the white room pulled to and sealed itself shut, severing her Interface connection.

It was like being in GRID. She turned, saw that she was standing at the edge of a hi-tech igloo, about the size of her sauna. A curved, domed wall reached over the top of her head, seeming to glow within, like sunlight passing through the igloo's walls.

There wasn't a single light fitting, just the soothing brightness emanating from the room's surfaces, warm, and calming. In the curved wall behind her, Esh made out a small indentation of some kind. She walked nearer, and realised that it was a soft white seat built into the wall, padded with suede. She sat down, and felt as though she was sinking into the cockpit of the most comfortable spacecraft in the galaxy. In the hazy brightness across the room, she discerned a large, white screen in the spherical wall.

The room was silent, a silence she realised she'd never heard before. An utter absence of sound, not even the ting of one atom colliding with another. She was isolated; deafness hung around her ears.

She sat thinking, relaxing, staring at the white screen.

So this was it. The Corporation wanted to sever her from Interface. No access to the outside world. Just this incredible hi-tech igloo to talk to her parents.

'Would my parents appear on that screen?'

She sat on the sofa in the living room beside Heavey.

'We'd pipe them in on a secure link,' he explained. 'You'd talk to them on a unique connection wired directly between their house and the Safe.'

'The Safe?'

'That's what we call the white room.'

Esh stared from the living room's circular window, at the deep, luminescent night. She didn't say anything to Heavey about the call she'd received as she left London, nor about knowing that this house had belonged to the Khaki Girl. Heavey was right about the threat to her from the Team, more than he knew. If the voice in London had come from the makers of the iVerts, it meant that they'd already got to her, and her position had been put in danger. Cutting herself off from the Net, though, she'd be untouchable, she'd speak to her parents through the dedicated link in the Safe, and no one could reach her. Not for the first time, she wondered what Kristin would make of all this. Probably some acerbic comment that would have put everything in perspective, taken the edge off the trepidation Esh was feeling right now. For a moment, just thinking about Kristin calmed her.

'I need to think about this,' she said.

'Of course,' said Heavey. 'This is important to us. You understand.'

Esh nodded.

'Okay,' he said.

He got up, and gave his driver and bodyguards a wave outside, waiting by his dark stretch saloon.

'Let me know tomorrow,' he said. 'You need to get some sleep.'

Recog

She woke up before Maria.

Barefoot, she walked down the spiral staircase to the ground floor and tried not to make a noise. She checked the time on EyeScreen. 06:15. Everything was silent, no one was up except the birds.

She found the kitchen, overlooking the garden. There was juice in the fridge. She poured a glass for herself and opened the doors to the terrace, stepping out and breathing in the air, to look over her grounds.

The trees and lawn were mottled with sunlight, the garden spreading out in front of her as if she'd woken up in a magazine.

If the Team got to her, as they'd got to the Khaki Girl, she'd lose all of this. She'd be back in London, with nothing.

Taking her off the Net might isolate her. But what was the worst that could happen? The campaign launched in three weeks, and the product would unveil a week after that. That meant a total of four weeks severed from the Net, in which time she had all the sumptuous luxury of this house to enjoy.

It seemed like a small concession to the Corporation, and importantly it safeguarded her against the chance of losing everything.

She looked across the garden, tranquil in the cool, fresh air, birds chirruping and the sprinklers ticking in semi-circles. Excitedly, her eyes travelled to the tall tree and bushes behind which lay the grate. Over that wall, just out of sight, Marcus was living next door.

She finished her juice, left the glass by the sink, and went outside to the pool, where she dived in and swam a hundred lengths.

Maria had made breakfast by the time Esh climbed out of the pool. She ate, showered, and dressed in a vest, some shorts and a pair of flip-flops she'd plucked from her huge closet, then made her way across the lawn.

Reaching the door in the wall, she stood at the iScan and it opened to the Pagoda beyond. Under the shade of the roof, she walked along the gravel paths leading from one building to the next. In the middle of them rose the Hub, full of activity at barely seven in the morning.

She found Heavey chatting on the sofa with Nathan and Gus, in the same glass room where they'd sat yesterday. He saw her, and instantly came down.

'Esh, you look great.'

She smiled.

'I just had a swim.'

She glanced at Gus and Nathan nattering busily upstairs, and turned to Heavey.

'I'll do it,' she said.

He reached out to touch her shoulder.

'I've told our lawyers about your condition,' he said.

'They've agreed. There's going to be no problem.'

Esh swallowed as Heavey continued to rest his hand on her shoulder.

'Thank you, Esh. We appreciate this.'

He took her to one of the outhouses of the Creative Pagoda.

'Esh, this is Steveland.'

His room was crammed with dozens of shelves littered with pieces of technological junk. She watched him searching chaotically for a piece of equipment in the jungle of hardware that only he seemed to know how to navigate. Somewhere in the mess was what he needed.

'Hi, Esh,' he said.

He was too busy with his own thoughts to register her presence right now. He looked as hectic and idiosyncratic as his studio. Incongruously in the LA sunshine, Steveland wore dark, heavy clothes, his hair messy, a little greasy, as though he'd been dragged out of bed to come to work. He was a little screwy and goofy-looking. As he rifled through the strata of junk in his workshop, Esh instinctively felt like smiling.

'Yes,' he said, addressing the piece of equipment he'd finally tracked down.

He turned to Esh by the wall.

'Easier if you sit down,' he said.

He grabbed a chair, and Heavey brought over a stool for Esh.

Steveland sat, and with unexpected precision began to arrange the black boxes he'd procured from his shelves on a small table between them. None of the boxes bore a brand name. They couldn't be bought in shops. This was Steveland's very special, private collection.

'Okay, here's the score,' he said.

He spoke frenetically as he worked.

'The Interface chip will have to stay in your Ear. I can't remove it without surgical procedure, and I'm not a surgeon. Where is it, by the way?'

Esh touched her right ear.

'Right. I'm going to disable it, kind of like an electronic analgesic, except it's permanent. When we boot you up in a few weeks, someone'll have to insert a new chip, but that's not a problem.'

'Have you done this before?' Esh asked him.

'No,' Steveland replied, picking up his first device from the small table.

For the next five minutes, he eyed her as if she were an intricately designed robot, not speaking once as he brought the devices up to her face, controlling them all from a small panel in his EyeScreen.

Heavey stood by her for support.

'I didn't know you were allowed to do this,' she said.

'You're not,' Heavey whispered. 'But we're doing it anyway.'

She looked up, and saw him give her a collusive wink.

Suddenly, Interface was gone. She was in the world but outside the Net. She blinked, gave her head a shake, and looked around the room.

'How is it?' Heavey asked.

She stood up, walked around as if trying on a new pair of shoes. It felt weirdly liberating. No EyeScreen. No Interface.

'I should tell you something,' Steveland murmured.

She turned to him as he packed up his devices.

'Your Ear Chip is a latent transmitting device. Even severed from Interface the chip in your Eye can be tracked. So I've killed them.'

'Killed them?'

Steveland wrapped a cable round one of his boxes.

'If someone knew your ID code they could trace your chip and find out where you were. So I've disabled it. If you go missing, we won't find you.'

'Steveland,' Heavey grinned. 'She's not going to go missing.'

Heavey looked at Esh as if Steveland were being overdramatic.

'Told you it was permanent,' Steveland mumbled.

'We're going to back up your Identity right now,' Heavey assured her. 'Every byte. Steveland's going to have it secured and kept right here on disk, where no one can touch it. Right, Steveland?'

Steveland carried on storing away his things.

'Sure.'

'From now until the launch we're going to keep you very safe,' Heavey said. 'We won't be able to track you, but we won't need to. Because you're going to be right here.'

Suddenly, Esh felt the vulnerability of being unhitched from her surroundings. She could feel what it was like to be a NAP. No access to anything. No connection. Just a body adrift on the planet.

She turned to Heavey.

'So what now?'

He led her back along the path to the Hub. At its outer wall, Esh saw everyone waiting inside.

'You're going to meet the crew,' he said.

The double doors opened in front of them.

'They've been dying to meet you,' he whispered. 'We've been working with your image while we waited for you to arrive.'

As he led her into the Hub, Heavey put his arm around her.

'People,' he announced.

The thirty-one people in front of her smiled. She noticed that Gus and Nathan weren't there, and turned to see them sitting in the glass room upstairs, on their own.

'This is Esh,' Heavey said, holding her by the shoulder.

The entire crew said 'hi' with their eyes.

'She just arrived from London yesterday,' he said. 'Try and go easy on her. Steveland's taken her off Interface.'

Light laughter rippled through the crew.

Heavey led her towards them.

'I'm going to take you through everyone,' he said, presenting her to the youngest member of the crew, a short guy with scruffy hair. 'This is our team assistant.'

'Carl?' Esh said.

Carl smiled, puzzled.

'How do you know my name?'

'Heavey pointed you out yesterday.'

Carl looked to Heavey for clarification. 'She's using Recog, right?' he asked.

'No, Carl. We just took her off Interface. She's got no software.'

Carl looked at Esh, and pointed to the girl on his right.

'Who's this?'

'Tanya,' Esh replied.

An amazed silence came over the Hub.

'What do I do?' asked Tanya.

'Market feedback for Asia.'

The crew audibly gasped.

'My God,' Tanya said, and pointed to the guy beside her. 'Who's this?'

'Paul,' Esh replied.

The crew whooped.

'What do I do?' Paul smiled.

'You work on the US brand strategy team.'

Paul turned, stunned, to Heavey.

'This for real, Heavey?'

Heavey's hand rested on Esh's shoulder.

'Bona fide, Paul.'

'You really not using Recog?' Paul asked, as the crew laughed.

'No,' she replied.

'So who's on my team?'

Esh scanned the thirty-one faces.

'Sandy,' she said, pointing to a girl at the back. 'And Brice. And Michael.'

She pointed them both out.

'Jesus,' said Paul.

'Hey, who am I?' a guy at the back called out.

The crew fell silent, and turned to him.

'You're Barney,' Esh told him. 'The media planner for Japan.'

Esh told each of the team who they were, leaving them astounded by her ability to remember all of them.

She looked round and, standing in the Hub's gallery, leaning casually on the handrail and watching over everything, were Gus and Nathan.

'Hey, who are those two?' someone asked.

A quiet chuckle passed through the crew. Gus and Nathan looked neither impressed nor amused. Esh had named everyone but them.

'Gus and Nathan,' she said.

'Yeah, but which one's which?' someone heckled.

The crew laughed, and a few people started clapping.

'I don't know,' Esh replied.

Suddenly, the crew burst into their loudest applause yet, howling at the two creatives standing on the gallery.

Nathan and Gus responded with nonchalant shrugs, but the baying continued ever louder. Without intending to, Esh had just scored her biggest hit. Regardless of the fortune the Corporation had spent retaining these skatewear-clad brain-boxes, Heavey allowed the crew's good spirits to flow, at the expense of the two guys looking down at them from on high.

Gravity

'You blew them away,' he said.

He led her through the Creative Pagoda towards the BlueCube, where they were going to shoot the campaign, Gus and Nathan following behind.

'Esh,' Gus called. 'You like autistic or something?'

Heavey turned to him. The four of them stopped on the path as Heavey glared at Gus, and spoke with such control it made Esh freeze.

'If you disrespect Esh ever again,' he said, 'you and Nathan will find it hard to work in this country for the rest of your lives. Do you understand?'

Gus stared back, shocked.

'Do I make myself clear?' Heavey demanded.

Gus turned to Nathan for help, but Nathan remained silent.

'Sure, Heavey,' Gus muttered.

Heavey stared him down, and turned forwards.

'Sorry, Esh,' he whispered. 'I'm really sorry.'

He didn't mention the incident again. For the next few

hours Esh was made to stand behind the glass screen of the BlueCube, accurately described. It was a sound-proofed isolation booth in the shape of a cube, and had incandescently glowing blue walls. It was designed to film her from every angle, and then mutate the footage in any way they chose. Heavey stood with Nathan and Gus behind a glass screen, giving her occasional commands over an intercom, while Steveland sat between them controlling the BlueCube's console. Heavey asked her to perform facial expressions and to answer rudimentary questions about her age and interests, while Gus and Nathan looked on.

'What's your name?'

The light of the room dazzled her. She was cut off from daylight, suspended in this strange, perpetual blue.

'Esh,' she replied, hearing her own voice in her ears.

She felt all the more aware of Interface's absence. She was standing in this strange brightness, severed from everything, and through the reflection in the glass, she could make out Heavey blending into her own outline.

'Who are you?' he asked.

She guessed it was midday. As she left the Creative Pagoda, her eye instinctively shot to the empty space where her EyeScreen had once been, but it was hollow, revealing the empty world outside.

She'd been given the rest of the day off. As she step-ped into her garden, breathing in the smell of flowers, she looked around.

Miguel, Felipe and Fontàn must have been on a break. Her grounds were empty, silent, fresh, and alive. She crossed the lawn towards the high wall. As she'd wanted to yesterday but hadn't dared she crouched in the bushes, walked through to the clearing and slid down the ditch to the foot of the wall. Leaning against the grass, she put her eye to the grate.

She looked into Marcus's garden, hearing her own breathing against the wall, but couldn't find him anywhere.

Suddenly, she heard a thwack. She looked up, tried to find the source of the sound. Half-obscured by the tree in front of her, she saw him on the roof of the house, in profile, a golf club raised behind his turned shoulders. He was gazing into the distance, tracing the trajectory of the golf ball he'd just dispatched to the scrub of the hills below.

After twenty seconds he resumed his position and fired off another.

He seemed totally unaware of everything around him, not another sound or event disturbing the Zen-like concentration of his shots.

She smiled, enjoying the restful sight of Marcus sending off golf balls into the void. But there was something sad about the exercise too, something lonely about the sound of that hollow smack of golf ball in the air.

He'd been here for five years, without another soul to entertain him.

'Marcus!' she hissed through the grate.

He didn't hear, and patiently lined up another shot.

She didn't want to attract attention on either side of the wall. But she wanted to see him.

'Marcus!' she hissed.

He twitched, noticing a sound, but then ignored it, and jiggled his legs, adopting the swing position.

'Marcus!'

He looked up, scoured his garden, searched in the tall trees around his house and amongst the bushes by the wall.

'Psst!'

His eyes turned to the grate. He'd seen her, she knew it, even though he couldn't have made her out. He dropped the golf club, and disappeared from the roof. A minute later, he appeared at the front door of his house and came over.

'Esh.'

He leaned against the wall, smiling.

'What are you doing?'

'What were you doing?' she asked.

Marcus smiled his beautiful Interface smile, and turned to the house.

'Practising my swing. I'm getting good, Esh. Few more years of this and I'm going to have to turn pro whether I like it or not.'

'Will they let you?'

Marcus rolled his eyes.

'No. But hey – I didn't want to be a golfer anyway.'

'What did you want to be?'

He grinned at her again, amused by her questions.

'Well,' he said, 'you mean apart from becoming the digital representation of the world's biggest remote internet portal service?'

He tapped his finger meditatively against his chin.

'Dunno. I just didn't imagine spending my twenties hitting golf balls off the roof of a hideaway mansion in the LA hills.'

Esh wanted to laugh. He was funny and charming without even meaning to be.

'So how did you imagine your twenties?'

'Hang on,' he stopped her. 'I want to know about you. What brings the English Girl to LA? I'm just some Chicago teenager who ended up becoming the face of Interface. You're a banker, a genius. Why have they got someone as formidable as you hiding out in the compound?'

For a second, Esh felt helplessly swept away by his charm, his smile, his warmth. The more he spoke, the less he became like Marcus.

'Who said I was a genius?'

'I did,' he said. 'I can see it. You were clever at school, weren't you?'

He eyed her.

'What makes you say that?'

'You have a seriousness. You're playful, light. But you also have something a little uptight in there, as if you've been working hard for years and you're still not quite sure how to relax.'

His perspicacity disarmed her. He looked at her fondly, but he'd given a name to something she'd never chosen to identify.

'You're probably right,' she said.

'It's very attractive.'

Something shifted subtly between them. She felt as if she'd lost her footing, with Marcus suddenly seeing through her like that. But it didn't matter. That was the strange thing. It felt comfortable losing her grip.

'I was thinking,' he said.

He looked at her for a moment, then suddenly glanced off into his garden, before turning back again.

'Would you like to come over?'

Something uncertain hung in Esh's stomach. She felt strong, more alive, and yet more fragile than she'd ever felt before.

'I'm not sure,' she said. 'Am I allowed to?'

Marcus smiled, peering at her.

'No,' he shrugged. 'We're not even meant to know the other lives here.'

He spoke with quiet resignation. Esh didn't say anything, the nervousness in her stomach growing more intense.

'Hey, I'm sorry,' he said putting his arms out.

'No,' Esh said. 'It's okay.'

She felt oddly determined. She felt timid, confused, unnerved, but also wildly, inexplicably self-assured. 'No, I'd like to,' she said.

The two of them looked at each other through the grate. The wall between them ran the perimeter of their gardens, rising as high as the trees.

Esh looked up, and had an idea.

'What time do your staff get off?' she asked.

'Around nine,' Marcus said.

'Mine too.'

She looked upwards, and then turned her eyes to Marcus in the grate.

'I'll come over about nine-thirty,' she said.

Marcus gaped at her, amazed by her sudden determination.

'How are you going to make it over?'

'By tree.'

Esh studied the tall tree arching over their mutual wall, reckoning it would be a cinch, even in darkness.

'You sure?' Marcus asked, a little concerned.

Esh reassured him with a grin.

'They can take a man and turn him into a digital creation so lifelike he looks like the real thing,' she said. 'I, on the other hand, can climb a tree. It's in our genes. Don't worry. All our ancestors climbed trees.'

Marcus gazed at her, smiling.

'Esh,' he said. 'I think I can see why they picked you for your campaign.'

She climbed excitedly up the side of the ditch. Crouching in the bushes, her heart beating, hardly believing that she'd had the guts to go through with what she had, she looked out and checked the coast was clear. There was no one there and she stepped from the bushes light-headed with triumph.

Suddenly, up ahead, she spotted two figures on the wall. It was Gus and Nathan, dangling their legs over the ledge by the Pagoda, ten metres off the ground. How had they climbed up there?

She walked towards them, watching them gaze down at her.

'What are you doing up there?'

They sat and stared.

'Heavey said we could come up here,' Gus said defensively.

He turned to Nathan and mumbled something she couldn't hear.

'Why are you looking into my garden?'

Gus and Nathan turned to her.

'We're getting inspiration,' Nathan answered.

'From where?'

'From you.'

The two creatives smirked at her.

'Hey, do you know which of us is which?' Nathan asked.

'Yes, you're Nathan,' Esh told him blankly.

He fell silent, and she knew she'd stumped him.

'So Heavey said you could snoop on me?' she asked.

Gus and Nathan lifted their heads and gazed straight over her.

'Hey, we're working,' Gus said with self-importance. 'Is that okay?'

Esh watched them for a few moments. She decided to let it go. If sitting on her wall looking into her garden was what did it for them, so be it.

She walked off, leaving the two geniuses sitting alone.

'What time is it?' she asked Maria.

Her eye had glanced automatically at EyeScreen for the time. This was going to be a hard habit to lose. She turned to Maria, and saw her looking at a clock on the kitchen wall.

'Nine,' Maria told her.

She hadn't noticed that clock before. Didn't Maria have the time in Interface?

She ate at the kitchen table, after Maria had asked where she'd like to take dinner. On the veranda? By the pool? The TV?

Right here at this table would be great, Esh told her. Immediately, Maria had tried to make herself scarce.

'No, please,' said Esh. 'Stay.'

Maria turned to Mano by the stove where he'd just finished preparing Esh's meal.

'Both of us?' she said.

'Please.'

She'd wanted to eat in the kitchen normally, with Maria and Mano around. Sitting and eating, she listened to Maria doing the washing-up in the sink, while Mano leaned against the stove in the corner, drinking a glass of water.

'How old's your son?' Esh asked.

Maria turned off the faucets.

'Twenty-one.'

'What does he do?'

Maria picked up a towel, began drying her hands.

'He's ill.'

She swished the towel around her small, strong hands, then straightened it neatly on its rail. As she rested against the work surface briefly, Esh realised she'd never seen Maria just stop, for a moment, and relax.

'He has a blood disease,' Maria explained. 'He's in a special clinic where they give him excellent treatment. They're doing everything they can.'

Mano stared vacantly while Maria spoke, taking tiny, never-ending sips of water. Maria realigned the towel on the rail.

'Very sad,' she said. 'But he's in good hands.'

Esh quietly finished her plate of food, and Maria came to pick it up.

'Good?'

'Delicious.'

Esh looked up at Mano, who responded with a small, ceremonious nod. Across the kitchen, Maria washed the plate in a flash.

'Okay,' she said, turning to check the kitchen was in order.

She left with Mano, and looked at Esh one last time.

'Goodnight,' she said. 'We'll see you in the morning.'

Esh listened to Maria close the door to her apartment. Mano had already left by the back door, to the front gates where his car had been waiting.

The house was quiet, empty.

She waited another minute, eyeing the kitchen clock, then turned off all the house lights, downstairs first, then up, to make it look as though she was going to bed.

In the darkness, pierced by the ambient glow of the SkyBoards from the windows, she crept downstairs and out of her front door to the garden.

She stood breathing, listening to the silence, making sure no one was in her grounds, and when all felt quiet she set off.

She scaled the tree, only now appreciating how tall it was. The ground was a long way below and she tried not to look down, hauling herself up from one branch to the next, until she was high enough to reach across and get a handhold on the wall.

She couldn't believe she was doing this. Breaking out of her house, meeting Marcus. What exactly was she expecting to happen? It was dark, there was no one around, and she suddenly had to confront the reality of what she'd arranged to do.

She sat on the top of the wall, ten metres up, looking for a way down. Trees reached to her height on Marcus's side of the wall, but they were all too far away. She shifted carefully along the ledge, looking for a branch close enough. She reached out and tested the strength of a protruding branch. It was solid, would hold her. Shifting her weight from the top of the wall, she suddenly dangled in mid-air, suspended from the branch. She swung her legs, building up momentum, and found a branch with her feet.

'Esh!'

She saw Marcus down in the shadows.

'You okay?' he asked.

Her heart pounded, thirty feet up in a tree.

'Fine,' she said. 'Won't be a sec.'

She grappled through the branches, levering herself down the tree's length, and jumped the last few feet, landing right in front of him.

'Impressive,' he said.

He looked at her as she brushed off her hands and turned to see him in the glow of the SkyBoards, the face she'd seen a thousand times.

'I can't believe you're him.'

Marcus stood breathing, an arm's reach from her.

'He doesn't exist, Esh. He just happens to have the same name and to look like me.'

For an instant, Esh wished sorely that Kristin had been here to hear that.

She smiled at him, feeling his nearness. Without Interface, she felt the isolation of her body, standing here before him.

She wanted to touch him. It was the first time she'd wanted someone. She felt almost scared to reach out, afraid of what might happen, of it being suddenly real. But the stillness and the safety of the moment drew her in slowly, irretrievably.

She lifted her hand, and invisibly touched his hip with her fingers. He was solid. There was someone there. She looked into his eyes, and saw his face coming towards hers. In response, she reached out her hand and placed it on his other hip, as he placed his arms round her waist. She pressed herself against him, felt his body against hers. He moved his arm around her back, held her, and face to face, they kissed.

'I can't believe I've just kissed a collection of polygons and digital skin-tones,' she said.

Marcus laughed quietly.

'Hey, I've just kissed the English Girl,' he said. 'And I don't even know what product she's advertising.'

They eyed each other in the half-light, not knowing who the other really was. It felt as if neither of them quite existed. For the first time in her life, Esh didn't feel weird holding a guy, resting her face near his, their arms round each other. He'd kissed her as if it had been her, not just anyone, that he was embracing.

She felt a whirl of air snap round them.

'Cold,' she said.

They squeezed each other, keeping themselves warm.

'We could go inside,' he said.

Esh felt the warmth of his body transferring to hers, the solidity of his form. She was afraid still, nervous of what she didn't know, sensing that Marcus knew this somehow. He held her, not tightly, just guarding her.

'I'd like that,' she said.

The house was dark. But even in the shadows, it still looked similar to hers. It was the same layout, the same living room and wide staircase. They kept their arms round each other's waists as they walked in. It felt so new, so strange, holding someone else like this, walking with her arm around a man and gripping him to her. But it didn't feel odd, that was the thing. She wanted to keep herself tight against him. They walked in darkness together, up the staircase, not switching on any lights, silently wanting to keep the moment shrouded in darkness. Esh's feelings thrilled her, the fact that in every moment she felt comfortable here, alone with him.

They walked along the hallway to his bedroom at the far end of the house. Thin slats of light from the SkyBoards came through the windows of his room, but other than their faint glow the room was dark. Marcus reached back with one arm and closed the door. They stood with their arms around each other. Slowly, they turned their faces, and started to kiss again. Holding each other tighter, they started to move across the room. Esh kept wanting to open her eyes, to see him, to believe it really was Marcus. But she lost herself in the growing desire she felt absorbing her, kissing him, feeling his mouth, his body against her.

They lay on his bed and she felt the weight float from her body, as she stretched out beside him. For a second she stopped kissing him. She wanted to look at him. She saw his eyes looking at her from the faint light. She breathed in, suddenly smelling the scent of his body. It wasn't cologne, but him. She felt as if she knew him from that scent in a way that seeing his face or speaking to him for a thousand days could never have told her. It was his physical being, this amalgamation of data breathing and gazing at her. She shut her eyes and moved her face towards his, letting her cheek brush against his skin. Searchingly, she traced her lips over his face, putting her mouth against his, kissing him, his softness, squeezing herself to him as if she were finally doing something for which she'd waited her entire life.

III

Evo

Launch

It was gone eight.

She sat on the edge of Marcus's bed and looked at the clock he'd put on her side of the bed.

'I've got to go,' she said.

Through the window, on the other side of the wall in the garden, the day was beginning.

'What's the time?' Marcus mumbled from the bed.

'Eight.'

She pulled on her shoes, turned and saw him opening his eyes.

'What are you doing tonight?' he asked.

'I don't know yet.'

'Will you come over?'

Gazing at him, she thought about how she'd come here every single night for the last three weeks.

'There's going to be a launch party,' she said.

Marcus looked at her sleepily from his pillow. Even with sleep fogging his eyes, she could see the fondness shine from him.

She leaned over, hovered her face above his, and kissed him.

'See you later, Marcus.'

'Good luck.'

They closed their eyes, kissed, and Esh touched his hair.

'Got to go.'

She gave him one last kiss, stood up and crossed to the door. Opening it, she waited in the doorway and looked along the corridor, listening for any signs of life. This was the gauntlet she ran every morning, escaping Marcus's house, climbing back into her own, without a single member of either her or his staff spotting her.

Her ears reached for the tiniest sound.

Nothing.

Esh turned to Marcus, blew him a kiss, and silently closed his door. She darted along the corridor, reached the stairs, and stopped on the top step, listening again. She homed in on the kitchen. Even if Marcus's housemaid was down there, she could still risk making it to the entrance without being seen. She knew it could be done, because she did the same thing in her own house, creeping past Maria to pretend that she'd been asleep in her bed.

She heard a cup tinkling. She crouched, crept down the staircase, peering through the banister to watch for anyone appearing from the kitchen. This was the worst part, taking these steps down the staircase, hoping that no one would appear. How many times could she get away with this? Coming over at night, after everyone had gone to bed, was fine. But these morning missions made her heart thump.

She made it to the bottom of the stairs, and sprang across the marble floor, out of the door and into the garden. She kept moving, slipping round the house's wall, scanning the garden. She stopped. Taking a firm, quick breath she made the dash across the lawn from the house to the wall. Amongst the trees, she turned to check the windows for peering faces, and then moved to the tree that reached across the wall. She climbed it quickly. She knew every grip and handhold. At the top, she slipped off onto the wall, and shifted along to the tree on her side.

She surveyed her garden, looking for Tony, Mikey, Clive or André on a patrol, or Felipe, Miguel or Fontàn in the bushes. None of them had started work. She slinked down the tree, moved deftly from branch to branch, and landed on her side of the wall. Crouching in the bushes, she checked the garden and house for activity, and when all was clear, finally came out and walked across the lawn.

For another day, she could forget about being caught. Another day. She'd swim in the pool, sunbathe, work for a couple of hours in the BlueCube, then go for an afternoon jog.

It was only knowing that she'd go back to Marcus's each night that made the quiet isolation of her days bearable. Every time she saw LA through the gaps in her trees, down there in its hazy grid of lights, she felt the gaping distance between her and the world. The high red wall around the garden, the gates at the bottom of the garden, the wall around the compound, it had all subtly closed in.

Another peaceful day in her house, the garden filled with aromatic smells and the sound of birds, the sun hitting the wall at the end of the drive. This was where she spent the day missing Marcus and everything about him.

She stepped off the brow of the lawn onto the driveway, heading for the front door. Everything inside was quiet. She pushed through the entrance, and made straight for the staircase upstairs.

'Esh.'

She stopped, turned to Maria.

'Hi, Maria.'

Maria looked at her seriously.

'Can I show you something?'

'Sure,' Esh replied.

She stepped off the staircase, followed Maria to the kitchen, and suddenly, as they reached the door, Maria turned to her and pinned her against the wall, taking Esh's cheeks in her hands and holding her face.

'You have to be careful,' she whispered.

Esh tried to shake her head, pretending that she hadn't understood, and immediately Maria squeezed her, gripping her harder to make her listen.

'The Khaki Girl,' she whispered. 'She was here.'

She stared at Esh with her big eyes. Esh nodded.

'She died, Esh.'

Maria shook her head, suddenly trying to stem the tears that came to her eyes. She whispered desperately.

'Don't mess around, Esh.'

Esh nodded again.

'They won't let you mess up.'

She held Esh's head in her vicelike paws. Then she let go, wiping the back of her hand across her eyes, and walked off.

Esh stood against the wall, stunned. Maria knew. She'd probably known about Marcus for some time, and instead of telling anyone had just warned her. The mention of the Khaki Girl after all these weeks made her shudder. What had happened to her?

She took a shower, feeling relieved and simultaneously panicked that Maria knew about Marcus. The urgency of her warning scared her. She kept looking across the bathroom at the corner where the Khaki Girl had probably died. Maria was protecting her. But it made Esh feel in even more danger than she'd previously imagined.

When she came downstairs, Heavey was waiting for her in the living room.

'Nervous?' he said.

'No. Why?'

Heavey grinned.

'The launch,' he reminded her.

Esh pulled herself together, forced a smile.

'Yes, a little, I suppose.'

'Only natural,' Heavey told her. 'We're all going crazy trying to tie things up. I just wanted to let you know how it's going to go tonight.'

He looked at her excitedly.

'We're going for full spectrum domination, Esh. There's almost nowhere in the world the campaign will not reach tonight. The next seven days will be nothing less than awesome. And it's due in no small part to you.'

She tried to play along with his enthusiasm, still too startled by Maria's warning to say anything.

'Tomorrow, I'm going to tell you what the product is, Esh.'

He looked at her seriously. Esh felt butterflies filling her stomach.

'It's time for you to know, especially after tonight's launch.'

He looked at her, and she automatically responded with a nod.

'Eight o'clock tonight, we go live,' he said. 'I want to organise some kind of party for the crew to watch it together. I was thinking of doing it here?'

Esh felt so tense she would have agreed to anything.

'Sounds fine,' she said.

Heavey cocked his head and gave her a smile.

'Great.'

Throughout the day, Maria pretended their conversation had never happened. As Esh lay outside by the pool, she thought feverishly.

What was she supposed to do? The thought of never going back to Marcus seemed impossible. She'd be left totally alone. He was her lifeline, the very beating of time that made her days pass. She knew the risk she took by spending every night in his bed, but she couldn't see any other way of living in this place. She knew that her secret was safe with Maria. She had to take care, not get sloppy, as Maria had warned her.

She looked up at the translucent SkyBoards in the sunshine. In the corner of the sky she suddenly spotted Marcus's face in the Interface campaign, looking almost as delicious and beautiful as he did in real life.

The ad shimmered for a second. Marcus's face shuddered, and the image on the SkyBoard warped from reality into an iVert, happening with the same ominous sense of unease with which a dream turns into a nightmare. He gave her a cheery, moronic wave, a big cartoon grin daubed over his face, and a cartoon rifle appeared in his hand. He put it against his head, pulling the trigger. His head exploded in a comic splurge of blood and brain, and a scrawl of childlike letters appeared across the mess: *INTERFACE! YOUR GATEWAY TO ANOTHER WORLD!*

And then the iVert disappeared as if it had never happened.

Dark space

It had grown dark. Mano and Maria served champagne by the pool, while Isabèl and Manuela carried round trays of food. The thirty-five Hub workers stood talking and drinking on the deck, where Mano had lit lanterns to illuminate the clear, beautiful night. It was 19:55 on a warm October evening.

Esh watched Heavey doing the rounds of the crew, making sure he got to speak to everyone before the campaign launched, to thank them each individually.

In the background, she could hear the loudspeaker that the crew had set up by the pool so all of them could listen to the launch together.

Five days earlier, she'd been told how the launch would permeate news TV in the days preceding lift-off. Later that day, she saw it with her own eyes.

'*A major new advertising campaign*,' said the American TV news presenter, '*launches this Friday, twenty hundred hours Pacific Standard Time. I'm told we're in for something of a real surprise.*'

He turned to his co-hostess and grinned.

'*Yes, Gerry,*' she smiled. '*We're in for a treat.*'

Esh looked over at Heavey, watched him moving through the crowd, patting each member of the crew on the back.

She looked up at the sky, feeling sick with nerves. All week she'd asked the crew for a peek of what they had planned. But all she received in response were enigmatic smiles. 'It'll be a surprise,' they said.

She looked over the SkyBoards, in a glance counting no less than eleven concurrent FMCG ads. They were sky-wide, peddling their perfect complement of boy-band personalities: George the blond leader with his pally grin, Larry the gentle giant with his thick neck and bear-like eyes, Dwight the nutty outsider with his crazy hair and wild eyes, Dirk the dreamboat with his shy-guy frown and brooding good looks.

And then there, in the middle of it all, she saw Marcus gazing from space. If she'd still had Interface he would have spoken to her now, whispered in her Ear. She missed him, suddenly missed Interface, missed having access to her Music files and Movies, her Photographs and address book. The sky above her was dead, responding neither to her Ear nor Eye.

Suddenly, something grabbed her attention. It was the smallest detail. In an FMCG commercial for Juice, the four of them grinned and sucked on their straws. But the banner above their heads was wrong.

'*Sucking Your Souls, People!*'

An iVert, right now.

Heavey put his hand on her shoulder.

'Okay?'

She looked down, heart beating.

Suddenly, the chattering around the pool grew fainter. The lights seemed to dim. Esh turned to the lanterns that Mano had lit, but if anything they seemed to glow even brighter. It was the sky that was growing dark.

Everyone looked up.

For the first time in their lives, the SkyBoards switched off one by one, leaving the night sky black, revealing the stars behind them.

'Jesus,' someone said.

A deep gentle voice came from the sky, the kind of voice you might have imagined Santa Claus having. Soothing, avuncular, a balmy, all-knowing American storyteller, speaking brightly and dreamily from the night.

'*We have invented a machine*,' he said.

The sky hung in perfect darkness, the stars glimmering anciently.

'*You do not have to build it, because it will build itself. Beginning from a single component, it will evolve into the most complex piece of machinery the world has ever seen. If it ever breaks, it will repair itself. If it is faced with a problem, it will solve it. If it runs out of power, it will generate more of its own.*'

Nothing happened. The SkyBoards remained blank.

'*Whatever environment it encounters, it will adapt to it more successfully than any organism that has ever existed. When it is faced with a task, it will learn how to perform that task without instruction. It will evolve automatically, advance and improve through every moment that it lives.*'

At the Western tip of the sky something was starting to happen. The SkyBoards were switching on, row by row, lighting up against the sky. When they reached a third of the way across the sky, their colours began to change.

Dark masses of colour appeared on the SkyBoards; each screen was covered by a different shape. They were moving as one in a sky-wide image.

Esh took a sip of champagne.

The last visible SkyBoard lit up, revealing a single, panoramic image before everyone's eyes. For the first time ever, the SkyBoards had been synchronised by NetSync to distribute a collective image over their screens.

It was Esh, looking down from heaven in the simple black vest she'd worn on the first day Heavey had taken her to the BlueCube. She stretched hundreds of miles long out in space, looking out from the white background that had been pasted in behind her in the BlueCube. She brought her hand to her mouth, cleared her throat, and gazed ahead, the largest single image that had ever filled the sky.

Gradually, she faded from the sky, and the darkness of space hung above them. Into its blackness three white letters materialised slowly.

e s h

'*She will exceed everything we have ever done,*' said the Storyteller.

The three letters twinkled in space, as the Storyteller's voice floated off, and then her name faded from the sky.

Heavey put his hand on her shoulder. Behind him, the whole crew turned towards her, holding their glasses of champagne, and let out a cheer.

'I need to tell you something,' Heavey whispered in her ear.

His hand pressed her shoulder, and he moved her away from the pool. Esh looked back at the crew, all cheering, waving. She felt numb.

'I've got some news,' he said.

Like an automaton, Esh let herself be led to the house, too stunned by the image in the sky to do anything. She knew that she'd never forget that moment, not for the rest of her life.

She stumbled over the paving stones towards the house, as behind her the crew carried on cheering. Heavey opened the entrance door, waited for her to enter. Outside, the crew suddenly became a poolside murmur.

She felt the calm and peace of her house for a moment. Turning to Heavey, she saw him looking horribly nervous. Behind his head, the SkyBoards were lighting up again, one by one.

'What's the product, Heavey?'

Heavey stared at her.

'Not a good time,' he replied.

She searched his unreadable eyes.

'There's been some news from London,' he said, and her heart sank. 'Your parents are waiting for you in the Safe.'

She felt sick, outside her own body, as if she was back in the BlueCube, sealed off from everything. She could sense the night squeezing them inside its vastness.

'You need to go, Esh. Your parents have to speak to you.'

*

She descended the stairs to the Safe. All she could think about was the SkyBoards, her image across the horizon, as big as the sky.

Standing at the door to the Safe, watching its white rubberised surface, the iScan read her and the door opened soundlessly in front of her.

She stepped inside, the door sealed itself shut, and she took her seat in the pod in the wall, facing the screen where she'd spoken to her parents every afternoon.

Mum and Dad came into view on the white screen, both looking tired, distraught, five in the morning in London and they hadn't slept.

'It's Grandad,' said Mum. 'He's in hospital.'

Esh sat in her slot in the wall, barely able to think.

'What's happened?'

'He's had a fit.'

'What kind of fit?'

'We don't know. They're doing tests.'

Mum looked more distressed than Esh could remember.

'He's in a coma.'

'Is he going to be okay?'

Dad looked sadly at her from the screen. 'We have to wait and see, Esh.'

He tried to smile, to make things better. Esh's heart beat furiously with the desire to suddenly do something, be there, take care of them. She felt it rise from her body, the urge to be back home in London.

'I can't believe it.'

Everything tangible seemed to be slipping away, seeing herself in the sky, Grandad having a fit. He'd been fine when she'd last seen him, healthy, on his feet. Suddenly he was in hospital, comatose.

She looked at Mum and Dad, looking small and frail. Mum peered up and smiled at Esh, trying to patch things over.

'How are you, Esh?'

'I'm fine, Mum.'

But she was lying too. She felt too panicked to be upset about Grandad. She felt herself bouncing from the sky, to the ground, to the sky.

'We miss you, Esh.'

Mum and Dad gazed at her.

'I miss you too,' she said.

When she stepped back outside, there was no one by the pool. The party had been cleared away, the crew had vanished as if the launch had never happened, and the sky looked as it always had, its caravanserai of ads moving steadily over the earth.

She walked around the pool's edge, breathing in the night air, the smells of the hills and her garden. All around, the crickets sang.

She tried to clear her head, but the image of her covering the sky filled her mind. The thought of Grandad hounded her, unreal as a dream. She couldn't stand the idea of him in hospital, lost in a slumber from which he might never wake.

She stopped, and turned to look at the house. All the lights had been switched off, and Maria had gone to bed. Mano had been driven home.

She turned to the pool and moved her eyes over the lonely water, watching the SkyBoards glow in the slow, gentle ripples.

She checked that the house was silent one last time, and then crept towards Marcus's wall.

He was waiting for her at the top of his staircase, his arms open and ready. They hugged in the darkness.

'My God, you were awesome,' he whispered. 'I couldn't believe it was you.'

Esh didn't say anything. Marcus instantly sensed that something was wrong.

'What is it?'

He pulled back, looked at her.

'My grandfather's in hospital.'

Marcus held her.

'He's in a coma. They don't know what's wrong with him.'

'Are you okay?' he whispered.

She shrugged, and he squeezed her.

'Come on,' he said.

Even in the darkness, he could see the pain on her face. He led her to the room, and closed the door behind them, then they sat down together, and held each other in silence.

'You okay, Esh?'

She nodded, savouring the warmth and nearness of him.

'I feel like I'm not here,' she said. 'As though I'm outside myself.'

Marcus squeezed her, understanding, remembering how it felt.

'Grandad's going to be okay,' he told her, and he held her all night.

Evo

'Such terrible news about your grandfather,' said Heavey.

They sat in the glass room together above the Hub.

'Our people let us know as soon as he was found.'

'Your people?'

'They're in touch with your parents, to do with the Safe. I wasn't even sure if we should worry you with this. We're taking care of him.'

Esh was momentarily surprised.

'Who is?' she said.

'We're paying for his treatment,' Heavey explained. 'The Corporation wants to take care of your grandfather. We're giving him the best medical attention in the world.'

'Can I see him?'

Heavey peered at her for a few seconds.

'Let's just see what happens.'

She glanced outside at the Hub, at the crew working away beneath the screens broadcasting the launch around the world.

'The security issue looms over us,' he said. 'In seven

days everyone on the planet's going to know what the product is, which makes this a very sensitive time. However, it's only right that you have some idea of what we're doing now. The impact of this thing is going to be huge. It's the reason the Corporation has waited so long to make an announcement. It has waited for the right moment to introduce the product to the market. In a sense, the campaign isn't even about the launch. It's about introducing the *ideology* before we ever release the product.'

Heavey's eyes narrowed.

'We are seven days away from the most important revolution in human technology for the last two thousand years, Esh. It will change everything, from the way we live to the way we view ourselves. What I'm about to describe will signify the most important social and scientific step that the human race is ever likely to take.'

Heavey breathed in slowly, and his voice quietened to a whisper.

'It's called Evo,' he said. 'It is a system of pre-embryonic genetic therapy that will allow couples to determine the make-up of their children before they ever reach single-cell stage. It will be the most liberating, beneficial technology the world has ever known, and as such it needs to be exercised in the most responsible, ethical manner possible.'

Heavey sat back in the sofa, crossing his legs.

'The Corporation has spent nearly two decades perfecting this technology. They decided a long time ago to acquire total and universal control over all genetic enhancement patents, to ensure that they were developed in the correct way. The Corporation has placed the most stringent regulations upon itself throughout its research and development programme. They wanted to perfect this technology on a mass, commercial scale so that they could offer the whole planet the benefits of genetic enhancement at once. That is what our campaign seeks to convey. We are staging an unprecedentedly far-reaching launch to make everyone aware of what Evo is going to offer us.'

Esh's eyes moved back to the crew in the Hub, all functioning as a unit, performing their tasks, going through their processes, collectively generating the campaign on the screens behind them.

'The technology itself won't hit the streets for at least another two years,' Heavey said. 'There's going to be no blitz, no rush to market. With most technology, you let it grow and develop, bringing out an early version then introducing better versions as you go along. But with Evo we're launching at full capacity. The things Evo can do will blow your mind. When we unveil it in seven days, the launch is going to be purely conceptual – there'll be nothing to buy for a long time. This is simply a way of phasing Evo in.'

Esh looked at Heavey, suddenly overwhelmed by everything, the campaign, Grandad, and now how inconceivably huge the product was.

'We needed someone like you to make Evo look as exciting and natural as possible,' Heavey said. 'It's the reason we chose an individual over a range of people, because we needed to show that Evo is about being unique, about being special. You had every attribute we could possibly have looked for in someone, Esh. We're going to teach you everything about Evo, how it works, where it came from, how it was produced, how it was developed. We want you to understand it all.'

She looked at the floor, couldn't stop thinking about Grandad suddenly. What did all this technology matter in the end? She was losing her grandfather.

'You have everything, Esh,' Heavey said.

She looked up, met his eye.

'We've studied everything about you. Your development as a child. Your school records, your academic achievements, and physical abilities. We know all there is to know. And no one even comes close to you.'

Esh looked into the Hub again. From everywhere around the globe, the screens above the room transmitted the opening sequence of the campaign, showing her standing in her black vest in the BlueCube. By tonight, everyone on the planet would know who she was.

'I want you to come to understand all that Evo's going to do,' Heavey said. 'The clock's ticking now, and you should be in on the action.'

He stood up, led her out of the room. Stepping onto the gallery, Esh noticed a few members of the crew look up and see her.

All of a sudden, the amount of money the Corporation was going to pay her finally made sense. Twenty years of funding, secrecy and research invested in her, the future of the biggest product the Corporation had ever released depended on her. Her fee, given how much Evo would eventually generate in profit, was suddenly not so crazy. The security guards. Why she wasn't allowed contact outside this place, why the Corporation were so paranoid about the slightest thing happening to her. They had everything riding on her, the girl from East Stratford they'd decided would embody everything about Evo.

'We have a lot to get through,' Heavey said, patting her shoulder. 'But you're the woman for the job.'

Red light

Walking out of the Hub, she stopped on the pathway and saw Steveland walking towards his studio. He was as lost in thought as ever. He never seemed to care much what the rest of the crew was up to, always absorbed as he was in his own world and thoughts. Steveland was the best, Heavey had said. He understood Net systems better than anyone in the world. He'd even helped to develop the Safe and the technology in the BlueCube.

She watched him heading for his hut in the Creative Pagoda, and followed him.

Steveland was taking down a couple of pieces of equipment from his shelves and seating himself in a swivel chair. He laid out his equipment and began working, and Esh quietly let herself in.

'Hi,' she said.

Steveland looked up.

'Hey, Esh.'

He eyed her for a moment, not seeming to mind her presence, then gave her a smile and went back to work.

She pulled up a seat.

'Do you know what the product is?' he asked.

'They just told me.'

Steveland sat with shoulders hunched.

'Pretty crazy stuff, huh?'

Esh murmured in agreement.

'What do you think of it?'

Esh cast her eyes around his room, full of technical debris that he seemed to have amassed from the entire history of the world.

'I think there's nothing we can do about it,' she replied.

'I think you're right,' Steveland chuckled.

As he worked, Esh thought about Evo. She knew in her gut, just from the way Heavey had spoken, that it had been decided a very long time ago that Evo would take over everything, come what may.

'You know, when motorcars first arrived on the planet,' Steveland said, 'they had men walking in front of them holding red flags.'

Esh watched him applying himself to his work.

'Why?'

'To warn people that the car was approaching, and to limit the vehicle's speed.'

Steveland laughed again.

'Now the red flag's a marketing campaign.'

In her garden, Esh saw Mikey and André on their morning patrol, walking in their light-coloured suits under the patches of shadow. In the far corner, Miguel, Felipe and Fontàn tended the bushes in their grey overalls.

She walked into her house, and Maria came up to her excitedly.

'Come,' she said, and led Esh into the living room.

On the TV was a shot of a swimming pool, divided into racing lanes. It looked like an old home movie. There were eight swimmers racing each other, and in the centre a single figure slicing through the water ahead of the others. As the figure in the middle gained distance, the camera zoomed in, and the central swimmer filled the shot, powering through the water, hardly making a splash. The sight was beautiful, graceful, the swimmer's limbs pulling effortlessly through the water. Then suddenly the swimmer touched the end of the pool, and looked up.

Esh recognised herself at the age of six or seven, pulling off her goggles in the pool at Ford and looking around, searching for the other swimmers, only to realise they were trailing far behind.

The close-up lingered on her young face.

'*She has never been sick in her life,*' the Storyteller said.

The shot closed in on Esh, dripping with water.

'*Because that is the way she was born.*'

Esh's image melted from the screen, and the three letters of her name appeared, slowly disappearing, until the screen went black.

She needed somewhere calm and quiet where she could think, somewhere isolated.

She walked down the stairs to the basement, iScanned through the wide, white door, and sat down in the soft suede seat in the Safe.

What had she done? They were using her life in the

campaign. In an instant, she understood the nature of what was about to happen. She and Evo were inextricable.

They were bringing the hi-tech miracle of Evo down to earth. They were going to make Evo look like the most natural thing that had ever happened. And they were going to do it through her.

Behind the money, lay the reality of Evo.

She sat staring at the blank screen of the Safe, silent, cocooned. It was all now set in stone. The campaign had begun.

The light in the top corner of the screen suddenly turned green. She watched as her parents came online.

'Esh, were you waiting?' asked Dad.

'I was here anyway.'

'We saw the launch,' he said.

Her parents smiled weakly, glowing from the screen in the radiance of the Safe's walls. When Esh had first arrived she'd felt so close to them here, in this room. But now, they looked so tired and drawn.

'Is Grandad okay?'

Mum looked at her.

'He's not doing so well.'

'He woke up,' said Dad.

'Woke up?'

Esh's heart leapt with hope.

'But there's brain damage,' said Dad. 'He doesn't know where he is.'

'Did he say anything?'

'No,' said Dad. 'He's not speaking.'

Esh watched Mum staring helplessly into her lap.

'The Corporation have been fantastic,' Dad told her, giving Mum's hand a squeeze. 'Grandad's in the best unit we've ever seen.'

He smiled humbly, holding Mum.

'We're very grateful,' he said.

When she came out of the Safe, the sun was dazzling. She stood in the hallway, and saw Maria pop her head out of the kitchen.

'All right, Esh?'

Esh felt numb, and hollow.

'My grandfather's ill.'

Maria watched her with an understanding, a sympathy between them that they couldn't openly acknowledge.

'They'll take care of him,' she said.

Esh nodded, appreciating the comfort. She saw Maria glance over her shoulder at the clock in the kitchen.

'Have to get back to work.'

'Do you not have Interface?' Esh asked.

It had been troubling her. She'd noticed Maria never used EyeScreen.

'No,' said Maria.

'Did they cut you off the Net?'

Maria eyed her, the two women standing and looking at each other.

'I've never had Interface, Esh.'

Esh stared and suddenly, from Maria's look, she finally understood.

They were NAPs. Maria, Mano, their son.

'The Corporation gave us our lives,' Maria said. 'They brought us here and took care of Samsòn. They gave us homes, and our jobs.'

Esh couldn't believe it. It was a crazy fairytale.

'How do they pay you? Without Interface?'

Maria shrugged, smiling at Esh's refusal to accept.

'They don't pay you?'

Maria shook her head.

'Then how do you leave this place?'

It was too much. Maria saw the incomprehension on Esh's face.

'We don't leave,' she said. 'The Corporation have given us everything we need.'

Isabèl, Manuela, Felipe, Miguel, Fontàn. They were all NAPs. Her staff had nothing. They could never leave unless the Corporation specifically sanctioned it.

All day, they quietly hurried around her. Silent, efficient, and deferential.

Esh thought about the amount of money she was going to receive in six days, how much she was going to make from Evo. And she knew that, with room to spare, her fee could have given an existence to every NAP on the planet.

Her house went quiet as night fell. Maria went to bed, Mano was picked up by his car, and Esh climbed over the wall to Marcus's house.

She found him sitting on the deck outside, and sat down beside him, kissing him, and putting her arm around him.

'You've been in the sky all day,' he said.

He held her, and watched her in the glow of the SkyBoards.

'They're making you famous.'

She sat up closer to him and glanced up, seeing both their faces in the heavens.

'Have you really never been sick?' Marcus asked.

'No,' she murmured. 'I don't think so.'

She peered at LA's lights in the distance.

'I know what the product is, Marcus.'

He turned to her.

'They're going to bio–engineer people. Couples, before they have babies, are going to choose what their babies are like. That's what they're selling.'

Marcus stared at her.

'Jesus.'

'This thing's going to be huge,' she said.

He watched her for a while.

'That's why it's you,' he said.

'What?'

'You're perfect.'

She held his eyes. She didn't feel any more comfortable hearing it from him than from Heavey.

'It's just the way the Corporation wants me to be seen,' she said. 'They need to believe that there's someone out there who's unlike anybody else.'

Marcus smiled at her.

'But you are,' he said. 'You've just seen yourself in a huge ad campaign, appearing all over the sky, and instead of thinking it's amazing you've seen straight through it. When the Interface campaign kicked off, it blew me away. It left me speechless. But you've got bored with this in a day.'

Esh stared at him, thinking.

'It's the way I am, I guess,' she said.

'Exactly,' Marcus smiled.

'It's just marketing.'

'It's you.'

'They could have chosen anyone.'

'But they didn't, they waited for you, you even told me that.'

'That's the way Heavey talks, Marcus. It doesn't mean anything.'

'But it's true.'

'What is?'

'You're not like anyone else, Esh.'

She turned, and stared past the trees at the lights of LA. Beside her, Marcus's presence felt so warm and comfortable. Suddenly, for some reason, she wondered about all the mansions around them, who was in them, how many of them were hidden away here in the compound.

'I don't want to be different,' she said. 'At school everyone made me feel like I was a freak. But I'm not. It's the way I am.'

Marcus held her tightly.

'Esh?' he said.

She turned to him, and gazed at his face in the light.

'You've just described how every person on the planet feels.'

Chaos

'Morning, Esh.'

Heavey smiled across the glass room in the Hub.

'I want to explain Evo to you. In its most basic application, it's going to be able to screen diseases and congenital conditions in everyone born in the future, which means that a huge spectrum of human afflictions will disappear overnight. The human genome is about to change, and the Corporation consequently sees Evo as a universal tool for humanity, not as some exclusive perk reserved for the super-rich. We're launching this to the planet, for the benefit of all. This is the next evolutionary step in human development.'

Heavey's passion was evident, yet carefully restrained.

'I'm no scientist,' he said. 'And yet the moment I knew what Evo could do, I understood it. Evo isn't about science. It's about what we are. That's why we didn't even tell Gus and Nathan what the technology was, to begin with. We just told them to come up with an original way of selling the idea of being human.'

He watched her carefully from the sofa.

'Individuality is at the heart of Evo,' he said. 'The real magic of Evo isn't simply its impact on the future health of everyone on the planet. It's the unlimited potential that it's going to create for individuality. Taking the genetic material of two donor parents, Evo matches them in a traditional method, but from that point on the true power of Evo begins to appear. The Corporation has created a panoply of genetic characteristics that Evo can enhance and promote at the pre-embryonic stage. We can influence eye colour, hair colour, physical build, gender, intellect. But you can't just tweak this, tweak that in total isolation. The genius of Evo lies in its ability to manipulate the genetic identity as a whole, taking the individual as a unique being.'

Heavey leaned forward, and placed his fingertips together.

'This is the truly fascinating dimension of Evo. It's what the Corporation has taken so long to develop. When the Human Genome Project was commenced, it laid down a map of the entire human genetic structure. But it barely scratched the surface of what Evo can now do. What the Corporation perfected was the effects of genetic manipulation on the human organism as a whole. The human system is a subtle, sophisticated structure. You can't just alter one part and not expect knock-on effects to others. But that is what Evo controls. We have a basic package of enhancements which everyone will receive through the medical establishment, things to which every human should have a right. Given time and the proliferation of the technology, those benefits will become standard. But running in tandem will be the general, commercial application of Evo in which people will enter programmes of genetic therapy for their children. When they do, though, they'll be guided very carefully through what Evo can and cannot do. Evo merely provides us with the tools to influence genetic enhancement. It cannot build prefabricated souls. People's children will still be their natural progeny, they'll still share their parents' genetic characteristics. They'll just have an extra set of advantages. They'll be healthier and stronger, screened for predispositions to physical and mental disease. But this is what nature has always achieved. Each generation of humanity improves on the last. Genetic improvement is inbuilt to evolution. And that's where Evo takes its power from, simply making the power of nature accessible to everyone.'

With a small smile, Heavey parted his fingertips and opened his palms as though to demonstrate how powerless he was.

'Evo cannot predict how your child is going to talk,' he said, 'or how it's going to feel at school, what kind of friends it's going to make, or what profession it's going to go into. It can't do anything like that, because it can't alter the intrinsically chaotic nature of human existence. The human character responds to its environment, to the choices of the individual, to chance and coincidence, and there is nothing in the world that can change that.'

Heavey peered brightly at Esh.

'Look at me,' he said. 'Look at you. We don't get to choose how we're born. We turn up the way we are and make do with what we are. But if you had the choice, wouldn't you choose the best qualities for yourself? Isn't that what you'd pick for your child if you could decide? These are things to which everyone should have a right. That's what Evo's going to enable for everyone.'

Heavey gazed at her.

'Two years from now our clinics will be phased in as flagships of Evo. They'll open in the States, in Europe, the Far East, the Middle East, Asia, and eventually one day in Africa. Above and beyond our own clinics, we'll also regulate the technology like a franchise, making it available to the world's public medical resources. People in any part of the world, however poor, will have access to Evo, administered by hospitals and medical facilities all over the planet. The Corporation is passionately committed to making Evo as widely available as possible. It will take decades, not years, to implement this programme. But in the long-term there won't be a person on this earth who hasn't benefited somehow from Evo. That's why everyone's got to know about it. Eventually, it will become as normal as brushing your teeth or taking an aspirin. That is how revolutionary and how fundamental Evo is.'

Heavey's eyes were sharp with solemnity.

'You're going to bring Evo to the world,' he said. 'Through you, the world's going to see that Evo isn't there just to make the genetically rich richer, and the poor poorer, but that it's the greatest force for good there's ever been.'

He stared at her.

'We're going to show the truth,' he said.

'Of what?' Esh asked.

'Of how amazing your life is.'

She stared back at him for a moment, but couldn't bear the glint in his eyes. She turned and looked out of the Hub. The sunshine filtered through the Pagoda, dappling the paths weaving together the studios.

'I'm me, Heavey,' she said.

'You're special, Esh.'

She turned to him.

'I understand this is difficult,' he said. 'I know the pressure that comes with this. It can be an unchosen advantage, one that marks you out from your peers. But I want you to remember something. Evo is the most important technological product the world will ever see. It is the largest commercial investment the Corporation has ever made. And they've entrusted the entire future of that investment in you. Think about that, Esh. I want you to think about it for just one second.'

He left a gap of silence for her to think. She looked out of the Hub's glass wall, feeling the pull of Heavey's eyes.

'You're about to become the highest-paid face of any product in history,' he said. 'The Hub and the Pagoda have been purpose-built for us. No expense has been spared. And at the very top of it all, at the culmination of two decades of investment and research, the Corporation chose you to carry its message.'

Esh stared out of the Hub at the red wall surrounding her garden.

'You're the one,' he told her.

Esh felt an icy stillness in the room, and couldn't say where Heavey's marketing fantasy ended and where her incredulity began.

'So what?' she said.

She meant it. What did it matter?

'People can be born with the most amazing abilities,' he said, 'and still squander them all. Why? Who can say? It's just human nature. But you, Esh, have excelled at everything you've ever done. You were born with exceptional gifts, and you did everything with them that you possibly could. That was your own doing. And that is what the Corporation was astounded by.'

The star pupil. The model student. She'd come all this way from London, from her destiny at the Bank, to hear the same thing she'd always been told at school.

'Did you know that your immune system is unique?' Heavey said.

She looked up.

'What do you mean?'

'It's something immunologists look for when they're battling a new disease. They look for a single person who has an immunity to that disease, so that they can study what that person has that no one else does. It's a matter of pure luck. That person will always be an exception, a magical part of nature, a sudden mutation who appears to allow the human race to grow in new directions and to develop new aptitudes. You are that person, Esh. Biologically, everything about you is perfect. Everything is perfectly balanced and calibrated inside you, protected by the hardened cocoon of the most efficient immune system there has ever been. No one else has it, Esh. You have the strength to fight off anything. You will never get ill.'

'There are other people like that,' Esh protested.

Heavey smiled sadly.

'No,' he shrugged. 'There aren't.'

He watched her sitting defiantly before him.

'You don't even have pre-menstrual syndrome, Esh.'

She didn't meet his eye. She wanted to tell him it wasn't true. But she knew it was. She stared at the ground, feeling vulnerable, alone.

'How do you know?' she asked.

'We know everything, Esh.'

Something trembled inside her, making her trapped, afraid.

'We know you're a virgin,' he said.

Esh looked up, and froze.

'We had to,' he said. 'So we'd know there was no risk of infection, no skeletons waiting in your closet.'

He eyed her urgently.

'You've led the perfect life, Esh.'

She stood on the gallery, watching the bank of screens over the Hub. In the midst of them she noticed an image in the campaign.

It was video footage, shaky, and filmed from a distance, of her lying by her pool next door, stretched out on her sun lounger in her bikini. The camera wobbled as it zoomed in, showing her as she stood up and looked into her pool.

'*She's just a normal girl*,' said the Storyteller.

She looked pure and innocent, strong, athletic.

'*With an IQ of 211.*'

Slowly, the shot faded to black, and the three letters of her name appeared. After what seemed a long time, they dissolved from the screen.

Gus and Nathan were sitting on a bench on the far side of the room. Everyone else in the crew was always so busy, but those two looked perpetually like they had nothing on their hands, as if their job literally entailed hanging out all day.

Esh walked round the gallery towards them. They saw her coming, looked up.

'Who was filming me next door?' she asked them.

Gus and Nathan observed her, unbothered by her question. Gus slowly turned to Nathan, looking for a reply, then turned back to her.

'Heavey said it was okay,' he shrugged.

'He said it was okay to spy on me?'

Nathan squinted.

'He pretty much allows us to do what we want.'

'Even film me in my garden?'

'Yeah,' Nathan replied.

'Why?'

'We wanted a closer look.'

'Of what?'

'Of you being you.'

'And what's being me?' she said.

Gus gestured in her general direction.

'It's pretty cool,' he said. 'Seeing someone hanging out by a pool, doing nothing much, but then they're totally intelligent.'

'We thought that was funny,' Nathan added.

'Like kind of a shock?' said Gus.

'What did Heavey tell you about me?' she asked them.

Gus and Nathan swapped a glance, then turned to her.

'Not much,' said Nathan.

'Have you seen my life story?'

'Heavey just gives us bits of information when we come up with ideas.'

'So where did you get my IQ?'

'We came up with it.'

'You made it up?'

'Heavey told us what number to use.'

They stared at her for a while. Esh gazed past them.

'Why, what's your real IQ?' Gus asked.

Esh looked down at him.

'Doesn't matter,' she said.

She walked into the airlocked room of the Safe and heard the door slide shut. Sitting in the suede-lined seat in the wall, she waited, and watched the red light in the corner of the screen.

The strangeness of the silence enthralled her. She felt as if a nuclear blast could have decimated the compound above her and she'd never have heard it.

The light in the screen turned green. Her parents appeared on the blank white wall, sitting beside each other and looking out.

'Hello, Esh,' said Mum.

'We're seeing you everywhere,' said Dad.

'They're talking about you on TV, there are articles about you in magazines.'

Esh looked at them on screen, and felt as if they were talking about another world.

'I'm finding it weird,' she said.

'It must be strange,' said Dad.

'They've been telling me things,' she confessed.

Mum and Dad's expressions changed.

'What sort of things?' asked Dad.

'They've said there's something different about my immune system?'

'Really?'

Both of them had gone a little still.

'What do you know about it?' Esh said.

'What exactly did they say?'

'That my immune system's different, that's why I've never been sick.'

Mum and Dad looked at her.

'It's true,' said Mum.

'What?'

'That you've never been ill.'

'Is that so strange?'

'It's unusual,' said Dad.

'Why? Did the other kids get ill?'

Dad looked at her, and nodded.

'Of course,' he said.

'But I didn't?'

'No.'

'Why did you never say anything about it?'

'It's not the kind of thing you tell a child,' said Mum.

'Why not?'

'You don't point out what's different about them.'

'So I *was* different?'

Something in Esh suddenly wanted to know everything, needed to hear it from her parents.

'You were different in so many ways,' Mum told her. 'You were so much quicker than other children, you learned so fast, everything you did was absurdly advanced.'

She looked at Esh nostalgically.

'Your abilities were incredible, Esh. But we never wanted you to feel odd or out-of-place, so we tried not to draw attention to it. We wanted you to feel as normal as you possibly could.'

Esh's heart beat faster.

'I wasn't normal?'

'You were extraordinary,' Dad said with a smile.

She hadn't wanted to hear this. She'd wanted them to tell her that Heavey had been making it up, twisting the story for the sake of Evo.

'You were always so healthy,' Mum said. 'You never got sniffles and fell over like the other children. I don't remember you even hurting yourself. It seemed as if you knew how to take care of yourself from the very start.'

Mum gazed at her from the screen.

'You know you hardly cried as a child?' she said.

'Really?'

'I can't think of a single time.'

Esh couldn't remember it either. She suddenly knew it was true, something she'd failed to notice simply because it had always been absent.

'They said I'll never contract a disease,' she said. 'That I'll never get ill.'

Dad stared at her curiously.

'Strange,' he said.

Esh suddenly noticed Mum looking upset.

'Mum, are you okay?'

Mum's hand trembled. She wiped her eyes, lifting her head.

'Grandad's going to die,' she said.

Dad's arm squeezed round her.

'They've done the tests. There's nothing more they can do.'

Esh sat in shock, feeling herself floating.

'When will he die?' she mumbled.

'We don't know. Could be any time.'

Esh felt time stopping.

'I don't understand,' she said.

She gazed at Mum and Dad, and they stared back at her.

'What's wrong with him?'

'We don't know,' said Dad.

Esh watched Mum crying beside him.

'You said they'd done the tests?'

'They have.'

'So what's wrong with him?'

'We can't tell you,' Dad said gently.

Esh watched him on the screen.

'Why?'

'They won't let us say.'

'Who won't?'

'The Corporation. They said it's for security.'

'What security?'

'We don't know,' he faltered.

Suddenly Esh wondered who was listening to them.

'Who's stopping you talking, Dad?'

'The people helping us at the hospital.'

'What did they say?'

'They don't want you to know what's wrong with Grandad.'

'Why?'

'Because of something to do with the campaign.'

Esh felt as if someone was uncoiling a thick black rope inside her, drawing it out of her, metre by metre.

Mum sat sobbing by Dad, and Esh wanted to reach out, and hold her.

'I need to see Grandad,' she said.

Mum and Dad looked at her. 'Will they let you?'

'I don't know.'

She needed to go to London, urgently.

'But I'm going to try,' she said.

Her parents vanished from the screen. The silence filled her ears. As she gazed into the unreal glow of the Safe's white light, it felt as if this small pod was keeping her hidden away from the world.

She didn't understand how Grandad could have gone from being so healthy to so decrepit in such a short time. How could he be dying? What was wrong with him? The Corporation didn't want her to know.

She could hear her own blood and thoughts flowing through her head in the silence. They'd cut her off. No Interface. No escape. She needed to see Grandad, and to find out what was wrong with him.

She found Heavey in the middle of a meeting with the strategy teams. She stood at the door of the conference room, behind his back, and the crew members in the meeting looked up to see her. Heavey turned round.

He excused himself from the room, and came out.

'Okay?' he said.

'My grandfather's dying.'

Heavey looked concerned.

'I know,' he said.

'What's wrong with him, Heavey?'

Heavey sighed.

'It's confidential,' he said.

'This is my grandfather.'

'I know.'

He stared into her eyes.

'I need to know,' she told him.

'I'm sorry,' he replied. 'I can't tell you.'

'Why not?'

'I'm afraid that's restricted too.'

Esh ground her jaw.

'I know how upsetting this is, Esh. But it's for your own sake.'

'I have to see him, Heavey.'

'I understand. But we can't let you do that.'

'Why?' she strained, raising her voice now.

'Because we're too close, because the campaign's in full swing.'

'My grandfather's dying.'

'I know. I'm sorry.'

'You're sorry?'

Heavey glared at her.

'This is a terrible time.'

'You have no idea.'

'Esh,' he said. 'You've got to face your responsibilities. You're one of us now.'

He nodded towards the crew.

'You're the most vital part of this entire campaign. If we let you out into the open now you'll be vulnerable to attack. And we can't take the slightest chance of you being harmed. We have too much going on.'

He spoke to her directly, as a colleague.

'I know how hard this is. Christ. It must feel terrible to be so far from your grandfather right now. But we're taking care of him, Esh. We're doing everything we can for him.'

'What's wrong with him, Heavey?'

'I can't tell you, Esh.'

'Why's he dying?'

'It would compromise you.'

'Compromise what?'

Heavey stared at her blankly.

'It's my health, isn't it?' she said.

Heavey didn't answer.

'You want to hide what's wrong with my grandfather because you're worried it'll make me look bad. There's something wrong with him that I shouldn't have?'

'Please, Esh.'

'That's it, isn't it?'

'We're trying to save him,' Heavey told her.

'Then tell me what's wrong with him.'

'I can't.'

'I have a right, Heavey.'

Heavey let out a hot, exasperated breath.

'You'll know soon,' he said.

'When?'

'When the time comes.'

Heavey re-entered the conference room, leaving Esh alone on the gallery. She stared at the ads on the Hub's screens, at the footage of her in the BlueCube, the sequence of her in the swimming pool, the shot of her getting off her sun lounger. And then a new image.

She walked nearer the bank of screens to see. It was a shot of her head and shoulders at the age of four, looking innocently into the camera.

'*What's your name?*' a voice asked her.

'*Esh,*' she replied.

'*How old are you, Esh?*'

'*Four and a half.*'

'*How far away's your next birthday?*'

Esh's hair was soft and dark, her face small and angelic. But there was something about her that wasn't childlike at all.

'*Eighteen weeks, three days,*' she responded.

157

'*And what will you do for your birthday?*'

Esh stared into the camera, shrugged.

'*Depends. Probably spend it with my parents.*'

The shot faded, and her name appeared on the screen in small white letters.

'*At the age of four,*' said the Storyteller, '*Esh possessed the physical and intellectual ability of a twelve-year-old.*'

The letters slowly dissolved from the screen.

'*But then, Esh was never a normal child.*'

She walked to Steveland's studio.

'Steveland,' she said, stepping in.

He turned in his chair.

'Hi.'

'Can I talk to you?'

'Sure.'

He pushed a chair towards her.

'What's up?'

'Is there any way of me sending a message from here without anyone knowing?'

Steveland's face darkened, teetering between curiosity and anxiety.

'Who do you need to speak to?'

'My lawyers.'

He watched her, thinking.

'Why?'

'I'm cut off, Steveland. I don't have access to anything. I need to know how much freedom of movement I'm allowed under my contract. My grandfather's dying in London and Heavey's told me I can't see him.'

Steveland understood.

'Ask Heavey to talk to your lawyers,' he suggested.

'I can't. I have to do this in secret.'

Steveland peered at her.

Esh couldn't believe she was doing this. She had no tangible reason to trust Steveland, just felt that he was someone she could turn to. She'd even thought of asking her parents to contact her lawyers, but something had held her back, the suspicion that somehow, the whole time, everything she said in the Safe was being listened to.

'What are you asking me to do?' Steveland asked.

'I need to speak to my lawyers without a soul knowing about it.'

Steveland frowned, screwed up his face.

'So how are we going to do that?' he said aloud.

'I don't know,' Esh whispered. 'That's why I'm asking.'

She needed Steveland's legendary genius to come into play, right now.

'They monitor everything that goes out of here,' he said. 'Do you know that?'

Esh nodded. She'd always assumed that was the case.

'They'd spot a message to your lawyers,' he told her.

'Don't you control the traffic out of here, Steveland?'

He shrugged.

'I'm not God.'

'There must be a way round the system?'

Steveland lifted his fingers, cradling them round his chin, and thought hard, getting to grips with the conundrum. Suddenly he looked up at her, panicked, as if he'd just woken from a daydream.

'Shit, this is crazy,' he said. 'It's too dangerous.'

Esh watched him, still hopeful he might tip over to her side.

'They'd fire me, Esh. I'd never work again.'

She understood his predicament, genuinely believed he wanted to help her. But it felt as if a last small door had closed, shutting her into this place indefinitely.

He shook his head.

'I'm sorry, I wish there was something I could do.'

Esh smiled wearily, getting up.

'Thanks,' she said, and she left.

She iScanned out of the Creative Pagoda, into her garden. Over the brow of her lawn, she saw Tony and Mikey on a patrol by the bottom of her drive, walking along the perimeter wall between her and Marcus. They saw her, and waved.

She walked up towards the house. The desire to see Marcus hit her urgently. She needed him. Trapped, she wanted him more than ever.

Lifting her head, she gazed idly, uselessly, at the SkyBoards above her, as if they offered the slightest hope of leading her out of here. Ads for Evo were everywhere. Her image dotted the sky, spanning its huge horizon.

Suddenly, all the SkyBoards blinked off, and the sky appeared, stretching above them in an empty blue canvas. No one had seen the sky for years. For the second time in a week, the SkyBoards synchronised to reveal the heavens. And then a single image formed itself across the sky, just as it had for the launch.

It was a home video of a child, eagerly taking its first steps across a summery lawn, over eighteen years ago.

It was Esh, wearing a nappy and rompers.

On her lawn in LA, she watched herself in the sun-filled Californian sky. She'd never seen the footage, had never even known of its existence. She saw herself walking excitedly, around Mum and Dad's garden, transported by her new bipedal ability, so tiny, almost too tiny to walk, but balancing on her feet, as if she'd not been able to stay earthbound a second longer.

Vox

Esh walked straight into the Safe, not knowing what to do. She wanted to feel Marcus beside her, to bring her on an even keel again. She needed to hear her parents' voices, to have Kristin's company for just a few seconds. In that instant she would have given anything to feel her old friend's companionship. Those images of the campaign swung around her, haunting her, scenes from a childhood she couldn't remember unravelling across the sky. She wanted to lock herself away and disappear from here, forget everything she'd seen.

The air pressure bumped, and the Safe sealed itself shut. Listening to the silence, she let the hush of the vacuum pass over her, breathed in slowly, and stepped backwards into her seat in the wall, falling into its padded suede pod as if it had been moulded to her very shape.

The silence was pure. Spacelike. Like deafness.

She watched the corner of the white screen, waiting for the light to turn green. Were Mum and Dad at home? She had no idea. How was she meant to even know? Her communication with everything, everyone, had been restricted.

In the suede seat, she patted her thumb and fingertip together, making contact between the chips. But they remained inert, as lifeless as clipped fingernails. The external world had been switched off.

She looked at the blank screen, needing to see Mum and Dad, imagining how Mum must be feeling watching her own father die, lying unconscious and vegetative in hospital. Something in her just couldn't grasp the reality that Grandad was dying. She tried to imagine him now. But was it even him? This living corpse?

'Esh.'

She sat on the edge of the seat, and saw that the light in the screen was still red.

Someone had spoken.

She got up, and looked round the corner of the room. The white door was shut. Where had the voice come from?

'Esh.'

She turned round, her heart pumping. The voice was in the Safe.

'Hello, Esh,' he said. 'Do you recognise me?'

It was the young American who'd called her in the limo in London.

'How did you get to me?'

'I told you I knew where you were going.'

'Who are you?'

'Guess.'

The room was soundproof, empty.

'I don't know,' she said.

'Are you sure?' the voice chuckled.

Esh stood panicking, dumbstruck.

'Do you think they can hear us?' the voice asked.

He sounded alert, as if he knew precisely how much danger he was courting.

'This is the most secure communications device in the world' he said. 'The Corporation built it so no one could hear you. But they were so diligent about it they didn't even give themselves the ability to listen in on you.'

He let out an amused laugh.

'Why are you here?' Esh asked.

'To help you.'

'What do you want?'

'Nothing,' he said.

She looked around the Safe. How had they got in? Even knowing that she was coming to LA, how could they have known about the Safe, let alone worked out how to break into it? They'd made it, they had infinite reach. They'd finally infiltrated her in the compound, just as they'd infiltrated the Khaki Girl.

'Why do you think the Corporation have got you hidden away in this little space-capsule, talking to your parents, Esh?'

He could see her. He knew where she was standing.

'Why do you think that is?' he asked.

'To stop you getting to me.'

'Oh really?' he said.

He laughed, a bright, genuine, joy-filled laugh. Even panicking, Esh realised it was strangely infectious.

'No,' the voice said, turning serious again. 'They're freezing your means of communication to stop you getting out. Because they know that when the time comes, you're going to want to run.'

'From what?'

Esh felt the cold of the room shiver down her spine. She couldn't see the voice, but she knew it was telling the truth. Something in its calmness and confidence had won her trust almost since the very first time she'd heard it.

'In six days, Esh, you're going to become a huge liability to the Corporation. They're making these preparations in advance to control you.'

'I don't understand.'

'They're keeping you very safe, very shut away, because they know you'll try to escape.'

'From what?'

'From what they're about to tell you.'

Esh felt herself melting in the brightness of the room, hypnotised by the voice reaching out to her and opening up the world.

'What are they going to tell me?'

'We're not sure yet.'

'Then how do you know?'

The voice was silent for a moment.

'Because we're the Team,' he said.

She stood breathing, gazing into the empty room. The Team had found her. They'd known about her, followed her, from London.

'All we know is the Corporation is hiding a lot from you.'

'Like what?'

'What you are. How they found you.'

The voice remained calm, down-to-earth.

'But luckily we got to you before they took you off the Net.'

'How?'

'Because we knew they were waiting for you. We knew you were coming here.'

She breathed, frozen on the Safe's white floor.

'Have you heard of the Foundation, Esh?'

She didn't answer. Should she speak? She felt as if she was going to lose everything, that the end was inevitable.

'No,' she said. But it rang a bell, however small. 'Who are the Foundation?'

'Find out, Esh.'

'What do you want from me?'

She stared at the blank white screen, waiting.

'Why have you come?' she asked.

But the silence lingered, dull, and muted.

There was nothing. The voice had gone. The thought of stepping back into the world filled her with a panicked foreboding. She couldn't remember ever feeling scared, as she did now. When she'd been a kid she'd hardly ever asked Mum or Dad to comfort her, had never woken in the middle of the night and crawled into their bed, or asked them to stroke her to sleep and leave the light on outside.

But suddenly now, the mere thought of everything that waited for her beyond the safety of this little white room made her feel afraid.

It weighed in her, like a rock.

The Team knew she was here. They'd tracked her down and finally made contact, while outside Evo unfurled her life story across the SkyBoards, with every detail the Corporation had managed to extract from her life.

And all along, the Team had been watching them do it.

*

She moved across the glowing floor, and the Safe's door opened in front of her.

Heavey was waiting for her outside.

'What are you doing, Esh?'

He stood in the hallway, anxious.

'We've been looking all over for you. We had no idea you were here.'

Esh froze in front of him. They hadn't been able to hear her in the Safe. Heavey held up his finger and thumb, an inch apart.

'This close to calling security,' he told her.

He smiled nervously, shaking his head with relief.

'I want to talk to you about something,' he said.

He tapped her arm and told her to follow him.

'You must feel an awful long way from your parents,' he said as they walked through the house.

She felt too nervous to speak.

'I guess,' she mumbled.

Heavey stopped by her living room, turning and looking in her eyes.

'You must feel trapped. I can understand. You probably feel the need to spend time on your own?'

Heavey looked at her for an answer. She nodded, and he nodded back.

'You must be going crazy all cooped up in here.' He pursed his mouth in sympathy. 'The isolation. The security. The pressure of the campaign.'

Had Steveland told Heavey about her wanting to contact her lawyers? Was that why he was sounding her out?

'Look,' he said. 'There's something we want you to do, which might be great for you. It would involve leaving the compound for a night. We're still assessing the security situation and the potential impact it might have on the campaign, so it's not for sure. But we're thinking about it. It would happen tonight.'

Heavey heard Maria's footsteps behind him. He stopped, and glanced back at her walking through the hallway, waiting until her footsteps had disappeared.

'Come to the Hub,' he said, turning back to Esh. 'I'm going to explain.'

Nathan, Gus, Paul, Alice, Barney, Brice and Steveland sat around Esh at the long table. At the head of the conference table sat Heavey.

He spoke with a deliberately hushed tone, designating that everything he was about to say was never to leave the room.

'We're sending Esh to the Fall Oscars. The security implication of the strategy is enormous, so it hasn't been finalised. No one even knows Esh is in the States, let alone LA, so moving her out of the compound for just one night opens her up to being tracked and traced by anyone out there crazy enough to do so. We'd lose a lot of security leverage, but the Oscars, in terms of global coverage, is unparalleled. Showing up at the ceremony might coincide perfectly with where the arc of the campaign's hitting right now. The market's fascinated with Esh. We've developed her into a real, relatable phenomenon. People are identifying with her, begging for more, and if we give them one glimpse of her, it could give us all the buzz we need for the five days until launch. This could be perfect. But it's a risk.'

Esh looked at the crew's faces, and saw them all eyeing her eagerly. She felt like she was in a dream, seeing the momentum of the plans being assembled around her, and the fact that the Team had already directly gained access to her.

'Esh's security are planning contingencies for tonight just in case. If we decide to green-light this, we can do it on five minutes' notice. The Academy doesn't even know she might turn up yet. But if we need the window, it'll be there for us.'

Heavey steered his attention to Nathan and Gus.

'Guys?' he said.

The whole table turned to them, both looking as if they'd been hauled into a family conference neither of them had any interest in attending.

'What are your thoughts?' Heavey asked.

'What do you want me to say?' Nathan said defensively. 'Oscars is the Oscars. You get coverage. But it's unmediated, unprocessed. She'll just become real.'

'She's already real,' Heavey interjected.

Nathan lifted a finger.

'Different real. She's real like memory, like a fable. Take her to the Oscars and she'll become as real as any other celebrity. Very different.'

Gus shrugged his agreement.

'Perhaps that's what we need,' Heavey suggested. 'To gradate Esh's image from a remote, mythical desirability to a walking, talking desirability based in reality.'

There was silence around the table.

'The Oscars can give us that,' Heavey said. 'We've built Esh as a palpable entity already. She's a rounded, flesh-and-blood being. If we give a glimpse of her out in the open now, we could dazzle everyone.'

Everyone thought about it.

'I agree,' Brice piped up.

'Me too,' said Barney.

Gus and Nathan threw each other a look. They obviously felt that they were going to have to let the non-creatives go ahead and screw it all up.

'This'll make Esh tantalisingly real,' Alice said. 'No one's seen her in the flesh. If we let them take a sneak peek, they'll go crazy over her.'

Everyone looked around, bouncing ideas off each other, eventually coming to a consensus, and forgetting that Esh was sitting amongst them.

Her heart was beating as she thought about the Safe, and the voice of the Team telling her that, any time now, she was going to suddenly want to escape.

'Okay, people,' Heavey said.

He called order, and turned to Steveland.

'If we're going to do this, we'll to need to ensure Esh's security aspect,' he said. 'Is that something you can deal with?'

Steveland nodded without hesitation. 'No problem.'

'Good,' said Heavey.

He turned finally to Esh, and smiled.

'We'll let you know as soon as we have the decision.'

Heavey led her out of the room, holding the door open for her.

'How do you feel, Esh?'

He waited for a response, but she didn't speak. She looked across the Hub at the screens of the campaign, and for the second time watched the home movie which the Corporation had found, showing her first steps in the garden.

'If we take you to the Oscars, we'll have to be careful,' Heavey said. 'We're at our most sensitive right now. We can't afford any kind of attack on you.'

She watched her childhood on the screens.

'Okay?' he said.

She nodded silently, and turned to him.

'Is there something you want to do while you wait for the decision?' he asked.

Esh looked into his eyes.

'I want to run,' she said.

The high steel gates opened. Clive and André moved first, scanning the compound road, while Esh stayed back with Mikey and Tony. Clive moved right, cleared his area, as André moved to his left.

'I'm good,' said Clive.

'We're good,' said André.

Tony tapped Esh on the shoulder.

'Ready to go,' he said.

She felt Mikey and Tony's shadows follow her as she left her grounds. She stepped onto the road, Clive and André guarding her either side, and ran.

The same high wall, the same entrances to all the other mansions that she'd never seen, passed rapidly. She wanted to run everything out of her system, as if all her fear would be expelled in a quick lap of the compound. She wanted to run until the feelings escaped: the thought of Grandad in hospital, the voice in the Safe, the agony of Heavey not allowing her to go to London, the Corporation telling her parents not to let her know what was wrong with Grandad. She needed Marcus. She needed Kristin.

171

As the hill inclined, her momentum picked up, and she ran so hard there was nothing left to think of but the movement of her arms and legs. She tried to forget the continuous wall running alongside her, the gateways to the hidden mansions, the asphalt leading her back to her own grounds.

The road flattened out, bent slowly round, and as they came to the base of the compound she hit level ground, and maintained her speed from the hill.

Coming round the long, slow corner, she glimpsed the enormous steel gate to the outside road, thick enough to withstand a missile attack. She felt it loom over her as she passed. Nothing could get through it. No one was allowed to know what was on this side of the wall. Even she was never allowed to pass through unless her security guards were with her.

No one in the world knew she was here. Except for the Team.

They knew about the Safe, about the compound, the campaign. They even claimed to know how long the Corporation had been watching her life.

Why had they made contact with her now? If they allegedly had all the material from her Identity that they'd ever need, why hadn't they already sabotaged her in an iVert? What were they waiting for?

Suddenly, Esh wondered whether this was what had happened to the Khaki Girl. Had they lured her slowly, via the Safe, earning her trust the same way, only to find the footage of her in the bathroom and broadcast it to the world?

The campaign for Evo was in full flow, and yet they hadn't hit her with an iVert. They could have been watching her through the Safe for weeks now, and yet they'd only just made contact.

They said they'd been watching her for as long as the Corporation. But how long did that mean? Somehow, they'd found a way through. They'd broken through the Corporation's defences, just as they had with every iVert ever staged.

She kept running.

So the Team existed. They were flesh and blood. She'd heard plenty of conspiracy theories about iVerts being an invention of the Corporation, to create a gang of fictional rogues whom everyone could root for.

But it was true. The Team was real. And everything the Corporation had done to protect her – the Safe, the compound, deleting her Identity, taking her off Interface – had been in vain. Because the Team had found her.

She ran past the giant steel gate guarding the entrance to the compound. Her four armed security guards trailed her. Why? To protect her from what?

She thought about what the voice had said, and ran faster. Was it true? Was her security there not to protect her, but to stop her escaping?

She reached the house. A hundred metres behind her, André, Clive, Mikey and Tony staggered up the hill, exhausted.

She turned to see Heavey waiting for her up by the house. Even from a distance, she could see his undisguisable pleasure.

'You're going to the Oscars, Esh. We've been cleared.'
He gazed at her, hoping she'd share in his pleasure.

'We're leaving in three hours. We have to prepare you quickly.'

Esh looked past him, through the line of trees by the house, trying to make out LA in the sunny distance. She had no idea what it was like down there.

'Okay?' he said.

Esh pulled back her gaze, and looked at him.

'Who are the Foundation?' she asked.

Heavey held her gaze, and didn't flinch.

'Why?'

'I want to know.'

'They have nothing to do with us, Esh.'

'I never said they did.'

The tenderness in Heavey's eyes quickly disappeared.

'Why are you asking this, Esh?'

'Who are they? What do they do?'

Heavey glanced at the bodyguards approaching them on the driveway.

'Why are you asking this now?' he stammered.

'I want to know what they have to do with me.'

'They have nothing to do with you.'

'Then why not tell me?'

'Why, Esh?' he asked impatiently. 'What is it you want to know?'

'Whatever you're hiding from me,' she said.

In that moment, she could see it, watching him think desperately how to deal with this situation. He was guilty. The Team had been right. They'd allowed her to ask something Heavey didn't want her to know.

'We haven't time to talk about this,' he said.

'Who are they, Heavey?'

Heavey stared into her eyes, and instead of his joy

from a minute before, she could only see a watery kind of panic.

'I won't be drawn on this topic, Esh.'

'Then let me see my grandfather. You're already risking me leaving the compound tonight. You could take me to London under armed guard so I could see him before he dies.'

Heavey glared at her. He shook his head, and then turned to walk away.

'Have a shower,' he said. 'You're needed in twenty minutes.'

The dress

When she joined him in the Hub, he ignored her previous questions completely. She asked again, more forceful this time, but he simply shook his head.

'Security are rehearsing their movements right now,' he told her. 'They're checking the layout of the building, working out how to extract you quickly if anything happens. But you won't notice any of this. You just need to follow your nose. Don't worry about what you're meant to be doing or where you need to be. Just follow the brief we're going to give you and security will do the rest. There's an art to this thing. Security need to be with you every step of the way, but they'll remain invisible. The last thing we need is you looking like some priceless diamond that can't be let out the vault. You have to look natural, completely at ease. We've already got you looking great in the campaign. People sense the reality of you, and we need to preserve that. Tonight is about giving away just a little bit more of you. We want them to see that what they're getting on TV and the SkyBoards isn't fake. We want them to see you exactly as you are, which means not having four ex–Green Berets lurking around, ready to take a bullet for you. It has to be magical. You'll arrive, you'll walk the red carpet as if it's the most normal thing on earth, and that's it. No frills. No fancy stuff.'

He abandoned his casual pose on the sofa and looked intently at Esh.

'We're not doing any direct Evo placement,' he said. 'This will not be a brand event. It's the one thing Gus and Nathan are happy about. We're keeping this very simple. You don't have to do anything, no standing in front of the cameras and posing for pictures. That vibe is totally anti-you, and anti-Evo. This is not glamour, Esh. This is about being human. I want you out there having a good time. Though nothing can prepare you for what it'll be like. You'll just have to go out, and not let the camera flashes faze you. It'll feel like half a million TV presenters are trying to talk to you at once, but don't stop for them. Security will keep you away from those elements, so don't worry about the crowd. You're not on some diplomatic meet–and–greet. This is just you turning up at the Oscars, impromptu. You'll be on your own, there won't be any stars around, they'll have already entered the building. That's how we've arranged things, so you'll have a free run from the street to the theatre. Walk slowly, calmly to the theatre building. And then your job will be done.'

Heavey smiled at her from the sofa.

'There's nothing to worry about. We'll do a couple of practice runs in the outfit, but that's it. Just follow security's lead, and they'll give you the pace.'

He stared, and Esh then realised he was even more nervous than she was.

'Go and see Steveland,' he said, 'then we'll get you ready.'

'Hi, Steveland.'

He turned from his work bench as Esh came in.

'Hey,' he grinned.

'Heavey said I had to see you.'

'Sure. Take a seat.'

Still sitting, he pushed a chair towards her, and picked up a couple of devices he had waiting. Esh looked over the huge jumble of equipment stored on his shelves.

'Okay,' he said. 'Could you move a little closer?'

Esh shifted her chair forward as Steveland lifted a device to her temple.

'Bow your head a little.'

She obediently bent forward.

'What are you going to do?'

'I need to get to your Eye,' he said. 'I'm going to boot your Retina so we can use it as a homing device. It won't reactivate Interface or EyeScreen, but we'll be able to trace the chip. I'll programme it with a specific code so only we can find you. No one else will know where you are.'

Steveland sat face-to-face with her. As he looked over her brow, she felt a warm, light puff of breath from his nose.

'This'll be quick,' he said.

She kept her head bowed, and Steveland worked away.

'Steveland?'

'Mmm?' he said, concentrating now.

'I need to ask you something.'

Steveland pressed a pad attached to a wire to Esh's cheekbone.

'Go ahead.'

'When did you build the Safe?' she asked.

He held her temples to keep her head still.

'We built it for you,' he said, 'just before you came.'

'When exactly?'

'About six months ago.'

'It wasn't in the house when the Khaki Girl died?'

Steveland suddenly stopped, and looked down.

'How did you know about her?'

'I worked it out. I want to know how the Team got to her.'

Steveland looked amazed.

'We don't know,' he said. 'That's why we built the Safe.'

'Is there any way of breaking into it?'

He paused, and looked into her eyes.

'The Safe's inviolable,' he said. 'No one can get in.'

Esh peered at him, and for a moment she wanted to tell him that the Team had already got in. But she didn't know what would happen. If the Corporation found out, everything could end overnight.

Steveland hesitantly pointed at her forehead.

'Your Retina's active,' he said. 'If you disappear, we'll know where to find you.'

He looked down, and started slowly wrapping up the equipment.

'Are you sure no one can get to me?' Esh asked.

Steveland stopped what he was doing for a moment, and looked at her.

'You're invisible to everyone but me,' he said, and smiled. 'Have fun at the Oscars.'

*

Heavey stood beside her in one of the studios around the Hub. With them was a woman in her forties Esh had never seen in the Pagoda, pretty, but looking harassed, as if she'd been conjured out of thin air in a hurry.

There were no windows in the room. The only furniture was a dressing-table with a spotlit mirror, and an armchair sitting in front of it.

'We made this for you,' said Heavey.

He pointed at a dress hanging on the wall, created from fine, gold lace that made it look as though it weighed no more than five grams.

Beneath the dress was a pair of gold thin-strapped heels.

'They're your size,' he said. 'Try them on.'

Esh looked at the tailor-made clothes. When had they been made?

'Tabitha will help you,' Heavey said. 'I'll leave it to you.'

He politely exited the room.

Esh stood where she was. Tabitha began to help her undress, her hands subtle and deft as if Esh were barely there.

Standing naked, she watched Tabitha reach over to the dressing-table and come back with a gold slip, made from lace, in the same colour as the dress. As she put it on, Tabitha turned to the dress and carefully removed it from the wall, lifting it delicately from the hanger. In one smooth motion, she slipped it over Esh's body, as if she'd gauged every line and angle of Esh's shape in advance.

Esh stood in the dress. It felt like a layer of air.

Tabitha crouched at her feet, and slipped the gold

heels on. They were soft, and leathery, and felt as natural as extensions of her own body. A knock came from the door.

'Ready?' Heavey called in.

He entered, and looked at Esh in the corner, standing over six feet tall in her heels. She felt her own body exposed beneath the dress.

'My God,' he said. 'You look divine.'

Tabitha led her slowly towards the mirror, making her sit at the dressing-table. In her own reflection, Esh saw how beautiful the dress was.

'Tabitha,' Heavey said. 'Weave your magic.'

She looked into her mirror image, and didn't recognise herself. She'd been slowly transformed before her eyes, under Tabitha's expert touch.

Over each of her shoulders, Heavey and Tabitha eyed her in the mirror, studying her painstakingly. She looked like a movie star, a goddess. But everything about herself, her make-up, her hair, her face, looked to her as if they belonged to someone fictional. The reflection was her own, and yet she looked like a woman, like the perfect woman.

'What do you think?' asked Heavey.

Tabitha took a last, intense look over Esh.

'She's ready,' she said.

Tabitha's voice was warm and light. It was the first time she'd spoken. She helped Esh up. In her heels and her dress, with her hair immaculately arranged and made-up for the first time ever, Esh turned to Heavey.

He shook his head, moved almost to tears.

'My God,' he said.

Standing tall, dressed in gold, armour-plated with Tabitha's make-up, Esh felt superhuman. But inside the butterflies plagued her. She was scared of leaving the compound, felt afraid of being paraded in front of the world.

'Come on,' Heavey said. 'Your chopper's waiting.'

She walked around the Hub's wall, and as she passed she saw the heads of the crew members turn to watch her, all gathering at the window to wave her off.

Heavey led her to the door of the Creative Pagoda, and stood in front of the iScan with her. Over the wall, she could hear the high-pitched burring of a helicopter's engines. Heavey rested his fingers lightly on her bare shoulder, careful not to disturb the dress. Tabitha lingered behind them, holding a make-up case.

'Have a good time, Esh,' Heavey said to her.

His fingertips gave her a little pinch of encouragement, and he smiled.

'Go on,' he said.

He nodded towards the door, and she turned round. Her nerves were so intense she felt as if they were lighting up the lace of her dress, buzzing over her warm, bare arms. The Pagoda door opened, and Mikey and Tony were waiting on the other side. She could see the helicopter in the middle of the lawn, its enormous blades churning, André and Clive looking small as they waited beneath it.

'See you later,' Heavey shouted over the noise of the chopper.

She stepped through, and crossed the lawn in her heels, Mikey and Tony joining her sides like pilot fish as Tabitha followed behind.

She suddenly didn't want to leave the compound, but just to cross over the wall to Marcus on the other side, and be safe and alone with him. What was going to happen when everyone saw her at the Oscars? She couldn't face the thought of so many people staring at her, recognising her from the sky, from TV. She felt helpless, as though some terrible, invisible force was pushing her across the lawn towards the helicopter. She wanted to be hidden away in the Safe, shut off from everything. She wanted the Voice to tell her why all of this was happening, why Grandad was dying, why the Corporation was keeping everything from her. Blown by the gusts of the rotor-blades fluttering across her skin through the lace of her dress, she realised, in panic, that she was scared of going back into the outside world.

IV

The Foundation

IV

The Foundation

Dollhouse

They all wore headphones in the chopper to block out the noise – except for Esh, whose hair couldn't be spoiled. Tabitha sat behind her in the rear seat, watching the view, her silent chaperone. Tony sat close to Esh's left, occasionally jostling elbows with her, while Mikey and Clive sat to the other side, bunched in the central seat of the helicopter. In front, André sat beside the two pilots, giving orders to the rest of the security team through their headsets.

Esh watched as their mouths periodically moved to speak. She could hear nothing except the droning of the chopper. She tried to glimpse LA through the porthole blocked by Tony's frame, but could make out very little. She turned her head and looked through the surprisingly small windscreen between the pilots, catching details of the city in fragments, even more incoherent up close than they had been through the trees around her house.

The aircraft flew quickly over the city, so far up it almost felt they were skimming beneath the SkyBoards. The chopper's engines raged around her as she sat hemmed in by Tony, Mikey and Clive, keeping her untraceable, anonymous, secure.

She watched André turn to the other three guys and make a hand-signal that she translated as 'two minutes to landing'. She'd seen them use the hand-signals before, a shared habit from military days.

LA rolled indecipherably below them, streets and houses containing all the people who watched the SkyBoards day by day, gazing at the face of a girl called Esh in a campaign for a product that they didn't even know was about to change them.

The landscape of the city unscrolled as uniformly as a desert, an unknowable mass of blocks and grids, built for its invisible population.

She sat with bare legs in her heels, nothing between her body and the world except the fine gossamer of her gold dress. She felt naked, her heart beating at its regular pace, the cold of the cabin air wrapping itself round her body.

In front of her, André turned to Mikey, Tony and Clive again, and gave them a nod. 'On target.' They registered the command, focused on their mission, moving the subject to the rendezvous in complete secrecy.

She had four men protecting her, a wordless woman sitting behind her with a make-up case on the ready. Beneath their four jackets, Tony, Mikey, André and Clive wore their concealed weapons, ready to protect Esh, if necessary, with their lives. But not a single member of the personnel in the chopper looked at her. She was the asset, dressed in gold, the Corporation's commercial investment being ferried from one location to another under secure guard.

André lifted his hand and pointed to the ground for the others' benefit. 'Approaching the landing zone.' The chopper swooped towards the city, and the security team steeled themselves.

From the indistinguishable mass of the city, the Oscars Theatre suddenly rose up before them, two blocks off, a nucleus of light burning in the afternoon sunshine. Dozens of iBoards stood around the entrance, screaming with ads and movies, everything intense, illuminated, and yet suddenly from up here so tiny and miniaturised, the red carpet like a slim fishtail, the entrance to the Awards Ceremony looking as intimidating as the door to a doll's house.

They descended through a narrow crop of buildings, still a couple of blocks behind the theatre, and hovered gently till they landed on the street. Esh looked around, and saw that the entire street was devoid of cars and people, sealed off to create this secure drop-point. The only vehicle on the street was a long black limo waiting barely twenty metres away. With a minuscule bump, the chopper touched the ground, and her guards jumped out, positioning themselves quickly around the bird. Tony took hold of Esh's wrist, taking no chances with her obeying orders, and he gently pulled her out of the chopper, keeping her on her feet, and guided her across the tarmac towards the open door of the limo.

Beside her, André's eyes roamed robotically as he stepped in front of her and fed her through the limo's door, quickly lowering her into the vehicle as if there were a hundred snipers trained on them.

Tony followed her into the car as close as a jacket, and the limo door closed. He sat down in a jump-seat in front of her, while she had the long back seat to herself. In her film-thin dress, the cold leather of the seat spread across the back of her legs, as the smell of it climbed up her nose.

Tony's eyes moved instinctively, checking the surroundings. His head quickly turned as the opposite passenger door opened and Tabitha climbed in, followed by Mikey. Make-up case in hand, Tabitha slipped in beside Esh, and Mikey sat in the jump-seat next to Tony. In front of them, behind the driver's smoked glass plate, they heard André and Clive climb in, and the limo moved off.

They sat silent in the dark interior, black windows obscuring the world around them. Esh felt aware of her body, sitting in her barely opaque gold dress, her legs stretched out in front of her, her neck, arms and cleavage bare to the air. She was moments from stepping out in front of hundreds of people. The limo turned a corner, decelerated, then gliding on, pulled inexorably towards the Oscars.

She'd never felt this nervous. Not before sporting events at school. Not before exams. She looked in a panic at Tony, and saw his gaze fixed in the middle distance between them. He was focusing on EyeScreen. She'd even forgotten what it was like. She was sitting here, her body exposed to the air-con, with nothing connecting her to the world. These were her limits, barely covered by the diaphanous lace of the dress, with a signal beeping to the Corporation from her Eye.

Tony's focus remained on his EyeScreen, and he pointed at Esh.

'We're there.'

He reached for the door handle, and the limo crawled imperceptibly to a stop.

Tony opened his door, and jumped out, moving quickly to the side of the door, and waited for Esh to come out. He reached in his large hand.

'Your cue to go,' said Tabitha.

Esh turned, briefly looked in her eyes, and saw the make-up case waiting beside her like an undetonated bomb.

Tony clicked his fingers.

'Esh.'

She turned to the open door. She angled herself across the car, stretched out a leg, and reached for the ground. A booming came from the theatre. She stood up, and saw hundreds of people staring at her behind the barriers that had been erected on either side of the red carpet. Tony's fingers air-guided her out of the car, and made sure she didn't slip.

The iBoards around the theatre were blank, no longer showing ads or trailers, just greeting Esh's arrival in silence, as she stood on the red carpet. Ahead of her, the runway ahead was completely clear, just as Heavey had promised.

Tony's arm gently tapped her back.

She stepped forward.

As she did, something on the iBoards seemed to move with her. She looked across the screens, and saw them moving like walls of light in time with her.

Suddenly, she realised what they were showing. She hesitated for a moment, then stopped, and turned round on the carpet.

She'd sensed iBoards behind her as she'd stepped

from the car. The opposite side of the street was lined with them, all showing the same thing as the screens outside the theatre: a long shot of Esh in this very moment.

She saw her gold lace back turning to see herself across the street. Nearby stood two bodyguards, melding into the background. In the foreground stood hundreds of photographers banked around her, cramming to see her on the carpet, transmitting live to the world. She peeked up, and saw that there were no ads in the sky. It was her in the same broadcast as the iBoards over the street, in a huge dizzying vision across the sky, wearing her gold dress, gazing at herself on the SkyBoards. Wherever she looked, she saw herself looking at the very thing she was doing.

Camera flashes pinged. Esh looked down, at the hundreds of faces staring at her from the press. Tony's arm lightly guided her, and she moved forwards again, along the carpet, feeling the warmth of LA on her arms, seeing Clive and Tony disappearing behind her blind spots. The two hundred press members ogled her, laid eyes on her for the first time in the flesh.

Up ahead, she noticed a group of people waiting inside the building, crowding around the door like expectant children, all looking oddly familiar.

She turned to the faces of the two hundred photographers and broadcasters gaping at her behind the barriers. She would never forget the moment. It felt as if everything in the world had stopped. Outside, freed from the compound for the first time since she'd come to LA, she was suddenly looking at a world that she didn't recognise, but one that knew her intimately. The faces all stared at her, and smiled as if she'd been in their lives for ever.

She gazed at the people inside the building, all grinning as if they were her closest friends. Why did she recognise them?

She listened to the pack of voices beckoning her loudly from either side of the carpet, and moved along, in a dream, feeling that she could have closed her eyes right now and perfectly described everything and everyone around her.

She felt Tony, Mikey, Clive and André's presence growing around her. André and Clive moved ahead, and sleekly disappeared into the building. The canopy of the Oscars' entrance shaded her as the beaming faces gazed at her from the door. Then suddenly she realised who they were. She recognised them. Film stars. They'd entered the building, and were standing, waiting, just to catch a glimpse of her as she arrived. And in that moment, she knew that she was no longer real.

She passed the stars, Tony and Mikey hustling her rapidly into the building. André and Clive flanked her left and right, clearing the path ahead of them like a pair of minesweepers. She knew every face in the foyer. They all stared at her in the theatre's hushed environment, everything damped by the carpet underfoot. Everything sounded like a whisper, as if this was how stars spoke, in private tones that only they could hear. They stood on every side of her, craning to get a glimpse of her passing in the dress, cluttering the path as André and Clive tried to clear them out the way.

Tony and Mikey moved in her wake. Without

pausing, Clive and André made a path to the end of the hall and turned left into a doorway, André passing through first, and Clive staying back on guard. Mikey and Tony whisked her through, led her down a carpeted staircase. All the stars were gone. She was moving fast down a deserted stairwell, a brass handrail running along the wall, the security guards following her in a tight, hurried unit.

They descended flight after flight, meeting no one. At the bottom of the staircase, a corridor stretched off in both directions, and they turned left. The guards cosseted Esh, kept her moving, through a low–ceilinged hallway strung with emergency lights and closed doors leading to the left and right. They were in a kind of emergency exit system.

André moved ahead suddenly, gaining some distance on them. With a clunk, Esh saw light enter the hallway from the door he'd just opened to the outside. Her three bodyguards sped her along, and she turned to Tony, suddenly uneasy.

'Where are we going, Tony?'

He moved her on with unbroken velocity. They stepped out into a back alley, like the alley outside GRID where Esh had first met him. The walls of adjacent buildings rose high above them. There was just a single cramped route ahead, along the narrow passageway. No exit strategies, no escape points, no places to turn. André, Clive, Mikey and Tony crowded round her like a security blanket and bundled her along the alleyway, bunching round her like a group of refugees. Without any cue, from under their jackets, the four of them pulled out their weapons.

They stepped onto a deserted dead-end street. There was nothing, no one around. Her four bodyguards closed in, pinning her in, weapons floating ominously by their sides.

Esh breathed in, between the four pillars protecting her from the world.

'Waiting for the chopper,' Tony told her quietly.

'*At the LZ*,' André spoke into Interface.

The four guards looked in opposite directions, scoping the terrain. Out of the air, from behind the buildings, came the sound of the chopper.

'*Ready*,' André confirmed.

The helicopter descended over the buildings like a dark cloud. Waiting on the empty street, Esh's bodyguards moved her across the asphalt, and as the bird touched the ground, André peeled off and opened the side-hatch. Within a moment of the helicopter landing, she was bundled inside.

Tony, Mikey and Clive climbed in after her and sat either side. André jumped into the front with the pilots, and the chopper lifted off.

They rose fast over the rooftops, and LA disappeared below them. Esh tried to turn to see the Oscars and the blaze of the iBoards, but they'd pulled away now and were already flying back over LA. All she could make out were the endless anonymous streets lost in the maze, and the hills in the distance waiting to swallow them up.

Cell

As the compound in the hills grew nearer, she saw it in its entirety for the first time. It was set inside a natural bowl just over the promontory on which her house stood overlooking the city. The long road along which she'd been jogging could now be seen circling the entire compound, in a loose, wide ellipse. Within it lay the complex of mansions that Esh had never seen behind their identical entry gates and the long red wall, each plot separated from the next like a patchwork of English fields.

As they cruised in over Esh's garden, she spied the road far down on the left where she'd first entered the compound. The giant double-wall was clearly visible from here, the only discernible break in the wall surrounding the compound.

They sailed over the line of trees around Esh's house and she looked over the wall into Marcus's grounds, trying to find him. But the grounds were empty, his house looked deserted, and everything disappeared as her chopper descended into the garden.

They landed, and André, Mikey, Clive and Tony jumped out, waiting for Esh to disembark. She shifted along the seat, stretched down in her heels, and stood on the lawn. Across the garden, by the door to the Pagoda, she saw Heavey.

He waved at her.

She bent down to the ground, took off her shoes, and walked over the grass towards him, carrying the shoes in her hand.

She glanced up, and saw clips of her life everywhere. Every screen in the sky carried footage of her from throughout her nineteen years. There were scenes of her winning sporting events, sitting exams, accepting prizes, saying her first words, riding her first bike, swimming in a paddling pool, all interspersed with footage of her arriving at the Oscars that night.

Then she noticed a scene that she'd never seen before. She was sitting at a desk at the age of four. She couldn't recall this. An assortment of geometric patterns had been spread out before her, and she was studying them intensely. The shot changed, and the diagrams had now been removed. In front of her was a blank sheet of paper, over which Esh held a pencil, tracing out neat and definite lines.

When the view jumped again, she'd filled ten sheets of paper with intricate, complex patterns. Then the shot altered once more, and showed Esh's drawings laid out beside the geometric patterns she'd been shown. They were exactly the same. Ten times over, she'd copied the patterns from memory. The camera closed in on her four-year-old face, unsurprised by her own achievement. As the camera went wide again, it revealed a group of adults standing behind her, all peering over her shoulder as she sat in her tiny chair.

'Esh!' Heavey called to her.

He waited by the Pagoda door with his arms spread wide, as the footage in the sky disappeared. She was sure she'd seen something familiar.

'You're a star!' Heavey said. 'We're all waiting in the Hub.'

The entire crew had assembled on the open-plan floor to greet her. She saw them looking through the glass at her, as she arrived through the sliding doors.

'People!' Heavey said as he stepped in with Esh.

They erupted in cheers, clapped their hands over their heads, whistled at her return, while the footage of her appearance at the Oscars played behind them on the screens. She stood barefoot in front of them.

'Come on,' Heavey whispered to her.

He led her through the crew, towards the bank of screens.

'Steveland!' he called out. 'Play it again!'

They stood under the screens. Above them the footage showed her limo arriving, Tony jumping out of the door, standing to the side, and Esh finally emerging from the dark interior of the car in her dazzling dress.

As she stood amongst the press and her bodyguards, flashes exploded around her, and she began the slow walk along the carpet. Suddenly she stopped. A look of curiosity passed over her face. She turned instinctively to the iBoards on the other side of the street and saw the present moment being transmitted to the world.

'How did you know what was behind you?' Heavey said.

The crew murmured, discussing the footage for the twentieth time. On the screen, Esh turned her back and looked at her own image on the iBoards, seeing what everyone else in the world was seeing.

'That is one of the iconic moments of this century' Heavey said. 'On every newspaper tomorrow, in every magazine stall, on every news TV programme around the globe, that image will be sealed in people's memories forever.'

The camera flashes popped around her.

'You're a star, Esh.'

Esh looked at the crew smiling at her and she could tell, immediately, that the way they looked at her had changed, and would never be the same again. In just the few hours she'd been gone, something had altered for ever.

She'd seen it in the gaze of everyone outside the Oscars. At first she'd thought it must be a change in the way she was seeing everything, a long-term effect of being shut away in the compound for so long. But then suddenly she saw that it wasn't her perspective that had changed. It was the world's.

She'd stepped into the public arena for the first time, and everyone now knew her. It was in all their expressions, a look that she knew would stand between her and the world for the rest of her life.

A little glint behind the eyes. Almost a look of fear, uncertainty, not sure that the person you're seeing is real. Even the stars gathered at the door of the theatre had worn it. A distant, awestruck expression of knowing somebody you've never set eyes on before.

She could see it in the crew. They'd watched her on

these screens while she'd been at the Oscars, they'd seen her step out in front of billions of people, and turn in her gold dress to see her own image on the iBoards across the street. And in that moment, she'd become a star.

Returning to the Hub, she'd brought that stardom into the room. She would carry it with her wherever she went now, casting an ineluctable aura around herself. She was no longer the English Girl who'd turned up one day to shoot the campaign. She was the superbeing into which they'd finally transformed her; and even her creators were unable to look at her in the same way.

As she walked through them, the crew reached out to congratulate her, to pat her on the back, to touch her dress and hair.

'You can get changed in the hut where we prepped you,' Heavey said as he led her through the crew to the exit.

They stepped outside together and looked around. Everything felt peaceful and deserted, like a temple. The sun filtered through the Pagoda's roof. Shadows fell behind the surrounding huts. It was a warm, beautiful evening, the end of another day, everything precisely as it had been since she'd arrived.

'Esh,' Heavey said, turning to her earnestly. 'We've got your parents waiting to speak to you in the Safe. They want to say "well done".'

He looked into her eyes and smiled. Esh said nothing in response. She was thinking about the footage of her studying the geometric patterns. She needed to see it again, to check what she thought she'd seen.

'Thank you for everything,' he told her. 'You tired?'

Esh looked into his eyes blankly, and nodded.

'Yes, Heavey,' she said. 'Very.'

She changed quickly, then came out of the hut and walked to Steveland's workshop. She saw him inside through the window, sitting at his workbench.

'Hey,' he said as she came in. 'How's the diva?'

'I need to ask you a favour,' Esh said.

Steveland winced a little at the request.

'Have a go,' he said.

'Can you access an ad from the campaign for me?'

Steveland paused, and then winced a little more.

'Why?'

'You've got my whole Identity on database, haven't you?'

'Yes.'

'Well, there's something I'd like to see.'

'What exactly?'

'Something I saw in the campaign. A sequence of me as a kid.'

Steveland looked at her hesitatingly.

'Look, I don't know,' he said.

She could see him racked with worry, straining to help her in any way he could.

'Why do you want to see it?'

'Because it's something I don't remember.'

'What was it?'

Esh kept her look bright and unknowing, as if she'd just walked in with nothing more than curiosity in mind.

'It's me when I was little.'

'Doing what?'

'Can you get it for me?'

'I don't know.'

Steveland looked at the floor.

'I'm not meant to do this,' he murmured. 'I'm not allowed to show you stuff from the campaign.'

'Why?'

He looked at her anxiously.

'They told me I can't. You're not allowed to see any of the material.'

'From my own life?'

Steveland shook his head, helpless.

'I'm sorry, Esh. Really, I am.'

She iScanned through the door and came out into her garden. Walking across the lawn, she searched the sky for the ad. There were moments from the course of her entire life, but not the one she was looking for.

She walked up to the house, and found Maria waiting inside excitedly.

'Come and see the TV,' she said.

She made Esh follow her, to the living room where an ad for Evo was playing.

Esh was four, but this wasn't the footage of her drawing the patterns. She was looking into the lens of the camera as a female American interviewed her.

'*What do you think you'll do when you're older?*' the woman asked.

'*I'm not sure,*' Esh replied. '*There are so many things I like.*'

The shot dissolved, and cut to Esh arriving at the Oscars, standing on the red carpet, before the world's cameras. Her four-year old voice played over the top.

'*Can you imagine being nineteen?*' asked the interviewer.

'*It's such a long way away,*' Esh said. '*I can't imagine what I'll be doing.*'

The footage slowed down, to near freeze-frame. No soundtrack, just camera flashes bouncing off Esh's features, as the Storyteller's voice appeared.

'*We take ourselves on the most amazing adventure,*' he said.

Esh's image froze on the screen, and filled the shot.

'*In five days' time, her dream will become our own.*'

The shot slowly faded, and three letters appeared on the black screen.

e   v   o

'Your mother and father are waiting on the line for you,' Maria said.

Esh turned and looked at her. A moment later, she heard FMCG come on the TV in a Chicken Stick ad.

'Thanks,' she said.

She left, and walked down the stairs to the Safe, iScanning through the door.

The glowing white interior of the room greeted her, more comforting, more reliable than anything she'd experienced in the outside world. The white rubber door clamped shut, and the light in the empty white screen turned green, as her parents appeared before her and she took her place in the wall.

They hadn't slept. They looked worn out.

'Hi,' Mum smiled, but she'd had the warmth drained out of her.

'What time is it?'

'It's early,' said Dad. 'We just came back from the hospital.'

'We saw you at the Oscars, Esh,' Mum said. 'You looked so beautiful.'

Her voice quivered. Her head dropped, and Dad put his arm around her.

'Mum?'

She wanted to look up at Esh, but couldn't.

Dad looked out from the screen.

'Grandad's almost gone,' he said.

Mum looked like she was falling apart. Just as she had when Granny had died. So strange. Esh had spent her life seeing Mum strong, resilient, getting on with her work. But now she was sobbing.

'You need to come to see him,' Dad said.

'I know.'

'Will they let you?'

'I don't know. They've refused so far.'

The Corporation had the biggest product they'd ever committed themselves to, only five days from launch. Esh's family crisis meant little to them.

'Ask them again, Esh.'

She could hear a rising helplessness creeping into Dad's voice. It was the hardship of keeping Mum going, the strain of staying strong.

She needed to be there. Grandad was going to die before Mum ever had the chance to say all the things she'd wanted to say to him, and it was slowly destroying her.

'We need to get some sleep,' Dad said. Esh nodded. 'You looked amazing at the Oscars.'

Esh smiled, something trapped inside her throat, seeing Mum and Dad sitting in their living room far across the world.

'I have to ask you something,' she said.

'What?' said Dad.

She felt the padded comfort of the seat around her, her solitude in the cell.

'Have you heard of the Foundation?'

Mum and Dad looked blank, and a little surprised.

'Why?'

'Do you know who they are?'

Mum's eyes dipped to the floor.

'Yes,' Dad replied.

Her lungs filled suddenly. She hadn't expected this.

'Who are they?'

'They helped us when you were little.'

'How old was I?'

'Four,' said Dad. 'They came to visit you at school.'

'They offered you a scholarship,' said Mum.

Esh stared at them. Her seat in the wall, the glowing Safe enclosed her tightly.

'What scholarship?'

'Your scholarship to Ford.'

'They paid for me?'

'They paid for everything, Esh.'

Esh looked at her parents on the glowing white screen. It was impossible. She couldn't believe that they could be telling her this.

'I don't understand.'

'They gave you a chance to have the best education,' said Mum.

'We couldn't afford to send you to Ford,' said Dad.

'They did all this?'

'Yes,' said Dad.

Esh had never got angry with her parents. She'd never

raised her voice to them. But she felt furious in a way that she couldn't explain.

'And you never told me?'

'They said it'd be better.'

'Who did?'

'The Foundation.'

'They said it was best, Esh.'

'They told you? The Foundation?'

'The Foundation helped us with everything, Esh. They paid for everything.'

Esh's world caved in. The Foundation had been funding her all along. They'd been in her life for ever.

'How did they find me?'

'They came to your school.'

'Just like that?'

'They interviewed you.'

'And what did I do?'

'You sat tests.'

'What sort?'

'Verbal reasoning. Memory.'

'You never thought of telling me this?'

'You would have felt so alien to everyone at Ford,' Mum said. 'You'd have hated knowing that you were on a scholarship. No child wants to feel different.'

'Why did you never say? You told me Ford gave me the scholarship.'

'We didn't want you to feel special, Esh.'

'But I did.'

Somehow, she'd always known. She'd finally found out something that she'd unconsciously waited all these years to hear.

'Who are they? Where are the Foundation now?'

'They left us alone,' said Mum.

'You never heard from them?'

'No.'

'Who did you deal with? Who spoke to you?'

'Lots of people.'

'Americans?'

'Yes.'

'And what did they want?'

'Nothing,' said Dad.

Esh stared at Mum and Dad. They'd hidden this for so long, with no idea of what it really meant.

'They never asked us for anything,' Mum said.

A divide had opened up in front of her, and her parents were sitting on the other side of it. As they disappeared from the screen, she could barely process the thought that they'd spent her entire life keeping this truth from her. Why? A charitable organisation had sponsored her entire education without ever asking for anything in return. They'd never asked to meet Esh, only asked Mum or Dad not to let her know that she had a benefactor.

She felt an almost unbearable resentment suddenly towards her parents. They'd betrayed her. But why? It was as if the Foundation had never wanted Esh to know they existed. Who were they?

She walked up the stairs to the house. There was no one around. No security guards in the garden. Neither Maria nor Mano were in the kitchen. The house was quiet, and it had started to get dark outside.

She stepped out of the doors to the pool area. She

walked around the water's edge towards the line of trees in front of the house and, standing on the parapet, she peeked through the trees down the side of the hill.

The wall dropped a hundred feet to the no man's land at the bottom of the bare rock face. There was nothing down there, nowhere to go, no means of approaching the house, and no way of leaving, except by gravity.

Esh pulled back and looked out over LA. Across the city, the SkyBoards broadcast her image, depicting her entire existence in a montage of special moments. All the achievements that the Foundation had secretly funded. Passing exams and winning competitions, excelling at everything she did. It seemed like a grand performance that some alternate personality of hers had pulled off on her behalf, while the Foundation had waited behind the scenery, paying for her, watching her.

The word '*Evo*' was emblazoned across the whole sky, everywhere she looked. Her entire life fitted the campaign so well. On one side of the planet the Corporation had spent years developing its technology, while on the other Esh's life took its course, and now the two finally met, perfectly, on the SkyBoards over LA.

She'd never set a foot wrong. She'd never rebelled or screwed up. She'd never done anything less than remarkable.

The Corporation had seen that. They'd watched her and waited, just as the Foundation had been watching over her all these years.

How were the two related? Had the Corporation found her because of the Foundation? Had they used the Foundation to screen potential candidates for Evo?

Watching herself on the SkyBoards, she felt as if her

life had been destined to end up on those screens. Every moment of her existence had been sponsored and watched over to end up being told as a perfect story. But the more she watched, the less she felt that it was actually hers. It seemed like someone else's, a personal history of which she had no recollection.

The sky darkened over the city, and the SkyBoards grew more luminous. She tried to imagine living normally in LA now, with her life story playing above her on the SkyBoards. And it was impossible.

She stepped out of the trees and breathed the fresh, aromatic scent of the garden. She watched the glass and steel structure of her house absorbing and reflecting the evening light. Behind it, the garden dropped from view towards the tall entrance gates, and the Pagoda beyond the high red wall.

She hated this place. She hated how perfectly it contained her, how accustomed she'd become to everything here, the daily iScanning through the door to the Pagoda, speaking to her parents from the seclusion of the Safe, being constantly locked into the confines of the grounds, having her security guards shadow her, having the compound sever her from everything, cutting her off from Interface.

There was nowhere for her to go now. Her life in London was a distant memory, and life in the outside world, on her own, without security, was impossible.

She levered herself off the wall into Marcus's garden. With the light of the SkyBoards filtering through the branches, she stretched across the empty space and hung thirty feet up in the air. The leaves made a tiny rustle as she dangled, and she swung her weight towards the trunk, to find a grip amongst the branches.

She crouched in the top of the tree, and turned to Marcus's house. There was no one around, no lights on indoors. She sat in the crook of two branches, listening to the silence, moving her eyes across the darkness and seeing nothing stir.

She climbed down the tree, muffling her sounds, quickly reaching the ground. Turning, she looked for moving bodies, checked the silence again. All clear, she darted through the darkness towards the house. She made it to the glass doors and pushed through silently. Stepping across the entrance hall, she crept upstairs, padded along the corridor, and opened the door to Marcus's bedroom.

She heard the toilet flush, and Marcus appeared from his bathroom.

'Esh.'

His face lit up with excitement, she closed the door behind her. He came over and hugged her, and for the first time that day she felt real herself.

'I saw you at the Oscars,' he whispered into her hair.

She kept her arms wrapped around him.

'You looked like something out of this world, Esh, like a being from another planet. I was staring at you and trying to remember that it was you, but you looked like someone totally different. And then suddenly you looked around. On that red carpet in your dress, you took in your surroundings, and I suddenly recognised it as you. You were looking with that focus you have when you're observing something. You looked beautiful.'

Esh smelled him, squeezing him.

'I missed you, Marcus.'

She wanted to cry suddenly, relaxing in his arms, with the relief of finally being with him. They walked over to his bed and sat down.

'I don't know what's happening to me,' she said.

She glanced at the wall, at the light from the SkyBoards playing across the plaster.

'What do you mean?'

'I found out that some organisation I've never heard of has paid for my entire education. My parents never told me about it, and I don't understand why. I'm scared that they've got something to do with the Corporation.'

'Why?' Marcus asked.

'Because of all the secrecy, because of everything that's being hidden from me.'

Marcus held her close, and watched her in the darkness.

'I feel as if my life's being made up,' she said. 'I feel like I've been invented by the Corporation for the campaign. I don't understand what my life is any more.'

'They're just taking everything about you and moulding it to sell the product,' Marcus said. 'I know how it feels. It screws with your head, watching yourself, seeing yourself everywhere you look, you start to feel like you don't even exist. But I promise you that suddenly, one day, you realise that you have nothing to do with what you're watching, and it even makes you understand what you really are.'

Esh heard the words, and tried to find as much comfort in them as she did in the warmth of his body and the sound of his voice.

'They're keeping everything from me,' she said. 'Why

Grandad's ill, and who these people who paid for my education are. I'm scared, Marcus. I don't understand why so much is being kept secret.'

'It's just the way they work. They're paranoid. You know that.'

They were. They both knew it. And yet Marcus didn't know how horribly right the Corporation were, that the Team had already found her in the Safe, and the truth of it made her so afraid that she didn't even want to tell Marcus about the Voice, and what it had said, because she didn't want to risk embroiling him.

'I feel like I've never paid attention to my life, Marcus. I feel as though things have always been happening around me and I was just too asleep to notice.'

She looked at him in the shadows.

'I feel like I'm not here, Marcus.'

He sat close by, holding her.

'They're making me disappear. I feel like there's nothing inside me.'

Marcus put his arm around her shoulders, and tightened it.

'It's okay,' he said.

He lifted his hand and touched her cheek, then stroked her hair.

Esh looked into his eyes, and put her arms around his neck. They sat hugging each other, not speaking for a long time.

'I'm so tired, Marcus.'

They moved up the bed, pulling the sheet aside to get in. Slipping off her shoes and undressing in a blind tangle, she stretched out, and turned to Marcus, pulling up the sheet and billowing it out to spread it over them.

They put their arms round each other and held each other as close as they could, pressing their faces together, and fell asleep in the darkness.

Lockdown

'What was that noise?'

Esh woke up, saw sunlight streaming through the blinds. She climbed out of bed and moved to the window. Looking out, she couldn't see anything.

The noise was familiar. Loud, whinnying, mechanical.

'What is it?'

Marcus rubbed his face, then heard the distinctive rumbling. Esh turned to the clock on the bedside table and saw that they'd overslept.

'It's a helicopter,' she said.

She quickly gathered her clothes from the floor, hurried them on, and stepped into her sneakers. Turning to the bed, she leant down and kissed Marcus, holding his warm face between her hands.

'I hate leaving you,' she whispered.

He looked into her eyes, sleepy, beautiful.

'Go quick,' he said, kissing her back.

She clambered off the bed and moved to the door, then turned to Marcus.

'See you later,' she said.

Marcus waved, and smiled.

She blew him a kiss and opened the door, checked the passage, and stepped out, walking quickly along the corridor. She jogged down the staircase, looking around for Marcus's staff. Clear, she darted across the hall to the front door.

The chopper was even louder, clearer now. Something was going on. Something was happening in her house.

She ran across the lawn, reached the tree by the wall. At the bottom of Marcus's drive she heard people calling frantically to one another. She scaled the tree, losing no time, and turned her head to see Marcus's gates. They'd opened, and four men in suits were running into the grounds, wielding firearms. She clambered for dear life, trying to keep silent, and made it to the top of the tree. Scrambling onto the top of the wall, she looked down.

The chopper she'd flown in yesterday had landed on her lawn. More than two dozen men in suits stood around the bird armed with automatic weapons, and at the entrance of her house she saw Maria, Mano, Isabèl and Manuela gathered in their white uniforms, being interviewed by four men in suits.

Had Maria told them where she was?

She turned her head. On the grass she saw Heavey standing near the helicopter, looking strangely composed. People were walking up to him, asking him questions, but he didn't move a muscle. He stood still, casting his eyes around, looking for her.

The entire garden was swarming with people, streaming in and out of the door to the Pagoda, in and out of the house. There was no way of getting back in.

She turned to Marcus's house.

The four men in suits spread across the lawn with their weapons, and then suddenly crouched, taking up positions around the house.

It was her team. Tony, Mikey, André and Clive. They prepared to move. Tony gave André a signal, and André quickly jogged around the house. On cue, Tony gave a second signal to Mikey, to run round the other side.

Esh lay her cheek on the wall.

At the bottom of the driveway, another four men were guarding the exit, standing next to a black SUV on the compound road, bearing arms.

Suddenly, she remembered.

The chip in her Eye. Steveland had activated it. The trace had led them to her, sending them looking for her in Marcus's house.

She crooked her neck and looked carefully down the side of the wall to see if there was sufficient tree cover to climb down to her house unseen. It was impossible. They had every approach covered.

She turned, looked desperately over at Marcus's window. She couldn't see him inside. All four security guards had now entered the house. What were they going to do when they didn't find her?

Suddenly, the pitch of the helicopter whinnied louder. She turned her head, and saw it rise from her lawn, throwing a gust of wind over everyone. It took off above her house, and lurched forward, towards the city.

Suddenly, it swung round again. Swivelling in mid-air, it nodded its nose towards her and perched fifty feet up in the air, hovering over her.

She turned her head, and saw the people on her lawn start to walk towards her. Someone in the chopper must have made contact with them. They all looked up blindly into the trees, trying to catch sight of her.

She rested her chin on the wall. At the bottom of Marcus's drive, she saw the security men by the black SUV moving in her direction.

She stretched her neck, and looked up at the helicopter. Through the reflection in the windshield, she made out the two helmeted faces of the pilots, staring at her, keeping their visual on her as they directed the personnel on the ground.

She turned to the other side of the wall, but still couldn't see Marcus or her security team appearing from his house. She turned again, and watched all the people walking towards her, like lines of police officers searching for a child's body in a field.

Hot little hand

Heavey was the first person to enter the glass conference room. She watched him walk in with a newspaper under his arm and sit in front of her.

For over an hour, she'd watched everything that happened in the Hub. On the gallery outside, André and Mikey had kept guard without once turning to check on her, knowing that she had no way of escaping from the glass room.

She sat patiently for an hour without moving, barely expecting anyone to come and explain what was happening. An eerie calm had descended, partially obscuring the panic she felt creeping through her, not knowing what had happened to Marcus.

In the Hub, a steady commotion of people moved in and out of the sliding doors. They kept appearing under the Pagoda, seemingly from nowhere, and then entered the Hub, before leaving and disappearing into one of the surrounding studios.

As they were all wearing suits, it took her a while to figure out who were the security guards and who were the

Corporation executives. It was all in their demeanour. Security always wore the same look of intense concentration, the one that Esh had seen in her guards. Their eyes always moved around, tracking their subjects with invisible attention.

Every few minutes, the screens over the Hub played the footage of her at the Oscars. All the morning's news programmes carried the story. They showed her emerging from the limo, walking down the red carpet, and turning to see herself on the iBoards, again and again. She was so numbed by the sight, it no longer even looked like her. She could barely bring herself to watch it.

All the time, between one news spot and another, the campaign broadcast her life in a scattered collage of moments, linking them all together under the Evo banner. She was inseparable from the word.

She scanned the screens for the ad showing her drawing the geometric patterns from memory. She needed to see the group of people behind her, to check their faces. But the ad never showed. She watched the campaign continuously, for an hour, and saw almost every moment from her past reappear but that one.

Heavey stood looking at her for a second before sitting down. He pulled the newspaper from under his arm and laid it face-down on the table.

'The Corporation is here,' he said.

He sounded calm, as if nothing had happened. Shock, Esh thought.

'We alerted them to the fact that you were missing.'

He flipped the newspaper over, and turned it to her. Across its front page was a photograph of her standing in her gold dress at the Oscars, just as he'd predicted, her back turned to see the iBoards across the street.

'I came this morning to the house to show you this,' he said. 'But you weren't in.'

He clasped his hands together and looked through the glass wall at the Pagoda.

'They're going to grill you hard,' he said. 'They want to know everything that you did with Marcus, when you started going over to him, what you did with him, how much time you spent there, why you kept going despite knowing the risks. They'll keep going until they have everything from you. You'll do well to just tell them and get it over with. They'll leave you alone more quickly.'

He looked almost as though he'd come to terms with everything in the past hour.

'They won't let me go in with you,' he said. 'They want everything kept apart.'

Esh watched him, and thought he looked withdrawn, not quite himself.

'I've told them everything I know,' he said.

He gazed across the table, smiling.

'Which wasn't much, of course.'

Suddenly, he chuckled.

'You did a pretty good job of keeping this all covered up, Esh.'

He shrugged, as if there was nothing either of them could now do.

'I'm glad you're safe,' he said. 'For a while this morning, I started fearing the worst. And it didn't feel good, Esh. It's a relief to know you're okay.'

He smiled sadly and fondly at her.

She glanced at André and Mikey on the gallery, and down below in the Hub at all the Corporation people walking around in their suits.

'They want to see you now,' Heavey said.

She was led to a darkened room outside the Hub. As soon as Mikey and André had taken her inside, they receded, and left her alone.

Her eyes adjusted to the darkness. A man was sitting in a black armchair in front of her, opposite an empty armchair.

'Hello, Esh,' he said.

His voice was warm, soft. His hair was dark, and he seemed to disappear into the room in his black suit trousers and tieless dark shirt.

'Take a seat,' he said.

He had a kind, friendly expression in his voice. Esh took the seat opposite him, and looked around. There were no windows in the room, just the light of a couple of small spot lamps above them.

'How are you, Esh?'

'Good,' she said, for the hell of it.

'An exciting morning,' he replied.

He looked at her with a chummy, avuncular smile. Funny. She knew she was here to be grilled. Why the friendliness? She tried to meet his eye, and couldn't. There was something too measured and cool in him.

'Who are you?'

The man gazed at her, half-smiling.

'I'm from the Foundation,' he said.

He wrong-footed her, with a smile.

'You asked your parents about us, didn't you?'

221

Esh sat back. Had they listened to her in the Safe? Had they always been listening? No. They'd have known about the Team.

'We talked to your parents after you spoke to them last night,' the man said. 'They mentioned your question. Who told you about the Foundation?'

She paused, thought quickly.

'An ad in the campaign triggered my memory.'

The man stared at her, and then smiled.

'You remember everything, don't you, Esh?' he said.

As he smiled, a shadow fell over the top of his head from the spot lamp in the ceiling. He peered at her studiously, grinning.

'The little that your parents told you about us was correct,' he said. 'We are a charitable entity who offer financial assistance to exceptional children. We have a variety of charitable arms, and do a lot of amazing things. But the division of the Foundation who discovered you deal exclusively with gifted infants, concerning themselves particularly with helping families send their children to prestigious institutions. That is what we do. You were one of those children, Esh. You were the brightest we ever saw. It is how the Corporation found you.'

'They found me through you?'

The man nodded.

'It was the first place they looked.'

The Voice had known this. It had sent her in the right direction. It knew that the Foundation was linked to the Corporation, that the one connected her to the other, and that it was how the Corporation had found her.

'The Corporation have always been waiting for me?'

she said. 'They always knew that they were going to use me?'

'They were watching,' said the man. 'Watching how your life unfolded.'

'Why was I never told?'

'For a good reason,' said the man. 'To give you a choice. This way, you were given every liberty to accept or refuse the offer, having no knowledge that all your life the Corporation, through the Foundation, had indirectly paid for your education.'

Esh stared at him.

'Why did you do it? So you could watch over me?'

'The most wasteful thing in the world would be to let your talents have come to nothing, Esh. We did what we could, because we felt a duty to.'

Esh stared at him.

'You kept it a secret from me.'

'So that you wouldn't be prejudiced.'

'You imposed yourself on someone's life without them knowing?'

'Do you think it's an imposition?'

'Financing somebody's entire existence without their knowledge? Yes.'

'You had no choice over not being able to afford a good school,' said the man. 'And we changed that. Would you rather we hadn't?'

'I had a right to know there was somebody paying for my education.'

'What does it ultimately change?'

'Everything,' Esh replied.

She looked across the dim light at the man.

'If you'd known about us, Esh, you would have felt

indebted. That is what we tried to spare you from. We protected you, so that you would be free.'

'You didn't have a right to do what you did.'

'No. But we did it.'

The man sat under the light, staring at her.

'Think of the alternative, Esh. Imagine that we had done nothing, and just stood by as you failed to receive the education which you so badly deserved. It may be morally dubious, but the means outstandingly justify the end.'

She stared at the man in front of her.

'Who are you?'

He stared back at her, and gave her a shrug.

'I am here on behalf of the Foundation.'

'Why am I talking to the Foundation?'

'You're in a serious predicament, Esh.'

'What have you got to do with this?'

'We shoulder some of the responsibility for you. We originally found you, and were established by the Corporation for this kind of initiative. We are an autonomous body, Esh, but our wealth derives entirely from the Corporation. They created the Foundation specifically to separate their commercial ends from our charitable intentions. That is why they signed over their philanthropic arm, to stop themselves indulging in moral corruptness.'

'The Corporation paid for my education?'

'Indirectly.'

'So why are you here?'

'Because you're in a great deal of trouble.'

They looked at each in the stark light.

'The Corporation wish me to mediate,' he said.

'In what?'

'Important parts of your contract have been triggered by the current circumstances. The Corporation has earned the right to take any action it feels necessary to guarantee your security. The product will be launched in four days, and the sensitivity of that launch is immeasurable. The fact that you have been in contact with Marcus represents a breach of security which the Corporation cannot countenance. They will do everything they have to in order to preserve the integrity of the product.'

The man stared at her.

'We know that Marcus knows about Evo,' he said.

They'd spoken to him. Where was he?

'The information you possess concerning Evo was never meant to leave your confidence, Esh. Your actions represent the gravest breach of your contract, a breach that, unfortunately, forfeits many of your rights under that contract.'

'Which rights?'

For a crazy moment, Esh suddenly didn't feel scared. They had her locked up in the mansion already. What else could they do?

'You created much freedom for yourself within the Corporation's strictures,' he said. 'But that will now change. There will be no more room for movement.'

'What do you mean?'

'You will not be restored to Interface after the launch.'

Esh looked at him.

'They can't do that. It was done as a concession. I gave my permission because they promised to restore it.'

'That right has been rescinded, Esh.'

225

'You can't do this.'

'They have you at their mercy.'

The darkness of the room closed in.

'Where's Marcus?'

'You won't see him again.'

Esh felt the room getting colder, smaller.

'That's not possible,' she said.

'He is the face of Interface. You are the face of Evo. You will never be seen together.'

Sitting in the spotlight, his shirt creaseless, he told her the words as if they were hers to cut out and keep.

'Marcus has been translocated. You will not be able to find him.'

'I need to see him.'

'The Corporation will control you very closely. You have betrayed their trust and repercussions will naturally follow. Everything is provided for contractually. You have temporarily lost your right to freedom.'

Esh looked into the emptiness of the room. It felt like a dense black bubble.

'I want to see my lawyers.'

'That won't be possible. You have invalidated your right to external communication. The security situation is being assessed, and in order to contain any damage the Corporation is sealing you off from outside interference. That includes your lawyers. They have assented to the mechanisms which the Corporation has put into place, as stipulated by your contract. They will be informed of the Corporation's implementation of those mechanisms as and when they occur, simply to approve them.'

The man looked at her coldly.

'You're about to become one of the wealthiest women

on the planet. With the money you receive in four days will come a degree of responsibility that is barely possible to imagine until you're holding it in your hot little hand. It is more wealth than you can ever spend, Esh. The Corporation consequently needs to ensure that you have the requisite maturity and responsibility to own that money. So, for the time being, it will remain in trust with your parents.'

'For how long?'

'Indefinitely.'

Esh took a sharp breath.

'How long till I get Interface and my life back?'

The man stared at her for a long while. She needed some kind of timeline.

'Could be as much as a year,' he said. 'Maybe longer.'

She couldn't conceive of it. She gasped, and the man stared at her solemnly, acknowledging the weight of what he'd just told her.

'It's in the hands of the Corporation now.'

Zero

She was led out of the room into the sunlight, where Heavey was waiting for her.

'Esh. Are you okay?'

He looked grimly worried. Mikey and André followed behind her like oversized shadows.

'Guys,' he said. 'Give us a moment?'

Mikey and André nodded, and stopped ten metres away. Heavey looked into her eyes, and put his hand on her shoulder.

'Are you all right?'

Esh looked up, and tried to contain her emotion. She felt faint.

'It's going to be okay, Esh.'

She shook her head, trying to find the words.

'They won't let me see Marcus,' she said, her voice cracking.

Heavey nodded.

'I know,' he said. 'I've talked to them. They don't want you leaving their sight for a moment, but it's not going to be for ever. You're just going to have to play by their rules for a while. There's some hard time to do, but you need to stick it out.'

Esh felt as if her body were about to split and fall apart around her.

'I've negotiated something for you,' he said. 'They're not going to take away the Safe. They didn't even want you to talk to your parents, but I convinced them. We've got people in London speaking to your parents the whole time, they're not a security risk. I told them how tough it had been for you coming here, how hard it's been dealing with the campaign and the isolation, how you needed an escape valve. They didn't want to hear it at first, but I talked them round. With your grandfather in hospital, I said it was crucial that you have family contact. So they're going to let you keep the Safe.'

Esh could see Mikey and André's reflection in the glass of the Hub's sliding doors, waiting behind her.

'Get some rest,' Heavey said.

She looked at him, and saw his kindness, and concern. 'Okay?'

He squeezed her shoulder, then gave André and Mikey a sign, and they came over to escort her to the house.

Four security personnel Esh had never seen before were patrolling the grounds. They saw Mikey and André following Esh through the door from the Pagoda and nodded to acknowledge them.

She walked across the lawn with Mikey and André behind her, and noticed Felipe, Miguel and Fontàn working in the bushes by Marcus's wall. She walked towards them, to see what they were doing. Mikey and André followed behind, while the four new security guys suddenly perked up as she approached the wall.

She stopped by the bushes, close enough to see what Felipe, Miguel and Fontàn were doing. Mikey and André stood behind her. The three gardeners were crouched around the tiny grate where she'd first seen Marcus, and were filling it in.

She turned, walked up the driveway, Mikey and André following her.

She couldn't shake them off. She kept trying to understand that she'd never see Marcus again, but the pain of it was so great that it hadn't begun to filter into her. She would never spend another moment with him.

She reached the forecourt of the house, walked quickly through the doors, past Maria and Mano in the kitchen, along the hallway, and down the stairs to the Safe. Mikey and André followed hurriedly behind.

'Where are you going?' André asked.

'To the Safe.'

She kept moving, turned at the bottom of the staircase, and iScanned at the white door in the basement.

'We'll wait out here,' said André, as Esh walked into the luminous room.

There was no signal on the screen. She sat in the white suede seat in the wall, listening to the silence, with her head in her hands, and wept.

She felt as if there were nothing out there. This glowing white space was the limit of her world. Grandad was dying. She didn't know when she'd see Kristin, Mum or Dad again.

She cried, remembering every moment she'd spent with Marcus, everything they'd shared. It came to her as if in a dream. She wanted to go back and say so much, tell him how good he'd made her feel, how she remembered now what her life had been like before she'd met him, how he'd made her feel more whole, more human, more special than ever in her life.

She peered through her tears at the Safe, feeling as if it was a white star caving in on itself. The most beautiful man she'd ever known, who'd changed her life, who'd moved her heart unexpectedly, had gone.

'Esh.'

The light in the screen was red.

'I'm sorry,' said the Voice.

She looked up, through her blur of tears.

'You don't know what I'm feeling.'

'I know that you're in pain.'

Esh felt tears dripping over her chin.

'You're a bona fide star,' said the Voice. 'You've arrived now.'

'Why haven't you hit me with an iVert?'

The Voice was taken by surprise, and for a moment didn't speak.

'We're not going to do that,' he replied.

'What are you going to do?'

'We're trying to re-establish a balance, Esh. The Corporation has hijacked every means of control and communication available to the planet. We're trying to wrest some of that power back to restore it to the people.'

'You mean to yourselves.'

The Voice paused.

'You really think that, Esh?'

'I think the iVerts and your busting in here make you feel powerful.'

'And why's that?'

Esh sniffed, wiping her arm across her eyes.

'You're the ones doing it,' she said. 'You tell me.'

The Voice had no answer.

'What do you want?' she said, suddenly tired, exhausted with everything.

'We want to save you, Esh.'

'From what?'

'From the Corporation.'

'Why on earth should I believe you?'

'Did you ask about the Foundation?'

Esh took a breath, tried to swallow the desire to cry.

'Yes,' she said.

'And what did you find?'

She felt almost too emotional, too confused to think.

'You're using me, aren't you?' she said.

'For what?'

'I don't know yet.'

'Who do you feel more threatened by? Us or the Corporation?'

Esh stared at the mesmerizing whiteness of the room. She didn't even know the answer.

'You can't beat them,' she said.

'But we can,' said the Voice.

'How?'

'By winning the media war.'

The words could almost have come from Heavey.

'Who are you?'

'We're the little people, Esh. We're like you.'

'I thought I was a big star?'

'You're being manipulated.'

'Why?'

The transmission was so clear the Voice could have been in the room with her.

'The Corporation has been in your life since you were born,' he said. 'We've found traces of activity between you and them from your earliest days. What we want to know is why. Why have they been in your life so long? Aren't you asking the same thing? How much is everything that's happened to you a coincidence? How much was planned? How much was your life tailored and steered to bring you to this place? You feel it in your bones, don't you, Esh?'

'Why are you doing this to me?'

'Because we've seen your entire life. We've looked at everything that's ever happened to you, and you've lived your life just like anyone else, except that you were born with exceptional abilities and that the Corporation has watched you since the very day you were born. Did you know that, Esh? They were monitoring you, watching you, from the first day you set foot on this planet. Why? How could they know you were special? Why take so much care over you? Why show such interest in you? Why leave nothing in your life to chance? They've been there the whole time, Esh, watching you and protecting you. They paid for your education. Why? So they could watch you. They were waiting all these years to bring you here. Why were you worth so much to them? Why did they wait so long? We know so little, Esh, apart from the fact that the Corporation has controlled your life from the very start, been your guardian angel since birth. That's why we're here, Esh.'

'How do you know all this?'

'By looking. By studying every moment of your life, and seeing everything the Corporation has done to eventually bring you here.'

'You knew I was coming?'

'They organised it, and we watched them do it. They planned for your arrival years in advance and put everything into place, controlling everything, even losing you the job at the Bank so you'd come. It was damage control, in case you said no.'

'How can you know?'

'Why did they delete you, Esh? For the same reason they shut off your Interface, to stop you finding out anything about yourself. They knew that once the campaign started you'd want to look into your life and search through your past. That's why they shut you in this little white room under your mansion. They don't want you knowing anything about yourself that they haven't carefully vetted for you.'

They knew the layout of the house.

'Everything has happened to you for a reason, Esh. You were always going to come here.'

'You can't know that for sure,' she said.

'The Foundation was always going to pay you.'

'Pay me what?'

'How does this figure sound?'

The Voice paused, and quoted the precise fee she was going to receive.

'It's been waiting for you all your life, Esh. Your fortune has been kept in a trustee Foundation account for you since you were born. It's in your name, and was going to be paid to you when you turned twenty-one, regardless of what happened. They were going to pay you whether or not you came here, Esh. It's insane. That's the wool they've pulled over your eyes. They've made out that this was some out-of-the-blue offer that was going to change your life, but they were going to change your life anyway. That connection between the Foundation and the Corporation goes back all the way through your life. They were going to make you a rich girl whatever you chose to do.'

'No,' she said.

'We've seen it, Esh.'

'Then show me.'

'We can't interfere with this screen.'

'But you can see me?'

The Voice was briefly silent.

'Yes,' he said. 'We can see you.'

Esh stared at the empty white room.

'Who are you?'

'I'm a friend, Esh. They have everything they've spent twenty years working towards invested in you. They will not risk losing you. You need to be very careful how you proceed. Don't rattle your chains too loudly.'

She looked out, frozen in her seat.

'What do I do?'

'Sit tight. They'll do anything they can to contain you. If they need to, they'll shut you down. They did it to the Khaki Girl, Esh. They'll do it to you.'

'What happened to her?'

'She was in your house for two years, she had a lot of problems. When she finally lost control, the Corporation got rid of her.'

Esh panted. It was impossible. But this was what Maria had warned her about.

'You're too valuable to them right now, they're not going to make you disappear. But you need to make as little trouble as possible.'

She gazed into the Safe.

'I'm scared,' she said.

She waited, for a reply, for further information. But no answer came from the Safe, and she realised the transmission had ended.

Coma

Mikey and André were waiting outside.

'Heavey wants to see you,' said André.

She moved past him, as Mikey stepped aside to let her through. This was how it was now. Everything she did, everything she said, was going to be mediated through one of her security team.

'Where is he?' she asked.

'Living room.'

She walked up the stairs, and Mikey and André followed.

Heavey put down the magazine he was reading.

'Can we have a moment?' he asked the guards.

Wordlessly, Mikey and André retreated.

'Jesus,' he whispered, throwing them a sour look. He turned to Esh, and suddenly saw that she'd been crying. 'Hey.'

She shrugged, as he took a step towards her.

'Listen,' he said. 'I have good news.'

She looked up, saw his eyes filled with eagerness.

'You're going to see your grandfather.'

'I don't understand.'

'You're flying to London. The Corporation's had a change of heart.'

She filled with hope at the thought of seeing Mum and Dad, Grandad, Kristin.

'But it's a whistle-stop tour. We need you back in LA in twenty-four hours. You'll go. You'll see Grandad. You'll come back.'

She looked into his blue eyes. She was going to see Grandad. He was so far away, she could barely imagine him.

'Why?' she said.

'Compassionate leave.'

He smiled.

'I'm coming with you, Esh.'

Just as her heart was getting light with hope, she felt a pause. Something felt wrong. This situation didn't figure. Why would the Corporation be taking the chance of sending her to London just when they'd decided to shut her down in the house? They were planning something, something they wanted her to do.

Everything had been carefully arranged, from sponsoring her education to putting money aside for her years before they ever got in touch with her.

She was dealing with a million thoughts, trying to process one piece of insanity after another. If the Corporation had discovered her through the Foundation, it still didn't make sense that they would have paid her regardless of what happened.

How could Evo have been so important that they'd started planning the concept of the campaign when she'd barely been born? Couldn't they risk waiting to find the right person for the campaign? Did they need to have that person in place all along, years in advance, making sure that her life went to plan?

It was possible.

But as Esh's mind raced, it didn't add up, the patterns didn't match. How could they have been that meticulously forward-looking?

Nothing explained the money waiting for her since she'd been born. It meant that they'd appeared in her life, four weeks ago, to propose something that they'd always known was going to happen. And if it hadn't, they would have paid her anyway. Why? As compensation? For what? It was too titanic an amount to have formed part of her scholarship. Why pay someone so much?

'We're leaving this morning,' Heavey said.

Esh focused on him. She felt as if she'd disappeared, as if her body had wandered out of the compound without her.

'When did you know about me?' she said.

Heavey gazed at her, stunned, for a moment. He didn't seem to follow.

'When did they first tell you about me, Heavey?'

He looked at her with an air of sadness.

'Two years ago,' he said.

Esh's stomach sank. He'd known all along.

'How?' she said.

'I was working on other campaigns in LA. I got a call from someone at the Corporation, one of their representatives. For a long time they didn't tell me anything about Evo. All we did was talk generally, about contracts, and concepts. They said I wasn't allowed to know anything about Evo until we started work. Just like you,

Esh. Just before I signed my contract, they told me it was a biotech product, and gave me an indication of the campaign's budget. I knew it would be the biggest thing that I ever worked on. I signed up for seven years too. And then, slowly, they let me in on Evo. There was a lot of planning and strategising and then, eventually, they told me about you.'

Esh gazed at his clear, blue eyes. She couldn't believe he was saying these words for the first time.

'What did they tell you?'

'They said there was a girl in London, someone exceptional, whom they wanted to use. They told me everything about you. I couldn't believe what I heard, Esh. They described everything you'd achieved, your academic flair, your physical ability. When they told me you were perfect, I believed them. I saw images of you, Esh, all the footage that we're using now, I saw most of your life, before you ever came here. And I knew that you were like no one else on the planet.'

'Did they say they'd always watched me?'

Heavey looked at her sadly, pitying all she was feeling.

'They found you through the Foundation, Esh. They said that they'd decided to let you finish your education before making contact.'

Esh's body felt as though it was being slowly hollowed out. The Corporation had waited, and made decisions about her from afar all along.

'They said that you'd been kept in the dark as to your suitability, so that you'd have the freedom to choose what you wanted.'

Esh wanted to burst into tears.

'They took that risk?'

'They told me how much they were going to pay you, Esh.'

He gazed at her.

'It was generally assumed that you'd say yes.'

'You all lied, Heavey. You pretended to appear out of nowhere, when you'd been waiting and planning this for my whole life.'

Heavey stared at her, didn't respond.

'My whole life was a joke. Everything I did, all that I worked for, all the choices that I made, everything I tried out, it was all just passing time, going through the motions until this moment arrived. They had my whole life mapped out. They funded my existence and watched me fulfil their expectations.'

For a bizarre instant, she wanted Heavey to hold her.

'I'm a fool, Heavey. I've been a fool my whole life. Everything I did was just a piece of stage magic.'

'They did a wonderful thing too, Esh. They gave you the best chance in life, they saw how special you were and tried to nurture that, tried to do everything in their power not to infringe on your existence apart from assisting you. They could have left you in your state school, not interfered with your life. But imagine it. You needed to go to Ford, Esh. Do you remember your first school? Do you know how lost and lonely and frustrated you'd have been if you'd stayed? Try to imagine your life that way, without the Corporation's assistance. How would you be feeling today? Can you imagine your life without having fulfilled all the potential you have? You needed to be with children of your ability, and the attention and nourishment that Ford gave you, more than anything else. And the Corporation gave you that. I know you feel as if your whole life's a dream that suddenly you've woken out of, and you're pissed as all hell. But think of the alternative. The Corporation kept the truth from you, but they did it deliberately, so you'd have the liberty to choose your life.'

Esh peered hard at him.

'I never had a choice,' she said.

'You chose to come here, Esh. You chose this.'

'I was manipulated. It all happened behind the scenes, without my knowledge. People with choice have the facts. But I was never told. I was never told the truth about the Foundation. That would have been a choice. But I didn't know.'

Heavey gazed at her, with no answer.

'What are they hiding from me, Heavey? Why do they want me to go to London?'

'I don't know,' he shrugged. 'They want you to see your parents.'

He looked at her sternly. Her parents? Didn't he mean Grandad?

'Your grandfather's almost dead,' he said. 'This will be one of the toughest things you ever do. You can't imagine it.'

His expression softened.

'I've told the Corporation that I'm coming with you. You need somebody around you. I don't want you to be alone now.'

For a moment, he almost seemed embarrassed.

'I'll see you in a couple of hours,' he said, and left.

Jet

'We're going by car?'

Three identical SUVs waited on the drive, with a dozen security guards standing by their blacked-out windows.

'It's safer than chopper,' Heavey replied.

He followed André and Clive towards the central car, sandwiched between the two dummy vehicles, lead and back. As they approached, the twelve security personnel seemed to close in a little tighter around them. Tony and Mikey stepped forwards, and opened their passenger doors. Tony shadowed his arm around her as Mikey led Heavey to the far side of the car, and quickly lowered her into the car.

Her door slammed shut. She sat alone in the car for a second, and then Heavey climbed in the other side, sat beside her, and his door closed behind him. In front and back, the three security teams climbed into their respective vehicles, and the motorcade moved off down Esh's driveway.

On the empty compound road, they hurtled along

towards the double steel gates. Above the roof of the lead vehicle, Esh could see the high steel wall approaching. It slid open, and behind it the second wall followed suit in perfect synch, the two of them gaping open to let the convoy through.

The cars sped through the entrance, straight onto the highway. They turned the corner so fast that Esh had to grab the handle in the roof to hold herself. As she did, she turned her head. Behind them, sitting in the middle of the highway, she saw three police bikes holding back the traffic.

They drove less than a car's length apart and nine minutes later were pulling up onto the airstrip where Esh had landed just over three weeks ago.

They stopped metres from the jet. Esh saw the security guys in the front and rear cars get out and position themselves around the tarmac, encircling the SUVs to ready themselves for the principals' emergence.

Their doors swung open. Tony and André reached inside to guide them out, brooking no hesitation. The jet's keening engines filled the air, and Heavey and Esh were briskly ferried across the tarmac towards the plane's stairway, a dozen men in dark suits surrounding them. Tony and André led them up the stairs, as Mikey and Clive brought up the rear.

Everything was quiet. She stood in the white interior of the jet, two empty armchairs waiting by the window, beside a small table. The security team disappeared, leaving her and Heavey to take their seats.

Through one of the windows, she saw one of the

back-up teams entering the front of the jet. Outside, the three black SUVs drove away.

Heavey had ignored everything, and had sat down to make himself comfortable. Esh sat in front of him and buckled her seat belt, looking out of the window.

The ground had already started moving. The bare surroundings of the airfield angled round as the jet turned, and began taxiing towards the runway.

Peeking up at the SkyBoards she saw her face everywhere, as if she'd left it behind as a memento of herself. The jet suddenly halted, paused for a few seconds, and then it accelerated towards the end of the runway.

V

Rosebud

21

'Take this.'

Tony held out a huge down-filled jacket, as big as a sleeping bag, with a large hood and lining. She pulled it round her.

'It's cold,' he said. 'And it'll help disguise you.'

André hauled open the jet's door, and a stream of icy wind sucked into the cabin like some frozen guest who'd stood outside for hours. Esh hugged the jacket to her. It was inhospitable out there, like an Arctic wasteland.

'Okay,' Tony warned everyone.

As the plane's stairs hit the ground, Tony and André took the lead. Esh and Heavey were effortlessly hustled down the steps by the security team, the wind buffeting their faces as they stepped outside.

It was the dead of night. Esh followed security through the darkness, towards the waiting headlamps of three SUVs. Shutting their doors behind them, security jumped into the lead and back-up vehicles, and Tony climbed in beside the driver.

Heavey clenched himself with cold next to her.

249

'What time is it?' she said.

Heavey sleepily looked into his EyeScreen.

'Four a.m.'

The warmth of the car's heating fed through to them. Esh slipped off the hood on her jacket and looked outside. It was too dark to see anything. She was protected, behind glass again. The convoy moved off, quickly arriving on a main road, the three cars driving fast and bumper-to-bumper.

Tony turned round. 'Twelve minutes to the hospital,' he said.

He'd just received the information from security on Interface.

Esh tried to take her bearings outside. They weren't stopping for traffic lights, but driving as fast as humanly possible past the familiar street signs and shopfronts of England. It all looked homely, but alien. She couldn't recognise which part of London they'd arrived in from the anonymous airfield.

'Weird to be back?' Heavey asked her.

She nodded. She'd expected to feel at home, but it simply seemed like some strange land she'd been dreaming about all her life.

The convoy sped across a main junction at seventy miles per hour. Shooting past, Esh saw four huge iBoards showing her face on each corner of the cross-roads. Her twenty-five-foot face glowed at her in the cold night air.

'*There's Never Been Anyone Like Her,*' read the iBoard.

They turned onto a side road. The three cars took the narrow road ahead at speed. Where were they? They turned another corner, fast, following their pre-planned route.

Suddenly, the three cars pulled up. All around them, security guards jumped out of the lead and back-up cars and waited. A moment later, Esh and Heavey's doors opened and they stepped out of the car.

They were in a backstreet in the middle of nowhere.

'This way,' Tony said.

He led her to an unmarked door in the building just in front of them. Mikey, Clive and André followed her, and moved through the door behind her.

They stepped into a corridor of bare, fluorescent light. The walls were white, the floor green linoleum. It smelled pungently of hospital.

Along the corridor stood an elevator, its door already waiting open. Tony, André, Mikey and Clive stepped into the cabin around Esh.

'Hit twenty-one,' Tony said.

The elevator cabin was incongruously elegant, its mirrored walls smoked, its brass fittings and control panel polished.

Mikey reached out, pushed 21. The top floor.

'Where's Heavey?' Esh asked.

The elevator cabin ascended in silence.

'Downstairs,' said Tony.

She suddenly wanted him up here. She was about to see Grandad, still unable to visualise it. She was nervous about seeing her parents. Why? She didn't understand, but she felt butterflies merely thinking about it.

She watched the floor counter ticking above the door. All four guards stood compactly around her.

The elevator stopped. The doors slid open, and Mikey

and Clive led out, Tony and André coming out behind Esh. In all certainty, not one of them had ever set foot in this building, and yet they each knew exactly where they were going.

They followed the quiet, hotel-like corridor along its carpeted floor, past its dark red walls lined with paintings and flowers arranged in front of dimly lit mirrors. Everything was pleasant, and soothing. On either side of them, doors appeared at regular intervals, all identical except for a brass number plate on each. Everyone was sleeping. The corridor was silent. The ceiling hung low over their heads, with tiny spot lamps casting calming beams of light.

The corridor reached a T-junction, offering two possible directions. Mikey immediately moved to the right. They followed behind. The walls and carpet seemed to absorb every sound they made. Esh heard their clothes lightly swishing as they moved, but no one appeared from the doors, no noise emerged from the building.

They reached a left turn. A few paces ahead, Mikey suddenly came to a halt. He stood outside a door, and reached out his hand to the doorknob. He held it for a second, waiting, and then pushed the door gently open.

In front of Esh lay a small, darkened hallway. There was a dim light at the end, leading to a hidden room on the right. Before it, though, was another room just a few steps ahead on the left.

She stepped into the hallway. Mikey closed the door behind her. Round the corner of the first room, she saw Mum and Dad sitting in a small living area, a couple of empty coffee cups on the table before them. Their faces lit up.

'Esh.'

Dad got up, and seemed almost about to collapse as he spoke. He walked towards her, to hug her.

'Hello, Esh.'

He squeezed her hard. She couldn't believe how long it had been since she'd seen him. It felt so weird to be hugging him.

He let go, and stood away. He looked a little different, changed by lack of sleep.

'How are you?'

She nodded.

'I'm okay, Dad.'

He looked into her eyes. Beside him, Mum stood waiting. She came forwards and reached up her arms, putting them urgently round Esh's neck, and held her daughter for a long time without speaking.

'So good to see you,' she said, still gripping her.

Esh sensed a frailty in both her parents that she'd never noticed before. Something had been sapped from them. They felt brittle, like children. As Mum loosened her grip and moved back to look at her, Esh studied the room. It had its own kitchenette, a bathroom, every amenity to keep them comfortable.

'They brought you straight here?' Mum asked.

'Straight from the plane.'

They'd whisked her here so fast she felt as if she'd hardly arrived. She looked around, taking off her huge jacket. Everything was covered in the comfort and luxury the Corporation had provided for her parents.

Dad caught her eye. He glanced at the room by the end of the hall.

'Grandad's in there,' he said.

Esh turned to the dimly lit area, feeling timid. She'd come all this way. But suddenly she didn't want to see him.

'Come on,' Dad said, reading her thoughts.

He put his hand on her shoulder and led her through the hallway. She stepped into the dim room ahead of Mum, nervous of what she was going to see.

His bony body was outlined beneath the sheet which had been draped over him. He lay with his eyes closed, his arms crookedly laid out either side of him. Esh had never seen him asleep before. Setting eyes on him like this felt like an imposition. They'd dressed him in a white hospital tunic, too flared for his bare, skinny shoulders. His skin looked wan, too insubstantial to cover his body. He looked like a child in the tunic. Under the sheet, his body looked shrunken to half its size. Just below his waist, she could make out the meagre lump of his genitals protruding from his silhouette. He was prostrate, helpless. His head resting motionlessly on the pillow, he looked serene and expressionless.

In an instant, without time even to think, Esh understood exactly what was in front of her. She could see Grandad dying. The simplicity of it stared at her plain and unadorned. She realised how uncomplicated it was. His biological form was ending, like an engine losing its power, gradually turning off its functions.

Esh, Mum and Dad stood at the doorway watching him. Machines were set into the wall behind him. Several tubes came from his nose, more tubes appeared from his arms. There were wires and sensors attached to his chest and head, all connected to a bank of monitors analysing him and measuring how alive he was. But the whole room, as tidy as the family room in the hall, was pointless. Inescapably, his body was leaving life.

As she gazed at him, she knew there was nothing left to say, nothing to do. She grasped the exhaustion that her parents were both suffering from. It wasn't so much an exhaustion of anguish and grief. It was a weariness of knowing there was nothing to say. The evidence was there, before them. The agreement between Grandad's life and body had been terminated.

Dad's hand rested on her shoulder.

'You okay, Esh?'

She felt hardly anything. She didn't even believe that in reality she was looking at Grandad. Grandad wasn't in this room. He was a part of her memory, a ghost living within her, and within Mum and Dad. She'd simply come to visit the empty stage on which he'd once existed.

'I'm all right' she said.

She turned to them, saw their concern for her.

'Do you want to say goodbye?' Mum said.

Half question, half request. Esh knew Mum wanted her to do this formally.

She turned to the bed, and walked towards the body. She stood over him, and reached out her fingers to touch his hand.

His skin was papery, warm. But he didn't respond to her touch.

She tried to remember him talking, the expression in his blue eyes. She recalled them speaking before she left for LA. She remembered how he'd always supported her, adored her, and treasured her, his only grandchild. But the memory existed in her alone. In the bed before her, none of it now remained. She stood with her fingers pressed on his hand, as if she was communing some kind of contact between them. But the moment, she knew, was one-way.

'Okay,' she said.

She lifted her fingers off his hand, and left.

At the end of the hall, a knock came from the door. She stood watching it, but no one came in. She turned to her parents, and saw Mum smiling excitedly.

'Open it,' said Mum.

'Why?'

'Go on.'

Esh turned to the door. She walked along the narrow hallway, turned the handle, and pulled the door towards her.

Standing outside with André, Mikey, Clive and Tony was Kristin.

'Esh.'

She wrapped her arms around her before the moment had even hit.

'What are you doing here, Kristin?'

'They told me you were coming.'

She crushed Kristin, didn't want to let go of her.

'How did you get here?' she asked.

'They picked me up.'

Esh let go, and looked at Kristin's face.

'So, *so* good to see you, Kristin.'

Her eyes teared up. She couldn't believe Kristin was in front of her. She pulled her friend by the arm, towards the hallway.

'Come in,' she said.

Tony put out his hand.

'Sorry, Esh. You've got to stay here.'

Esh looked back at Kristin, who understood even better than she did.

'They made me sign a contract promising I wouldn't reveal that I'd seen you,' Kristin said. 'I'm not even allowed to talk about anything we discuss.'

Esh shrugged, resigned to the lunacy of the security protocol.

'"I was never here,"' Kristin said, springing a pair of fat air-commas.

They started laughing, despite the seriousness of the situation.

'When did you know I was coming?' Esh asked.

'They turned up last night, with the contract prepared.'

Kristin cast an ironic glance back at the guards watching them in the corridor.

'You have some pretty scarily efficient people working for you,' she said.

Esh looked at her, unable to wipe the smile from her face.

'This is so crazy, Kristin.'

Kristin nodded.

'It's nuts.'

Esh reached out and held Kristin's arms, to remind herself she was there. But in that moment sadness descended through her, as the joy of seeing Kristin suddenly came face-to-face with the reality of how briefly she was going to be there.

'I started at the Bank, Esh.'

Esh smiled, ecstatic at seeing her. But the mention of the life they were going to have led together made her want to cry. She felt desperate, remembering the normal existence she thought they'd been destined for.

'I see you every day, Esh. It's so weird. You keep popping up on all the SkyBoards and appearing in my Interface. You're there the whole time.'

Esh gripped Kristin's wrists. She wanted to speak, but nothing came from her mouth. Looking into Kristin's eyes, her head suddenly flopped forwards.

'Esh?'

Esh's eyes filled with tears. She wanted to tell Kristin everything that had happened to her, everything about Marcus, about all the crazy places in her house, the Safe, the pool, Maria and Mano, about Gus and Nathan being wankers. But there was too much suddenly. She didn't know where to begin, and now that Kristin was finally in front of her, she couldn't speak.

She held on to Kristin. A gasp came from her mouth.

'It's okay, Esh.'

Kristin put her hands round Esh's face.

'It's going to be okay,' she said.

Esh nodded. The strength had gone from her neck. She couldn't speak.

She wanted to say '*It's so good to see you*,' but her voice didn't make a sound.

'Good to see your face, Esh,' Kristin said, saying it for her. 'They made you look pretty good in the campaign. But you're better close-up.'

Involuntarily Esh laughed. She looked up at Kristin smiling. Joy flooded through her again, and then just as suddenly the pall of darkness descended over her.

She glanced at the guards.

Suddenly none of this made sense. Why had they

flown her here? Why bring Kristin just to talk to her?

She heard a noise down the corridor. She turned, and saw two security guards appear around the corner, followed by Heavey and two more bodyguards.

She squeezed Kristin's wrist, as Heavey stopped in front of her.

'I'm afraid Kristin has to go,' he said.

Esh stared back.

'Why?'

'We have a room for you and your parents to talk together.'

Esh turned to Kristin. She didn't want her to go.

'These gentlemen will escort you home, Kristin,' Heavey said.

Esh gripped Kristin's wrists, wouldn't let go.

'Come on, Esh,' said Heavey.

He touched Esh's knuckles, trying to relax them.

'No,' Esh said.

'We don't have time, Esh.'

Tears streamed from Esh's eyes.

'I'll see you soon,' said Kristin, squeezing her hands.

They looked at each other, as Heavey reached out to take Esh.

'Got to go, Esh.'

His four security guards gathered round Kristin, and started walking her away.

'Bye,' Kristin said, turning to smile.

Esh watched her walk away. She couldn't bear it.

'Kristin!' she called.

Kristin turned her head, as the bodyguards led her round the corner.

*

'Come with me,' said Heavey.

He looked past her shoulder, at her parents coming out of the hallway.

'Hello,' he said, giving them a respectful grin. 'If you'd like to follow me.'

He led them down the corridor, Tony and Mikey by his side, André and Clive bringing up the rear.

'Where are we going?'

'They have a room for us to talk,' Dad said.

'About what?'

Heavey and the security team hurried them along.

She was escorted into the room with Mum and Dad and then left alone, as Heavey and the guards waited outside.

The room was as simply and elegantly furnished as the waiting room beside Grandad. There were a few armchairs and a sofa, and vases of fresh flowers.

Her parents sat either side of her on the long sofa. Dad reached out his hand and placed it on Esh's knee, looking nervous.

'You know that Mum and I love you very much,' he said.

Esh turned to him. As she did, she felt Mum take hold of her hand.

'We love you more than anything else in the world,' Mum said.

'What's happening?' Esh said.

She felt Mum and Dad gaze at her.

'It's about Grandad,' said Mum.

Esh looked up, and met Mum's eyes.

'The Corporation want us to tell you.'

'Tell me what?'

Mum looked at her seriously.

'That Grandad's disease is hereditary.'

Esh looked at Mum, trying to divine her expression. And then suddenly, her stomach sank, as she finally realised what it was.

It was the reason they'd flown her all the way here, why they'd fought so hard to withhold the news from her, why they'd even brought Kristin to console her. It was the reason they'd kept everything secret, why they'd hidden all this information.

It was the chink in her armour, the single defect of the perfect girl they'd found for Evo. She'd inherited Grandad's disease. One day, at an unknown time in the future, she would develop the same condition as Grandad and die in the same way as him, comatose, unconscious, and gradually losing her functions.

She would die like this, and they knew it. Discovering the truth, the Corporation had shown Esh the mercy and compassion of bringing her to London so that her parents could tell her the news in person.

'I didn't inherit the disease,' Mum said.

Esh stared at her, and in the sadness of Mum's eyes she saw the grief Mum felt at knowing she'd been spared, only for Esh to have been chosen, mother passing death on to daughter. She squeezed Esh's hand, her eyes filling with tears.

'And neither did you, Esh.'

Esh gaped at her, understanding nothing.

'When you were little, Esh, Dad and I got very sick once, when we were in France. We went on holiday to Normandy. Do you remember?'

Esh nodded. She couldn't recall the holiday itself, only the fact that they'd been in France.

'You weren't two years old, but you were up and walking and talking like a little person. You were such a joy, Esh. I think you were a fuller, rounder person than we'd ever met. From the very start, we loved every minute we spent with you. We would lie in bed holding you and watch you, talk about you, and you'd pay attention, listening intently to us before you even understood what we were saying. You were absorbing the world around you constantly.'

Mum smiled through her tears.

'We stayed in a little hotel in Normandy, where they had a restaurant. On our first night the waiter spotted you and thought you were terribly cute, a lot of people did. He asked you if you'd like to eat some bouillabaisse. You looked him straight in the eye and said "Yes." He laughed, surprised, but he brought you some in a child-sized bowl. We all ate it, Esh. You loved it. But that night your dad and I got sick. We were up all night. Everyone in the hotel who'd eaten the soup was ill. The hotel asked if there was a doctor, but there wasn't much Dad could do. He had some rehydration salts which helped, but we were sick as hell. The rest of the next day we stayed in bed, along with almost everyone in the hotel. Some of the kitchen staff had eaten the soup and were laid up too. The hotel practically shut down. Some time in the afternoon, though, the same waiter brought us some herbal tea and bread. I think he felt awful about us being sick. He saw us in bed, looking atrocious, taking it in turns to vomit in the bathroom. He left the bread for us and saw you sitting on the end of the bed, amusing yourself with your little word-games. You loved the fact you could speak. You were happy as anything. But he stared at you, realising that you weren't ill.'

Mum smiled at Esh, weeping.

'You were twenty months old, Esh. You had the immune system of an infant, and you didn't get sick. Every person in that hotel was laid out for twenty-four hours except for you. You didn't stop for a second, you didn't feel a thing. You took care of us as we lay there, trying to help us drink some tea, eat a little bread.'

Dad squeezed her knee. Esh turned to him, and saw him crying, looking at her in wonder. She felt her parents' devotion to her as if it was physically radiating from them.

'You were our hero, Esh. You were our star. You're unlike anyone we've ever known.'

Mum stroked Esh's hand.

'You don't have Grandad's condition, Esh,' she said.

Esh turned to her.

'Why not?'

Mum smiled, but it made her cry all the more.

'You are our daughter,' she said.

She tried to keep her lip from quivering. She wanted to pull herself together to carry on, but suddenly she couldn't hold it any more. She gasped, stopping herself from crying, and looked up at Esh.

'When you were very tiny, we adopted you, Esh. Dad and I had never been able to have children of our own, and you came to us when you were two months old. You were the most wonderful thing that ever happened to us.'

They both sobbed, holding Esh tight.

'We love you more than we can ever explain,' Mum

said, her jaw trembling. 'We love you more than we thought we could ever love anyone, Esh. You can't explain what it's like to have a child. It doesn't make a difference if it's not your own. To care for someone, to have their life depending on yours, to feel the joy of their every minute on this earth, is something I can't put into words. The joy that you have brought us has been boundless. We dreaded this day, Esh, we always knew how terrible it would be for all three of us. But we also knew that nothing would ever alter how much we have loved you from the very first day we held you.'

Mum and Dad held her hands, as if to stop her from disappearing. She could feel alternating waves of love and anguish coming from them. In a single moment, she suddenly realised how much they'd always felt for her.

The door to the room opened, and Heavey's face appeared in the gap. He looked at the two adults sobbing. He turned to Esh, saw her staring at him, and seemed caught up in a crisis of his own, looking at her with all the fondness and sympathy he could muster. But Esh knew that he'd also come with a purpose, to let her know as unobtrusively as possible that it was time to go back to LA.

Dark glass

The silence of London felt infinite. Esh sat in the back of the SUV staring out of the window, at the dark punctuated by streetlights and iBoards showing her in the Evo campaign. There seemed to be hardly anyone on the streets, as if everything in London had vanished.

Seeing her face reflected in the dark window brought to mind a switched-off TV screen. As she stared at herself, half inside the car, half outside, she felt as if she was melting into the dark glass separating her from the world. Periodically the car's heat twirled round her, whilst outdoors London's icy wind blew over the car as it raced through the streets towards the airfield.

Heavey sat on the rear seat beside her. She watched the streets outside, rigidly unable to turn or look at him. It was somehow his silence, and not the silence of the world around her, that oppressed her the most.

She watched London's darkness unfurling as they sped through the city where she'd been raised. Where had she been born? Who were her real parents? Why had they given her up? Everything that her parents had said came back to her. Temporarily, it had receded, drifting off into the darkness like some flotsam bobbing up and down on a wave. And suddenly it crashed over her again.

She wanted to obliterate everything she'd become, go back home, and lead a normal existence in London with Kristin.

The three SUVs zipped through the cold, safely cushioning their principal in the central vehicle. They pulled off the main road, towards the airfield. Heavey sat beside her, saying nothing.

They passed through an open security barrier onto the airstrip, where the jet was waiting, engines running, its inner cabin lit up in the darkness. She looked up at the SkyBoards as the cars pulled up. Where she'd once seen Marcus, George, Larry, Dwight and Dirk filling the sky, she saw nothing but herself.

They must have always known that they'd have to do this, bring her here for her parents to tell her that she wasn't their daughter, before returning her immediately to LA under armed guard.

As soon as her education came to an end, the Corporation knew that they'd approach her and ask her to star in the campaign, and that they'd then cosset her in so much security she would eventually forget what the outside world was like. They'd known that one day she would be worth more to them than all the money they'd ever paid for her.

The Foundation had known that she was adopted. It was possible that they'd even chosen her before she was born. But why? Did they need somebody without a past, without any traceable biological lineage?

The SUVs quickly drew up beside the jet. The

security teams jumped out and surrounded them. After an instant, Esh and Heavey's doors opened, and wind immediately blew into the car.

She stepped out in her huge, padded jacket and looked around. She could have sprinted away now, into the night, as far as she could make it. But her Ear Chip was still sending out its signal. She knew it was only a matter of time. Someone, eventually, would lead her back to the Corporation.

Tony, André, Mikey and Clive led her across the tarmac, sheltering her as she walked towards the jet. As Heavey followed in silence, she knew he had been aware of what the Corporation had scheduled to happen tonight.

She walked up the stairs to the jet, and Heavey's footsteps followed.

'You know everything?' she said.

Heavey looked at her across the small table by the window and nodded, the sky outside buoying them weightlessly over the Atlantic.

'Who am I, Heavey?'

'Not yet, Esh.'

'I have a right to know. Why was it me? Because I'm an orphan? Because I'd have no family history? You've hidden everything from me. You've lied and I want to know why.'

Heavey looked at her impassively.

'You're in shock, Esh.'

'Don't try to pacify me. I want to know why the Corporation chose me for Evo. Was it because I didn't have parents?'

Heavey took a deep breath, and didn't reply.

'What do you know about me?'

'I know everything, Esh.'

'Who are my real parents?'

She wanted to scream. Only the humming quietness of the jet stopped her grabbing him by the neck there and then.

'We're trying to reveal everything to you slowly,' he said.

'Who the fuck are they, Heavey?'

She stared at him.

'I'm not authorised to tell you, Esh. Someone else must tell you.'

'Who?'

'I can't say.'

'Of course you can't. This is bullshit.'

She raised her voice, enough to break the stillness of their flight. But Heavey continued to gaze at her calmly.

'You deserve to know the truth, Esh. It's not a very easy truth to relate, though. You'll be told everything in LA. You need to be patient.'

'Patient?'

She felt herself simmering, on the verge of hitting someone.

'You want me to be patient after I've been lied to?'

'You have to trust me, Esh.'

'Fuck you, Heavey.'

She turned to look out of the window. The SkyBoards glowed above them, covering the sky with her luminous image.

'I deserved to know all this so long ago,' she whispered, barely loud enough for Heavey to hear. 'Before any of this, Heavey, before I came to LA, before the Foundation paid for me to go to school. I deserved to know everything and you never told me. Don't ask me to trust you. You lied to me on behalf of the Corporation.'

Tears rose in her eyes. Inside herself, curled up tight, she felt a fury purer than anything she'd ever experienced. It was intense, more certain than any conviction she'd held. The anger was something sure, keeping her solid, and intact.

'I always felt that you cared about me, Heavey. You were kind and considerate. But you betrayed me. You kept everything hidden from me so that I'd end up here. It was even you who convinced me to cut myself off the Net so the Corporation would have me in its total power. You knew that, Heavey, you knew absolutely. On behalf of the Corporation, you've fucked me. And I'm going to turn that wrong into a right.'

Heavey stared at her, stunned.

'What do you mean?'

He looked at her, hoping for an answer. But she didn't say a word. She stared out of the window, the luminescence of her own image in the sky lighting up her face.

One

It was morning in LA, a day after they'd left. As she stepped off the plane into the sunlight, she felt as if she'd spent the last twenty-four hours in darkness.

Security led them quickly down the steps, into the warm air, across the tarmac towards the waiting SUVs. Almost simultaneously the three security teams climbed into the vehicles and the convoy set off, speeding towards the compound on the highway through the hills of LA.

Esh sat in silence on the back seat with Heavey. Suddenly, in the iciness of the air con, Heavey spoke, having received a message on Interface.

'Someone is waiting to see you in the compound,' he said.

Esh didn't turn round. She looked out of the window, strong, lucid, and alive.

The Team had been right about everything. They'd tried to warn her, they'd tried to lead her to the truth she'd now discovered for herself. They'd said all along that the Corporation had been carefully manipulating her life, suppressing the truth from her, keeping her pliant and innocent. The Voice had even called to warn her in London. Piece by piece, moment by moment, everything it had told her had come true. So she had to believe that, as surely as she could on blind and unsubstantiated faith, everything it had told her was in earnest. The warning Maria had given her had been the severest she could have feared. The Corporation would stop at nothing to subdue her, if she now started to kick against the rafters. She knew that the Khaki Girl had been killed because she'd become uncontrollable. History was repeating itself with eerie perfection. She was as safely contained and hidden away now as the Khaki Girl had been before she'd died, before the iVert of her injecting herself had been broadcast. She'd let them cut her off the Net, sever her from the world, and render her as impotent as a NAP.

She didn't know how she was going to do it, or where she was going to go, or how she would survive with no access to the Net or Money. She didn't know how she was going to disguise herself and remain invisible. But she knew, with as much horror as resolve, that she had no choice, that she couldn't carry on with her life as it had become, that she was going to escape, as the Voice had told her she eventually would.

'They're waiting in your house,' Heavey said, receiving a message on EyeScreen. 'We'll be with them in a few minutes.'

They pulled off the highway, through the giant steel gate of the compound. Up the hill, along the high red wall, they passed the anonymous entrances of the mansions, contained within the compound's ring of security. At the top of the hill, they passed the gate to Marcus's mansion. His house looked abandoned.

Her entrance gates opened, and the cars in the convoy turned off the road onto the driveway. The sprinklers in her garden were tapping rhythmically, security guards were patrolling the grounds, Felipe, Miguel and Fontàn were trimming the lawn. The cars pulled up outside the front doors, and Esh was led from the vehicle to her entrance hall.

As she walked across the driveway, she looked up at the SkyBoards. And finally, in the middle of the sky, she found the ad she'd been waiting to see since the first time she'd glimpsed it. She was four, copying out the geo-metric patterns, in front of the adults who'd assembled to watch her display her gifts. And half-hidden amongst them, as Esh had first suspected, she saw Estella, looking even more beautiful than she did today, gazing down at Esh's form in wonder.

She walked into her living room at Heavey's bidding. Sitting on the sofa in the wide, light-filled room, looking as composed and elegant as she had the day they'd first met, was Estella.

'Esh,' she said, standing up.

Esh looked across the room, as at an old friend. Estella looked the same, though dressed in lighter clothing for the weather. Her mannerisms, grace, her self-possession were all there. It was dislocating to see her here, in her own house.

'Have a seat, Esh.'

Still the same unquestioning authority. Esh sat down in one of her seats, and with the sighing tranquillity of the garden and sunshine harbouring them, the two of them looked at each other.

'I want to tell you why everything has happened,' Estella said, smiling at Esh with her transparently green eyes. 'I want you to know that we didn't find you.'

She paused, and looked at Esh for a few moments.

'We never came looking for you, Esh. You came to us. It was always you. Before you were even born.'

There was a glow of intimacy in Estella's eyes which Esh now remembered from that day in her parents' kitchen.

'We waited so that we wouldn't interrupt your life,' she said. 'That was important to us, something we chose to do under the auspices of the highest authorities. We needed to protect you, but we left you as long as we could so that you'd have as normal a life as possible. We helped you through the Foundation's scholarship, as you now know, but we never patronised your parents with financial assistance. To this day, they have been frankly unaware of why we have looked after you. We vetted them, Esh, we chose them. They were the most good-hearted, responsible people we could find. They didn't know it, and neither do they now, but they were the two people whom we chose out of all those we examined. Of course, we tried to ensure that you would never run into undue danger or find yourself financially straitened, but we also did everything within our power to interfere as little as possible, to allow your life to proceed as normally and unhampered as it could. We left you to develop as a normal girl, Esh, under Mum and Dad's guidance.'

She peered at Esh with impassioned eyes.

'Who are my real parents?' Esh asked.

Estella's eyes smiled.

'We are.'

Esh gazed at her, understanding nothing.

'Who am I?' she said.

'What you *are* is something that we could never have given you, Esh. It is what you have become by yourself.'

Esh looked tremblingly into Estella's eyes, fearing what they concealed.

'I was the senior research director of Evo,' Estella told her. 'When the project was initiated twenty-one years ago, I was brought in to run what remains the most highly-funded project there has ever been. It was the most exciting enterprise any of us would ever work on. As pioneers, we knew the benefits and value of Evo before it ever bore that name. We believed in it passionately, and spent twenty years perfecting the technology that we are about to unveil. In a lab complex built for us in Utah, we commenced the greatest scientific venture ever undertaken, with effectively unlimited funding from the Corporation. It was their Ark of the Covenant, conducted in absolute secrecy, though we never once flouted international wisdom or convention. Everything we did, at every stage, was approved by US government. We did what we did because we believed in the wider historical and cultural benefit of the technology to the world. Our primary mandate was to create a prototype, to demonstrate the technology's potential. We wanted for nothing. We had the best minds and the best technology at our disposal, all concentrated in this one hothouse, in the most creatively explosive, exciting time of our careers. The programme evolved faster than we could ever have imagined. Within two years, we had achieved the prototype. It was one of those miracles, the kind of breakthrough about which science dreams.'

Estella gazed at her.

'When you were born, Esh, I decided to work at the Foundation to continue to oversee the work I'd been responsible for under Evo. I believed with all my heart in what we'd achieved. I believed in the value of what the Foundation could do for children who deserved an exceptional education. But I chose to work at the Foundation, above all, because I wanted to be close to you. It was my way of protecting you, Esh. I wanted to be able to watch over you, to look after you in some way. I have been near you since before you were born. I have watched you grow into the most beautiful woman you could have possibly become.'

Estella sat forward, her eyes watering.

'I was there, Esh, when you came into being. You were the single prototype of Evo's development programme, our exemplar of what Evo can do. You are alone in this. There are no others like you, and there will never be a 'you' again. We were committed under federal licence to produce only one specimen of Evo's full gamut. We have since perfected the technology that is embodied in you, on a mass-market commercial scale. But you were the first. You have no biological parentage. You are made from the most perfect genetic composites ever assembled, a fault-free genome generations ahead of the rest of humanity. Through Evo, human zygotes will still be created with the introduction of two parents, and then be manipulated and enhanced. But you were created perfectly, Esh. There was no sperm, no egg.'

*

Nausea shot up through Esh.

'It will take time to accept and understand what you really are,' said Estella. 'You need to learn everything about yourself, and that is why we are here, to teach you. You deserve to know who you are, and you deserved to live a normal life until that time came. But the time is here now.'

'You're lying.'

'No, Esh.'

'This is some bullshit invented for the campaign.'

'No,' said Estella. 'It's the truth.'

Her life was flashing before her eyes, everything she'd seen, everyone she'd known. School. Kristin. Mum. Dad. Grandad. Her scholarship. LA.

'It can't be real.'

'It's real.'

'You're lying to me.'

Estella didn't move. She watched Esh staring at her knees in despair, and then glanced at Heavey and beckoned him to come in.

'Esh,' he said. 'We need to show you something.'

Esh looked up, as he switched on the TV. The screen filled with a hazy video. There was no soundtrack, just footage of an enormous laboratory where scores of scientists worked in separate divisions, followed by a shot of them all grouped together for the camera. In the middle of them stood Estella.

The footage cut to a sunlit room, where a series of adults stood in casual summer wear, all watching a common object out of reach of the shot. At the end of the row was Estella again, looking young, serious, beautiful amongst the crowd.

The shot cut to a baby crawling by their feet. They watched attentively, some of them turning to their neighbours to make a comment. The baby crawled quickly, with agility, anxious to walk. At the end of the line she suddenly, instinctively turned towards Estella, who stooped down proudly to pick her up.

'I'd held you many times,' said Estella. 'You always came to me.'

Esh watched herself swaddled in Estella's arms on TV.

'You were only five weeks old, but already crawling like a one-year old. You were a marvel, Esh. You were more amazing than anything we could have imagined.'

Esh stared at the footage.

'Who's my mother?'

She heard how quiet and hoarse her own voice had become.

'We implanted you in a surrogate mother,' said Estella. 'You had no biological parents, only the woman who bore you to term. Her identity will always be kept a secret. She will never interfere with you, Esh, and you will never meet her.'

The camera zoomed in on Esh's five-week old face, smiling happily in Estella's arms.

'We gave you a life,' Estella said, reaching over and putting her hand on Esh's knee. 'We tried to give you every chance we could, and vowed that we wouldn't contact you until you had finished school.'

Esh turned her head, looked into Estella's warm, green eyes. She wanted to cry, for Estella to hold her.

'Who's my mother?' she said.

Her voice cracked, while Estella continued gazing steadily at her.

'You don't have one, Esh.'

She laid both hands on Esh's knees, looking into her eyes to comfort her.

'I have to go,' she said. 'You need to rest and take time to get used to this. There is so much for you to understand. I'm going to spend a lot of time with you, to help you and teach you all the incredible things that you are.'

She squeezed Esh's knees, and stood up. Turning on her heels, she walked out of the room, and left Esh alone with Heavey.

She looked up at him, hovering over her apologetically.

'You knew?'

Heavey nodded. Rising like a ghost from her own body, Esh stood up, and moved towards him, whispering directly to his face.

'You tricked me, Heavey.'

He peered at her an inch away. She breathed in slowly, feeling a cold, streaming wind swirl inside her.

'You lied to me.'

Heavey looked back at her, and nodded once more. The tornado suddenly whipped through her. Out of nowhere, a scream erupted in her body and she grabbed Heavey, shook him like a sheet of paper.

'You could have told me! You could have told me any time and you lied! I should have known, Heavey! You should have told me!'

He flapped between her arms. She screamed louder, yet it sounded to her no stronger than a tiny voice trying to make itself heard. She shook him, waiting for him to resist or fight or say something.

One

Tony and André ran over from the entrance and tore at her arms, trying to pull her off. She wouldn't come away, screaming at Heavey at the top of her voice. They tried to prise her hands from his shoulders, but she gripped him so tightly they could barely slip their fingers beneath hers. Mikey and Clive came running in, and seized her, the four of them tugging at her arms, trying to wrench her away. But she wouldn't let go.

Then they looked at each other, counted down from three, and in one motion yanked her off with all their strength, pulled her from Heavey, and dragged her out of the room, screaming, weeping, and yelling.

Sleeper

The house was silent. There were no sounds in the garden. Neither Maria nor Mano made a noise downstairs. It was as if they'd all been cleared out, just as Esh imagined Marcus's house being emptied.

She lay motionless, staring at the light on the wall, unaware of anything happening outside.

She wanted Marcus. She wanted him to kiss her and touch her, to make her feel as if she was here.

It was the first time her body had ever made sense to her, being naked with him, sleeping with him, as though she'd finally known why she was alive, and whole. She'd never experience the sensation of Marcus looking at her or feeling her again. Here, alone in the silence, she listened to her body automatically breathing, existing, pumping blood around her.

Her fire and anger had gone. When she'd shaken Heavey in her arms, she'd felt that she could have quite happily killed him, snuffed him out like a light. But now she felt drained of all energy. She lay on the bed, unconnected to anything in the universe, the passive observer of her own breath.

She'd achieved so much in her life. All along, she'd excelled, progressed, performed, done so many things. But there was nothing she wouldn't have given, right now, to be able tell Marcus that in a month she'd felt more with him than she had in her whole previous life.

At school she'd unwittingly fulfilled every expectation the Corporation had had of her. But deep down, she now knew she was nothing. She was simply this mind, inside a cage they'd built for her.

Steps came across the floor. Maria's white dress appeared. She was carrying something. She laid it on the small bedside table and sat on the mattress by Esh, nestling her bum against her legs. She rested her hand on Esh's shoulder, as Esh continued to stare at the beam of light on the wall.

'I've brought you some food,' she said. 'I'm going to make you eat something.'

She looked at Esh's eyes. They were dead, like an animal found on the roadside.

'I want you to eat a little, then I'm going to leave you in peace.'

Maria reached for the plate of buttered bread that she'd asked Mano to prepare, and rested it on her lap. Tearing off a little piece, she put a morsel near to Esh's lips, and waited. Nothing happened; then, spontaneously, Esh's lips slowly moved to accept the crumb, chewing on it cheerlessly.

Maria repeated the action, waited for Esh to swallow,

then tore off another piece of bread. Morsel by morsel, they got through the plate.

'Good,' Maria said, as much to herself as Esh.

She watched Esh in the stillness of the room, shaded from the day outside.

'Is there anything you'd like?'

Esh's eyes didn't move.

'I want to see Marcus.'

Maria stroked her.

'I know,' she said. 'I never told them about him. I wanted you to know that.'

Esh's eyes stared lifelessly, but she murmured quietly.

'Thank you.'

Maria continued stroking her for a while.

'Go to sleep, Esh,' she said.

Esh opened her eyes, and looked up at the blinds. It was dark. Night, the house still and quiet. Nothing had moved or changed around her, except the light. Like a fug everything came back to her, clouding her over.

She closed her eyes, and fell back into the same grey, continuous sleep.

'Esh.'

She looked out. It was still dark, and Heavey was sitting on her bed, touching her side.

'You need to come to the Safe,' he said.

Esh looked ahead at the blank, dark wall.

Heavey sat looking at her. In the darkness, the entire house had started to feel like a mausoleum.

'You need to come,' he told her. 'Your grandfather has died.'

*

Tony, Heavey and André escorted her to the basement. She couldn't tell whether it was night or day. She walked towards the Safe's radiance and iScanned through the door.

'We'll be waiting out here,' Heavey said.

She walked into the white light, and felt as if she was in a dream. The Safe seemed to hum around her. She sat in the white suede seat, looking for her parents on the screen. But the signal light remained red.

'Esh,' said the Voice.

They'd got her into the Safe to speak to her. Was Grandad dead?

'We're sorry about your grandfather,' he said. 'We jumped the queue ahead of your parents. The Corporation thinks there's a communications jam in London, so we have to be quick.'

Esh looked around and felt as hollow as the Safe.

'We know who you are,' said the Voice.

'You do?'

'We know you were adopted, and that the Corporation altered the first two months of your Identity to make it appear that you were born in London. You were actually born in Utah, taken to England two months later. Do you know this?'

The whiteness of the room washed over her.

'What do you want?'

'No, Esh. What do *you* want?'

She sat cocooned, not wanting a thing.

'I want to be left alone.'

'They're going to control you and keep you under wraps for the rest of your life, Esh. Your time's starting to run out. We've had word from our source that the Corporation's about to lock you down with security measures that will keep you in their sight forever. Our intelligence indicates that there's no intention of restoring you to Interface. They'll keep you cut off as long as they have to. The decision to tell you who you are was apparently taken at the last minute. It's a one-way ticket, Esh. Because now that they've told you, they know what a liability you are to them. They simply cannot afford for you to escape.'

The Voice paused, and left her lingering in silence and space.

'You have to decide, Esh.'

'What do I have to decide?'

'What you're going to do.'

The Voice paused again, and the silence and emptiness of the Safe engulfed her.

'We can help you escape, Esh.'

'How?'

'You have to trust us.'

Esh stared into the void.

'Why should I?' she asked.

'There's no why, Esh. You trust us right now. Or you don't.'

In her mind, the bubble of the Safe pulsed like a giant beating heart.

'What do I have to do?' she said.

'We have a contact in the Corporation, Esh, a sleeper. We call him Rosebud. He can help you to get out.'

'How do I find him?'

'We can't give you a name. You need to wait.'

'How long?'

'We're not sure. It depends on Rosebud's ability to move you.'

'Where is he?'

The Voice didn't reply. Was he here in the compound, amongst them?

'We'll be able to hide you from the Corporation, Esh.'

'How?'

'Believe me, they will never find you. We can make you as invisible to them as we are. But you'll never see your family or make contact with any part of your past again. That's how it works. That's the choice.'

Everything inside her felt swept away by the tide of what she'd become, this shell of what the Corporation had created. She had nothing left. No Marcus. No Kristin. No contact with Mum or Dad, beyond her visiting rights in the Safe. Her life was confined to this house, under the constant care of Tony, André, Mikey and Clive.

What would happen on the outside? However much the Team promised they could protect her, what would she be out there, without family, past, or money?

'I need some kind of guarantee,' she said, struggling for a solution.

'There's no guarantee, Esh.'

She looked at the screen, and the signal light had turned green. The Voice had disappeared. Her parents came into view, holding each other.

'He's gone, Esh,' said Mum.

She let out a sobbing laugh, suddenly relieved that it was all over.

'He would have been so happy that you said goodbye, Esh. It would have meant everything to him. He worshipped you.'

Esh looked at Mum and Dad, trying to understand them, struggling to see them as a pair of normal people.

'They've told us who you are, Esh.'

Mum suddenly broke down.

'We wish we were there with you,' she wept. 'We wish you weren't alone right now.'

Just hearing Mum say the words made Esh want to cry. And she restrained herself, because she didn't want that to happen. She didn't want to lose the hardness of her anger, the resolution that came from feeling so numb inside.

'Grandad knew that you were adopted,' Mum told her.

Suddenly, Esh's eyes filled with tears.

'You were his only grandchild. He loved you ever since you were tiny, treasured you, and adored you, more than he ever did me.'

Mum sobbed with the delayed realisation that her father had just died.

'Esh, he left everything in his will to you,' she said, smiling though her tears. 'He wanted you to be happy, to have everything that you'd ever desired.'

Esh's body shook uncontrollably. Tears streamed down her face as she looked up at her parents. In a huge involuntary rush, she thought of everything they'd done for her.

'Mum,' she said, her voice cracking up. 'He told me how sorry he was.'

Mum gazed at her in expectation and disbelief.

'What do you mean?'

'He told me he was sorry for how he neglected you and mistreated you. He knew how much you resented him and he wanted to say sorry, after Granny died. But I don't think he knew how. That's why he told me.'

Mum gasped, listening.

'When did he tell you this?'

'Before I left London, when I went to see him.'

Mum's chest heaved with new energy, as the relief and the shock burst inside her. Dad squeezed her, and turned to look at Esh.

'Esh,' Dad said.

In the Safe's brightness, Esh gazed at the two people who'd cared for her, loved her, and done everything for her since she was a child.

'We've just lost Grandad,' Dad said. 'We don't want to lose you too, Esh.'

Thousands of miles away, she sobbed alone in the Safe.

'We love you,' Mum said.

'We love you so much,' Dad cried.

She looked at her two parents holding each other, her body trembling.

'I love you too,' she said.

Kane

Heavey saw her come out of the Safe in tears, and took her in his arms. Weak, and shivering, she let him hold her for a long time.

She opened her eyes as he took her up the stairs, glimpsing the newly-risen sun through her eyelids. As they stepped into her entrance hall, she saw that the garden was bathed in daylight, the sprinklers ticking in every corner of the lawn. Felipe, Miguel and Fontàn were tending the grounds, security guards patrolling the borders, and Mikey and Clive stood guard outside her door.

'You're going to be okay, Esh,' Heavey said.

He walked her through the hallway, holding her with his arm, and turned to see if she was all right. She was still crying, her body shaking, but she seemed to be growing calmer, as the process of healing finally began.

'I'll need to take you to the Hub in a moment,' he said.

She looked up.

'Why?'

'I know this isn't what you want right now, but we

need to consolidate your security situation, make sure you're secure for launch. You'll be out in the open and you must be traceable to us. We're only two days away.'

They were locking her down. It was about to happen.

Heavey led her to the Pagoda, tracked by Tony and André. As they walked up the stairs to the conference room, he suddenly remembered.

'Hey, sorry you had to wait for your parents.'

Esh looked at the workers in the Hub, searching for Rosebud. How was she meant to find him? How would she have time before they locked her down?

'Sorry?'

'We had a comms problem in London. Jammed up the transmission for a while, took a little longer to connect you.'

Heavey opened the door in front of them, and took her into the glass room.

'I want you to know that we're going to take care of you,' he said, as he sat down on the sofa. 'We're going to help you through this transformation. We have psychologists trained for this kind of thing who will work with you, to help you overcome the trauma and begin to patch yourself together. This is going to be an incredibly hard time, but we will be there every step of the way. You're already a mature adult, Esh, so it's hoped that the psychological damage to you will be minimal. You're a remarkable, fully-formed person, with a strong identity and sense of self.'

Esh looked out of the room, scouring the Hub.

'You have to remember something,' he continued. 'We've watched you all your life. When we decided to hire you, it wasn't simply because of what you were born. It was primarily the person that you've become. We need you to be an ambassador for Evo, to travel around the planet showing people what you are and making them realise that you are as real, normal and natural as any other human being. That's going to be a huge responsibility for you, one that you'll need to be properly prepared for. That's why it's crucial that you understand exactly who you are.'

It was impossible. Rosebud could have been anyone. She needed a sign, an invitation to approach him.

'And what if I refuse?' she said.

Heavey sat on the sofa, calmly peering at her.

'You're under contract, Esh. If you don't work, you don't get paid.'

She blanked him and gazed at the Hub.

'You gave me poor parents on purpose, didn't you?'

It suddenly fell into place.

'You made sure we didn't have money so you could exert more control over me. You must have even decided that I'd grow up in England.'

Heavey looked relaxed on the sofa.

'The English education system is incomparable, Esh.'

'And it would make people take me seriously.'

Heavey paused, and nodded.

'There is that.'

They could have raised her anywhere on the planet, but they'd groomed her with this accent, creating the very impact that Marcus had reacted to the first time he'd met her. An American campaign featuring a British girl.

'I could have been anyone,' she said.

She scanned her eyes over the Hub, fruitlessly looking for Rosebud.

'Esh,' Heavey said. 'We have to conclude your security arrangements. The Corporation wants everything set in order. You need to see Steveland now.'

Tony and André escorted her through the Pagoda. At Steveland's studio, they stood outside the door and allowed her to enter alone.

Steveland turned chirpily as she entered.

'Hey. How you doing?'

Evidently no one had told him who she really was.

'I heard about your grandfather,' he said, suddenly more sombre. 'Sorry.'

Esh looked over his cluttered work surfaces, thinking of Grandad, of Mum and Dad in East Stratford, Kristin in Portman Square.

'I know you had to wait to speak to your folks,' Steveland said. 'I'm really sorry. We had some problems in the pipeline.'

Esh turned to him. The Team had pulled the wool over his eyes perfectly. They seemed to show almost total control in gaining access to her. But she was about to be tied down by the Corporation for ever.

'What are you going to do to me, Steveland?'

Steveland sat looking at her for a little while. Then he reached up into his shelves, stored across the room in the order only he knew.

'They want to put a twenty-four-hour trace on you. It'll make you permanently locatable, down to the nearest inch. After that, they won't even have guards around you. They'll be able to watch you around the clock, and see when you roll over in bed.'

He found what he was looking for and sat back down in his chair.

'I've been told not to put you back on to Interface, Esh. Indefinitely. The Corporation doesn't want to risk the Team ever getting to you. And they don't want you making contact with anyone outside the compound. You've become as big a security risk to them as whoever makes the iVerts.'

As Steveland's words reached her, Esh felt her body tingling, as if it was evaporating into the sunshine. The daylight suddenly felt too bright, like a giant standard-lamp that no one could ever switch off.

'Steveland,' she said. 'Is there any way you can not do this?'

Steveland frowned, seeing the plaintive expression on her face.

'I'm sorry. I have to.'

'Please,' she said.

'There's nothing I can do, Esh.'

Tears came suddenly to her eyes. She'd never begged anyone for anything.

'I can't stay here, Steveland. I'm begging you. They'll kill me one day like the Khaki Girl. They're never going to let me leave. I can't live my life in this prison.'

Steveland bit his lip. Unable to take the burden, he looked down at the ground and shook his head.

'I have to do this,' he said quietly. 'It's my job.'

Tears fell down Esh's face. She looked into the never-ending sunshine falling from the Pagoda's roof, covering them in invisibility. She sobbed with her whole body, as the sunlight blazed into her, sealing the air around her like an atomic explosion. She suddenly knew, in her heart, that she would rather die than live here.

'I have to do this,' Steveland said.

Esh looked down, weeping. She walked towards him and watched as he pulled over a stool for her.

Silently, she sat down, and gazed at the sun-reflected window, tears filling her eyes. She ignored Steveland's meticulous operations as he controlled his devices to enhance the frequencies and settings of her Eye Chip.

'There.'

He sat back, quietly put aside his equipment. The procedure he'd just performed, like many things he'd been asked to do, had been illegal. But sanctioned by the Corporation, there was nothing he wasn't allowed to do.

'We're done,' he said, as if the worst was over.

Esh gazed lifelessly through the window, and he stood up.

'I want you to have something,' he told her, reaching into his shelves.

She didn't look up or register a response. Sitting down again, Steveland placed an object in her hand. It was plastic, bulky.

She looked down and saw a digital watch.

Steveland smiled.

'For you to tell the time,' he said.

She stared at it, thinking of the clock that Marcus had kept by his bed. This was it. Her connection to the world.

'It's correct to within a tenth of a second,' Steveland told her.

It was a collector's piece, one of his hard-to-find items,

and he was giving it to her. The watch appealed to him greatly, particularly in its ability to show what it did so clunkily, with its big buttons and over-obvious functions.

Esh held it without interest.

'The gates of the compound are playing up,' Steveland said.

She looked at him wearily, wondering what the hell he was talking about.

'I've inserted a worm into the compound's security system that keeps triggering them open. You probably know that they're not meant to open at the same time. But we did it the other day, so that your convoy could get onto the highway quickly. Since then, it's been happening again and again.'

She gazed at the unassuming, tech-support aura around Steveland that no one had ever bothered to see through. He gave her a sly smile.

'I'm Rosebud, Esh.'

Her fingers curled around the wristwatch.

'You?'

He nodded.

'What have you done to me?'

'Disabled your Eye Chip. You're untraceable.'

She stared at him, barely able to believe that he was the one.

'We've got an exit plan,' he said. 'You have to go now, before they notice that your Eye Chip's not transmitting. Tell security you need to go for a jog. At twenty-one minutes past nine the steel gates will open simultaneously. You'll have to escape your security team, and make it past the sentry guards. But there's an emergency shut-down button just by the outer steel gate. Hit it as you run out, and the gate will immediately close. When you're on the highway, turn right.'

Her head swarmed with thoughts.

'Then what?'

Steveland reached out and attached the strap of the wristwatch to her hand.

'Keep running.'

She looked down at the time, in chunky liquid crystal. 08:41.

'What'll happen to me?'

'You'll disappear.'

'To where?'

'You have to go, Esh.'

Steveland glanced at Tony and André guarding the door.

'What will the Team do with me?'

'They'll explain when you find them.'

'Where are they?'

She felt as if she was crumpling. She gazed into Steveland's eyes for an answer, but he replied with the friendly face he'd always had.

'Run, Esh.'

'New watch?' Tony asked, suddenly keen to start up a friendship.

He followed behind her with André. As they passed the Hub, she glanced inside, and tried to maintain as inconspicuous a pace as possible. Upstairs in the gallery, she glimpsed Heavey brainstorming with Gus and Nathan. On the Hub floor, the crew moved around as they built the campaign to a climax, while above them

Esh's face appeared a dozen times over on the broadcasting bank of screens.

She reached the door of the Pagoda and iScanned into her garden.

'Is it okay if we go for a run?' she asked, turning to André and Tony.

'Sure' Tony smiled. 'Give us ten minutes.'

She waited in the entrance hall, looking at her watch. 09:01.

'Esh?'

She turned round, and saw Maria eyeing her from the kitchen.

'You're running?' Maria asked, with a frown.

Esh nodded. She felt the suspiciousness in Maria's eyes at her jogging so soon after all that had happened.

'Well, that's good,' Maria shrugged.

She wasn't being fooled. Somehow, she'd intuited almost perfectly what Esh was about to do, just as she'd known about Marcus.

'Be careful,' she smiled.

As Maria eyed her from the kitchen, Esh wanted to step closer and hug her, but stopped herself, knowing she would betray their secret.

'Thank you, Maria.'

Maria peered at her sadly, but fondly.

'We'll have breakfast ready when you're back,' she said.

'Esh?'

She turned round. Tony was waiting, with Mikey, André and Clive.

'We're ready.'

*

Esh tore past the mansions, too fast to even look over her shoulder. She listened hard for her bodyguards, having no idea how far behind they were. Her legs pounded, arms propelling her, body almost beyond her control, as natural and effortless as a motor. The body the Corporation had given her darted along the road, flitting beneath the shadows of the trees.

The road curved round, began the descent toward the compound's gates. She checked the watch. 09:18. Gates still out of sight. She turned and checked security's position. Forty metres away, fighting to gain ground.

She looked forward, sprinting. Suddenly the gates came into view, but with no sign of them opening. She lifted her hand, wind hurtling past her. 09:19. If she slowed down security would soon be kicking at her heels. But if she sped up and reached the gates too soon, she'd have to stop and wait, alerting them to her.

She ran with everything she had, giving herself distance from security to leave room for manoeuvre. She raised the watch to her wind-streaming eyes. 09:20.

The gates began opening, too early. She ran faster, no time to check security. She threw her body into space, moving like air, and reached the gate. Braking on the ground, she gripped the edge of the wall and spun ninety degrees right. The sentry guard who'd leaned into her SUV the first time she'd arrived in the compound was hulking in front of her, panicking at the gate opening. He fixed her with his startled eyes. She dashed to his left, and he reached out to grab her.

'Jerry!' he screamed.

She slipped through. Jerry stood at the outer gate,

back turned. Quickly he swivelled, but to the wrong side, as Esh wrong-footed him and lunged past, slamming her hand on the emergency button.

She vanished through the gap in the wall just as the steel gate shut around her, and a loud siren cried out within the compound. She turned right, and ran.

Cars screamed past, five lanes of traffic hounding her on the edge of the road, as she sprinted along the tiny stretch of grass between the highway and the compound's wall. She turned back to the gate, and saw that security hadn't made it out. How long till they got the gate open, and came running?

She turned forwards, saw iBoards on both sides of the highway covered with her image, the sky above her spread with her face. Jogging on the road, she looked anonymous, like a lunatic escaped from an asylum. But where to go? She had nothing on her but the clothes on her back and the watch on her wrist.

A black van tore past and stopped suddenly, ten metres in front of her, skidding to a halt on the side of the road in a cloud of dust. Its rear doors swung open and two men in balaclavas jumped out, came running towards her. She froze, and turned back to see the gate of the compound opening. The nose of a black SUV was just appearing on the road. Two pairs of hands grabbed her.

'Rosebud,' said a voice behind one of the masks.

The men hauled her to the back of the van, bundled her inside, and pulled the doors shut, as the van accelerated away onto the highway.

*

'Sorry, Esh, we're going to have to hood you.'

Before she saw the speaker, a soft black cover came over her head, and the van raced on, as she sat in darkness, bucketed in a soft, velour-lined seat.

'Did they see us?' someone asked.

'No.'

'Sure?'

'*Yes.*'

How many of them? She panted into the hood, looking around, blind.

A hand rested on her shoulder.

'Hello, Esh,' he said.

It was him, in front of her.

'You doing okay?'

The Voice sounded as warm and close as he always had in the Safe.

'I'm scared,' she said.

'I don't blame you. But you're going to be okay now.'

His hand left her shoulder, and she jogged sideways with the van's movements.

'Did Steveland disable your Eye Chip?'

'Yes,' she said.

'Good.'

Panting and frightened, she felt a little reassured by the Voice's presence.

'Where are we going?' she said.

'Somewhere safe,' he replied. 'Don't worry, Esh.'

Distractedly, she felt the velour of the seat beneath her. There were dimples in the upholstery, like an old-fashioned RV.

'How many of us are in here?' she asked.

Through the van's walls, she could hear the hum of

speeding traffic. They were driving fast, still on the highway.

'Four of us and you, Esh.'

'Where are the Team?' she asked.

The Voice chuckled, sounding as though the bedlam of helping her escape from the compound hadn't ruffled him one bit.

'Esh,' he said. 'We're it.'

Silence

The van turned, and lurched down a ramp. Outside, the noise of traffic vanished as they swung round a corner and suddenly pulled up. The sound of the engine cut out, and she heard it quietly ticking over.

The rear doors opened. Someone took hold of Esh and led her out of the van. She stood on the ground, smelt gasoline. The van's doors slammed, and the echo returned low and dull. They were in an underground garage.

A hand led her away, followed by footsteps. She stumbled, the world submerged in blackness, and a door unlocked in front of her. The hand steered her into a corridor. No more echo. She was conducted round a corner then made to stop as the sound of another door opened beside her.

The hand guided her into a room, and halted her. Turning her around, he reached up, and slipped off her hood.

She squinted in the dim light. There were four guys in front of her, chairs stacked by walls, furniture piled up around them.

'Okay, Esh?'

She blinked, looked at the four pairs of eyes in front of her.

They were all in their late twenties. Dressed in T-shirts, jeans, sneakers, not the kind of guys you'd have turned to notice in the street. But there was something instantly familiar about them. One of them was blond, with broad shoulders and a bright grin. The guy next to him was shorter and dweebier-looking, but full of mischief. His neighbour was taller and better-looking, olive-skinned, dark hair. And beside him stood the largest of the four, a huge guy with a barrel chest and a tree-trunk neck.

They stood looking at her.

'Good to meet you, Esh,' smiled the blond guy.

It was him. The Voice.

'Hello,' she said as if they'd met a million times before.

She looked at all four of them. They were so ordinary-looking. It seemed unreal. These were the guys responsible for all the iVerts, for terrorising the Corporation, for breaking her out of the compound?

The end result of her dreams was so surprising. There wasn't the slightest political fire in their eyes, nothing about them that looked threatening or imposing. They just seemed faintly amused by their status as guerrillas in the world, standing there looking at her with the same fascination that any other four guys in their twenties would have shown at seeing the girl from the Evo campaign.

'You look familiar,' she said.

The blond guy turned to the others and chuckled.

'Really?' he said.

The easy-going tone of his voice made sense, in the context of his confident, relaxed gestures and young, boyish features.

'Do I know you?' she asked them.

The four guys laughed heartily.

'I don't know, do you?' the blond guy asked back.

In a moment of sudden and absurd lucidity, she recognised them. They were just ordinary guys, wild cartoons reduced to the everyday.

'George,' she said to the blond guy.

'Pleasure to meet you, Esh.'

'Dwight?'

'You doing okay?' the dweeby guy responded.

'Dirk?' she turned to the good-looking guy.

'Hi, Esh,' he said.

'Larry?'

Larry, arms as thick as piglets, gave her a little wave.

It was them. On earth. The Team. FMCG.

'Have I gone mad?'

'Your eyes are good, Esh,' George grinned.

'What's going on?'

Her head spun, light and oxygen sucking from the room.

'We created FMCG,' George said. 'We invented them years ago, designed them and gave them a life, gave them our own names and faces. They were just a joke we did when we were at college, the ultimate consumer bitch boy-band working round the clock and selling their souls. We launched FMCG on the Net and the Corporation heard about them. They loved them, and sent us an anonymous message asking if we'd sell them the concept. We never met them. We negotiated the whole thing through lawyers, and cut a licensing deal that still earns us more money than we'll ever know how to spend. Well, except on creating iVerts and busting English girls out of high-security advertising complexes.'

George grinned, the whole thing a luscious comedy.

'Don't people recognise you?' Esh asked, reeling.

'We don't show our faces,' George said. 'It ensures our lifelong commitment to the Team. We can no longer live in the open world. We're cut off the Net, just like you. Our money travels from the FMCG licensing deal via a hundred sources, eventually being distributed to the wide, silent network we have working for us.'

'You don't have Interface?'

'We have nothing, Esh.'

George smiled affably.

'No one knows where to look for us. We live on the LA underground, without Money, without Identities.'

'How do you survive?' Esh said.

'Through our people inside the Net,' he replied.

Quickly, a pattern formed in Esh's mind, based on the memory of an old urban myth she'd never believed.

'Like the NAPs' black market?'

'Exactly so,' George concurred. 'That's how you're going to disappear. In fact, it's how you've already escaped. The Corporation deleted you, left you as invisible as a NAP. With Steveland's piece of handiwork, you've now passed beyond all their methods of detection. The only way they can get to you is by setting eyes on you or getting a DNA sample from you. But if you don't want them to, Esh, they'll never find you again. We can hide you. In time, we can even help you change your appearance, disguise everything about you. You're never going to be able to go back to your old life. But I think you knew that already. Right now, the person with all the power, Esh, is you. Precisely because you have nothing at all.'

'What do you mean?'

Standing in front of her in this dusty room hadn't diminished George's fondness for cryptic rhetoric.

'The Corporation have the mother of all products launching in two days and their principal's not even in their control. Do you have any idea how much havoc you're on the verge of creating? You have no Ear Chip, no Interface system, no Eye Chip to trace you. You've disappeared and become as untraceable as the day you were born. Our indications are that the Corporation will not pull back from the launch, even without you. They'll go ahead and run the campaign with your image, and maybe even pretend that you haven't gone missing at all. Which makes the fact that you're right here with us more and more powerful. We can invent you from scratch, even give you a new Identity once we've changed your physical appearance. That is your choice. You'd never be seen the same way. You'd no longer be you, you'd have to change into someone you didn't even know, and learn to conceal everything about yourself. Accent. Mental faculties. Character traits. You'd have to be vigilant for the rest of your life, as the Corporation looked for you. They'll never give up on the smallest possibility that you might crop up one day. You'd have to be totally invisible. We'd watch over you, Esh, and move you underground if things got hot. You'd always be under our surveillance.'

'Why?' she said. 'What do you get out of this?'

'Nothing,' he said. 'Except a favour.'

She gauged his expression, watching the impish thought behind his eyes. She tried to grasp the proposition he'd made. But in whichever direction her mind travelled, she felt that there was no proposition at all. Because if she left here, if the Team even let her go now that she'd seen their faces, she'd have to return to the Corporation. And she knew, with an icy panic rising up through her body at the mere thought of it, that she'd rather be no one, rather become somebody alien, than assume the form of the person the Corporation had created for her.

She'd have the features of an unknown woman. She'd be born again, vanishing into society and growing into a fiction of her own. The legacy that the Corporation had set aside for her in the Foundation's account would never become her own. In a couple of days it would pass to Mum and Dad, as she had requested.

'What do you need from me?' she said.

She stared at the four of them, wanting a bargain, seeing in all their faces the same mischievous look of curiosity and intrigue.

'We'd like to use footage of you,' George told her.

White room

Her face took over the entire sky, in a global media onslaught never before seen. Every SkyBoard and iBoard carried the launch, every TV channel and commercial break was devoted to the broadcast, as Evo launched simultaneously across the planet, announcing the news that Esh was the first human in existence to have been born with entirely enhanced and manipulated genes.

Her life was broadcast to the world, showing how she was created in Evo's research programme, how she was implanted in her surrogate mother, how she was born and then developed, manifesting at an astonishing rate all the characteristics that she alone had been given, the summation of evolution in one woman.

She appeared in every transmission on every SkyBoard and iBoard, even in the iVerts that popped up unremittingly as Evo launched to the globe.

The same footage kept playing all day, showing her seated inside a strange igloo-shaped sphere where she receded into an oval-shaped seat in the wall. The camera shot was fixed, and filmed her in the bizarre white brightness of her pod, the time and situations changing, but her position in the room never moving.

The footage was obviously clandestine, and had iVert written all over it. One minute Esh would be talking to somebody in the camera's perspective, and the next crying her heart out. Then suddenly she'd be normal again.

The scenes switched constantly, mimicking the montages of Esh's life in the campaign, except without banners or the Storyteller narrating Esh's genesis. The iVerts simply showed her undergoing an obviously harrowing transformation as she learned who she was within the strange, glowing confines of her pod.

Why was she trapped in this white bubble? Why was she always seated in that chair, pouring her heart out to the lens? The iVerts showed her successively joyful, hopeful, frantic, tearful, anxious, bewildered. The images peppered Evo's launch with stolen scenes from Esh's existence, her private turmoil in this strange little room that the Corporation had built for her.

Then at the end of the day there was a new iVert, as simple as the footage of her in the Safe, but showing Esh standing against an obviously digitised background to disguise her true location.

On SkyBoards and iBoards everywhere, Esh's eyes looked out from the screens, alive, pale and innocent, again mimicking the campaign's footage from the BlueCube. Careworn and drawn, she still looked vital, and beautiful. A ghost of a smile hovered around her, betraying a latent excitement inside, as she looked into the camera, and spoke.

'My name is Esh. You'll know who I am. I have

neither parents nor siblings. I was created by the Corporation from the great genetic cauldron whence we all spring, in order to demonstrate what Evo is going to be able to do for future generations of humankind. I'm told I'm something of a miracle, so here I am with a few words from our sponsors.'

She paused momentarily and cleared her throat, eyes blinking against the enormous glowing SkyBoards as she put her hand to her mouth.

'I'm nineteen,' she said, 'and until now I've lived in ignorance of my origins. The Corporation didn't choose to tell me anything about myself until very recently, with the result that I've spent most of my life assuming that I was just like anyone else, well, bar a few exceptional superhuman aptitudes. But the funny thing is that even without knowing any of this about myself, I still felt isolated, lonely, and distant from other people much of the time. Which isn't so surprising perhaps. Someone very close to my heart, whom I miss a great deal, once told me that this feeling is common to many human beings. So maybe I'm not such a freak after all. Which was probably intentional on the part of the Corporation, as I believe they wanted me to lead a relatively normal life, until the day they showed up on my doorstep in London and asked me to come to California to become the star of their ad campaign, before landing me with the bombshell that actually *I'm* the laboratory-designed human genetic exception Evo sought to produce.'

Again, Esh briefly cleared her throat, and then continued.

'Two days ago, I escaped from the Corporation,' she said, 'with the help of the industrious bunch of guys bringing you this transmission. The Corporation, sadly, don't have the first clue where I am. To tell the truth neither do I. But that's well and good, because I'm about to become invisible for a very long time. I may even disappear altogether. I'll still be amongst you, though, walking between you on the street, looking over your shoulder. Maybe in years to come when you've forgotten about me I'll suddenly pop back to say hi. By then, I'll look different. Evo will have moved on to ever greater capabilities, and the campaign will have evolved into something brand new. I imagine the Corporation will have extinguished me as the face of their product. But I'll still be here, one way or another. I'll be around for a long time. So for now, goodbye, and hello. And welcome to your world.'

The Genesis Code

John Case

ITALY: a dying doctor makes a chilling confession to the priest in a remote hillside village.

WASHINGTON, D.C.: a mother and her young son are savagely murdered. Their house is then burned down.

JOE LASSITER, the woman's brother, discovers a chain of similar killings around the world.

WHAT IS THE LINK? Who are the shadowy, merciless killers? And what is the Genesis Code, the secret so unthinkable that powerful men will do anything to ensure it remains in the grave?

arrow books

The First Horseman

John Case

In the Book of Revelation the Four Horsemen herald the arrival of the Apocalypse. When the First Horseman thunders forth, pestilence will spread throughout the land. For the First Horseman is plague . . .

WHY is a disease-ravaged village in North Korea razed to the ground, its inhabitants massacred by the army?

WHO are the shadowy terrorists willing to unleash epidemic and death on an unsuspecting world?

WHAT is the deadly treasure that has been ransacked for 80-year-old tombs n the Arctic Circle before an American scientific expedition can investigate their secrets?

For reporter Frank Daly this is the story of a lifetime. Yet the more he uncovers, the more dangerous the stakes become. Until at last he comes face to face with a shocking secret, pitching him into a harrowing race to prevent nothing than . . . apocalypse.

arrow books

**Order further Arrow titles
from your local bookshop, or have them delivered
direct to your door by Bookpost**

☐	**The Genesis Code** John Case	0 09 918412 5	£6.99
☐	**The First Horseman** John Case	0 09 918402 8	£6.99
☐	**The Bridge of Sighs** Olen Steinhauer	0 09 945198 0	£6.99
☐	**Fatherland** Robert Harris	0 09 926381 5	£6.99
☐	**Archangel** Robert Harris	0 09 928241 0	£6.99
☐	**Enigma** Robert Harris	0 09 999200 0	£6.99

Free post and packing
Overseas customers allow £2 per paperback

Phone: 01624 677237

Post: Random House Books
c/o Bookpost, PO Box 29, Douglas, Isle of Man IM99 1BQ

Fax: 01624 670923

email: bookshop@enterprise.net

Cheques (payable to Bookpost) and credit cards accepted

Prices and availability subject to change without notice.
Allow 28 days for delivery.
When placing your order, please state if you do not wish to receive any
additional information.

www.randomhouse.co.uk/arrowbooks

arrow books